THE
ABATEMENT MANDATE

R. R. BOXALL

CRANTHORPE
MILLNER
PUBLISHERS

First published by Cranthorpe Millner Publishers (2026)

ISBN 978-1-80378-341-3 (Paperback)

www.cranthorpemillner.com

Cranthorpe Millner Publishers

To everyone who read book one –
thank you all for taking a chance on the adventure.

For those of you who have come back for book two –
we journey together.

THE RESTITUTION OF YOUR SOUL LIES IN
THE INTEGRITY OF YOUR ACTIONS.

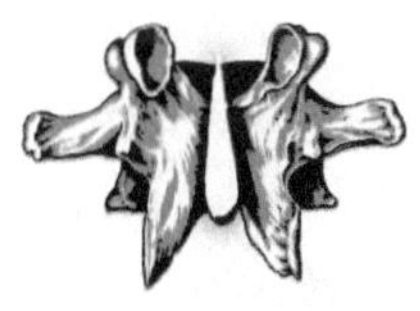

EXTRACTS TAKEN FROM THE PRIVATE MISSIVES AND SANCTIONS RECORDED WITHIN THE SENATE ARCHIVES

PRIVATE MISSIVE
April 2nd, one year after the Fall

To members of the convening Senate,

The evidence is now conclusive and irrevocable: to proceed on the current course would be to accept our annihilation. We will not survive a second winter such as the last. The only viable option is the immediate and radical reduction of superfluous elements within the populace.

Author: Unknown

SENATE SANCTION: ITEM 1 (A)

It is herein decreed the acceptable means of compliance for the necessary measures of population control within the Empire. These Sanctions give full autonomy and legal pardon for all actions taken in line with the proposed extermination policy. It is the majority agreement of all those who hold a recognised seat that the needs of the Empire outweigh the rights of her citizens.

SENATE SANCTION: AMENDMENT 1 (A.2)

Following the initial success of the Generation Project, additional funding shall be provided to the Scientific Wing of the Senate, awarded for the sole purpose of supporting new research into the long-term management of overbreeding and population growth within the lowland colonies.

PRIVATE MISSIVE

September 20th, 80 years after the Rebirth of the Empire

To members of the Senate currently in situ,

I address you directly and with the utmost urgency. The use to which you intend to put my work is a grotesque abuse of its design and is most reckless in the extreme. I caution you against such action, not simply due to its potential unknown reverberations, but above all because of the most heinous departure from morality such a use would incur.

Author: Dr Cornelius Alfredson

CHAPTER ONE
A YOUNG MAN'S FOLLY

Cornelius

Cornelius sat up straight in his chair, turning on the dirty yellow light that shone down from the lamp above his desk. The hour was growing late, but he couldn't stop now. The work was not yet perfect, and he knew it must be infallible this time. They already scrutinised his projects more than most, believing that a young man so newly out of the Educatorium had little to offer such learned academics as themselves. His back had begun to ache from the hours he had sat hunched over his papers, and there was a blister forming on his finger where the constant pressure of his pen had bitten deep. The scholars' rooms in the Capital were well furnished – usually Cornelius found them comfortable enough – but spending so long sitting like this would have caused any back to complain, no matter how well cushioned the chair. Still, it would be well worth the price of his discomfort, if they approved the funding for his work this time.

He ran his hands through his hair again, leaving it standing up at awkward angles. Then, realising what he had done, he tutted. The maid who cleaned the apartments was always telling him not to do that. She had explained, a little curtly, that it was hard enough to respect the ideas of a boy only recently out from behind his mother's skirts, and even harder when he looked as though he had been fast asleep in his bed mere moments ago.

Cornelius tried to smooth it flat again. It didn't matter to him what his hair looked like, but he knew the woman was right: such idiotic formalities always seemed to carry weight with the Senate. He wished then that he had made time for a haircut, but the thought had not occurred to him until now, and *now* was much too late to do anything about it. He made a note to ensure that his best shirt was pressed, and his shoes freshly polished, before the budget committee convened in the morning. He hoped that would be enough to detract from his lapse in grooming.

He scanned the papers before him again; the ink was still wet in places and he was careful not to smudge it. Surely, this time he had addressed all of their concerns. Then, finally, his promise of a better future would receive the resources it deserved. At the last convention, they had protested that it would take him away from his current project – *Botanicals and their Genetic Modification for the New Climate*. This latest proposal would have to remedy that concern. It shouldn't be too hard to convince them; after all, his modified seedlings had been thriving in their test environments inside the Capital's Scientific Wing for over a year now. Even the ones that had been shipped out to local villages had so far withstood the challenge. Of course, they were not infallible. Everything still had to follow the cycle of nature, and so by virtue were subject to her whims, but on the whole, they had begun to yield more crops than anyone had seen for generations after the Fall.

The young man's eyes narrowed. There were still loopholes to close; he could feel it in his gut. He just couldn't seem to find them on the page. Where were those hidden weak spots they would use to decline his funding request for the third, and what could be the final, time? He could not afford to leave anything open to interpretation in this last bid.

Pausing at the second paragraph, he nodded to himself.

There. He needed to be more specific right *there.* Scoring out a few lines, he added:

The maintenance of the modified seedling project can be successfully overseen by the interns currently within the team. I have in paragraph five, section three, named two such suitably qualified members of the current staff who have the abilities required and scope for such work within their ongoing remit. Even so, while I am engaged in the initial phases of the proposed project, I will at all times remain available for consultation and collaboration in the unlikely event that any new problems or challenges arise that have the potential to impact the former.

He knew the interns were more than capable of keeping the existing project going. It was well established now. This new work was different, though. Cornelius was quite sure that only he alone would be able to complete such a complex design; that without him, the *Pulmonis Botanica* project would remain a foolish notion that his peers would use as the punchline of their jokes at the next gathering. He knew what they all thought about his project, but he remained undeterred. Often, he would sit at this very desk, his thoughts miles away from the reports in front of him, as his mind worked furiously on one new problem or another.

He could not afford to let himself be distracted that way today; today he must remain focused on the task at hand. This time he would present a proposal so compelling that it would force the Senate to invest in his endeavour.

Sighing, he shook his head. It shouldn't be *this* difficult to convince them of the importance of his project. If only the old fools would open their eyes to its potential. When he thought about the resources the Senate had wasted, it made him baulk: the way they insisted on ploughing endless resources into the

Scientific Wing's military division, while his own department in Social Development barely had enough funding to keep the lighting on in the evenings. When would they let go of that old mantra 'might is right'? When had that mentality ever benefited a society in the documented history of the world?

He huffed, trying to refocus. He could not let himself be distracted this time – far too often he would think of an idea for only a moment, then lose half the night exploring each of its branching arms as they grew more quickly than he could follow. Not for this work, though. Not when this work could change the course of *everything*.

Cornelius hadn't slept. Smoothing his hair down, he carefully pressed his shirt and read his final draft aloud one last time. He smiled, pleased not to have found a single last-minute change to make.

As the large hand of the clock above him crept towards its peak, he stood in the corridor to the Great Hall, waiting. The four newest members of his team accompanied him. He had hand-selected each of them for this project and they had all beamed with pride at being chosen. He hoped they wouldn't find out that he knew not one of their names. Cornelius had a hard time remembering the names and faces of the staff in his department, but what he *did* remember was much more important. Looking at each of them, he nodded. *That one* never forgot to update a report; the one next to her was happy to be allocated any amount of busywork, provided he was shown how to do it first; the girl at the back was fastidious about standards and would make sure the others in the team followed any conditions Cornelius set.

He frowned as he looked upon the last member of his team. Cornelius had not been sure about him, but the young man had come so highly recommended that he'd waived his reservations. The boy was the one the others enjoyed working with. He was always cheerful and seemed to meld the other three individuals into a team. While Cornelius hadn't felt the need for a fourth member, the young man's effect on the productivity of those around him was undeniable.

There was a loud click as the lock on the doors slid open and the massive wooden panels began to swing inward into the Great Hall.

"This is it," he whispered, as much to himself as to the others.

Cornelius stood in the centre of the Hall, cold hard marble under his freshly shined shoes, while the unreadable faces of the committee looked down on him from their raised platform ahead. As soon as he read the project title aloud, a few of them began to snicker. A ripple of irritation spread through him. He cleared his throat and tried to ignore the hot flush that was spreading up his neck – he could not afford to let them rattle him this time.

So it had gone on for hours. They began by questioning each aspect of the work in turn, seeming desperate to find a way to discredit him. As he had expected, the most obvious problems had been addressed first, beginning with the fact that the botanicals he required didn't yet exist. In answer, he reminded the Senate how they had been sceptical of his abilities in the early years of the seedling project too, but he had spliced and grafted until whole new varieties of grains had learned to thrive in their new climate. He could offer his assurance that this time would be no different, citing several of the proposed flora he knew had the potential to achieve success.

Then there was the infrastructure. It was not just the

technical difficulty of building of such a complex design that the Senate took issue with, but the fact such a grand project hadn't been attempted since before the Fall, never mind after. Cornelius was undeterred by this line of questioning. The last time he had proposed it, he had thought his ideas would be enough to move them, however, he had quickly encountered the naivety of that. This time, he had employed the help of some of the engineering division at a considerable personal cost to himself. But it had been worth it. The labyrinth of tunnels and passages, the support beams and the ventilation shafts, were all mapped and charted on the parchment he placed in front of them. He watched their eyebrows rise at the drawings. Drawings that he knew made it undeniable that, in theory, the work was plausible.

Cornelius couldn't have said at what point the opinions in the room began to shift, but by the time he was reciting his well-rehearsed conclusion, he knew he had them.

"The *Pulmonis Botanica* Project will result in an intricate system of chambers and plant life, all working in a delicate balance. Once we have perfected the ecosystem, harmonising not only the soil acidity, but also the humidity and rate of photosynthesis within each ventricle, we will change the course of the world. The modified and enhanced botanicals shall line every inch of the organ, absorbing previously unfathomable amounts of the rank atmosphere. Not only will they filter it, but they will thrive on its rich, noxious stew."

Cornelius had written on his notes: *Pause to allow them time to consider this.* He could feel his excitement building and he struggled to follow his own direction before he went on.

"It won't be easy or quick, but, built deep under the ground, this creation will become the lungs of the Empire, breathing in the pollutants of the world and sighing out cleaner air than any have known in generations. Once we have perfected the initial design in the Capital, it is feasible that every town and village could receive such an installation. With the success of this project, science will finally have provided the answer to nature's vengeance."

Cornelius looked up from his papers, shocked to find every eye fixed on him, no longer mocking but in sincere consideration. After that, it had not even taken one full day for the writ approving the financing for his project to arrive at his office. The chairman of the Senate had placed it into his hand directly.

"Well done, lad." His tone had contained an odd mix of respect and warning. "You'd better be able to make good on it, but well done."

It had taken years of careful construction, and of course there had been setbacks, but for the most part, Cornelius had been able to deliver results that surpassed expectations, and often ahead of his deadlines.

It was only as the structure neared its completion that he discovered his folly.

He was not a man who considered himself to be naïve – he knew there was a darker side to the Scientific Division. He would have had to be blind not to realise that some within the Senate held fast to the old ways. Until those outdated philosophies died, there would always be those scholars who invested their talents not for the betterment of the world or the advancement of science, but instead to ensure just who would continue to hold the power. That was not the nature of his work, though. It was not a stain he had to bear upon his conscience the way some others did.

The first he knew that something had gone wrong was during his final examination of the structure's right lobe. As he neared the entrance of the pipeline that fed that compartment, his nephew had been waiting for him. Cornelius had never taken to Theodore – the boy was only slightly younger than himself and, although they had shared a number of classes in their time at the Educatorium, they had little in common. He thought his nephew was overly egotistical, and that his work paralleled too closely with the ambitions of the Military Wing for comfort. Cornelius hadn't known exactly what it was that his nephew worked on down in the labs, but that was not unusual. Many in his profession were secretive about their projects, fearful of imitators or outside interference. Even if Theodore had been inclined to discuss his work with his family, Cornelius knew those projects were classified and he neither expected nor wanted to know what kind of study that might entail.

So it was a most unwelcome surprise when his nephew led him away from his own endeavours and down into that dark world. The labs underground, too cold and sterile for a man who studied nature and life, were enough to make Cornelius feel uneasy. But as they descended further, he started to hear things. Shrieking and sounds of struggling, noises that made every hair on the back of his neck rise in apprehension. Theodore led him onward past it all, showing no more than casual indifference at the disturbance until they reached his office. Cornelius could see straight away that it was much larger than any in his own department of Social Development.

Theodore gestured for him to take a seat, but Cornelius did not want to sit. The artificial light buzzed irritatingly and everything within him wanted to be finished with this conversation so he could leave.

"Will we be long?" Cornelius asked, looking at his watch. He knew that was a gesture people used to imply they were short on time.

"Really, that all depends on you, Uncle."

Cornelius didn't even like the way the boy talked – oily and condescending, as though he alone knew anything of importance.

"Have you heard of the Generation Project?" Theodore continued.

"I have heard the rumours," Cornelius replied cautiously. The Social Development department was as bad as any other for gossip and speculation, but Cornelius did not want to embarrass himself by repeating the tall tales he had heard about such a ridiculous notion.

"Ah yes, the *rumours*. Horrifying, aren't they?" the younger man replied, bringing his hands together and interlacing his long fingers. "Well, of course they are only horrifying until you know the truth, and then they actually appear rather reasonable in comparison."

Cornelius took a seat, feeling that his legs might not hold him anymore. Something was happening – something bad – and he was about to find out just how bad it was going to be.

As the depths of the Generation Project were revealed to him, he protested, he threatened, he begged for Theodore to see sense. But by the time the sun had begun to set in the world above, Cornelius understood the true horror of it all.

The worst part, Theodore had saved for last. After explaining the need for the Generation Project to be abandoned, after the sporadic outbreak of Gen4 Immutavi, he had gone on to tell his uncle of the new 'mandate for population control'.

At last, they had arrived at the crux of it. Cornelius's *Pulmonis*

Botanica – the beacon of hope that could scrub the air clean of its polluting foulness – was to become the delivery system for a consumptive agent.

"It'll be nothing too dramatic, of course." Theodore was cold and clinical in his delivery. "Nothing that could incite panic. Nevertheless, the Senate has seen fit to implement a limitation of sorts upon the unmoderated duration of the lowland life cycle."

Instantly, Cornelius knew what that meant. The Senate could dress up the terminology any way that they liked, but he knew what poisoning a populace sounded like in any fancy language.

"It will be subtle enough not to invite examination," Theodore continued to expound upon the details. "The more susceptible will pass more quickly, while the stronger should have a little more time. But, all in all, the Empire has no need of an aging workforce – the group that is, right now, consuming her most precious and finite resources in exchange for a limited societal contribution. You understand."

Cornelius's mind was reeling. Yes, he understood the words, but what they *meant*? Surely, he had to be mistaken about what they meant. This was not the Empire he worked for. This kind of murder was not the work of learned scientists. He could feel Theodore studying his face. He needed to leave: he was giving away too much. Suddenly, he felt as though his nephew could read every thought in his mind through the expressions on his face – a skill that Cornelius had never possessed.

He stood up abruptly.

"This is all in complete confidence, of course," Theodore went on. "You have been permitted clearance to hear this information only due to the impeccable contribution your Tunnels will provide towards my project."

Cornelius could not bear to listen to any more of his nephew's vile ideas. He fled the tomb-like room, up through cold corridors, until he felt the fresh air of the night on his face. He stayed there on his hands and knees, retching until nothing but bile and shame poured out of him.

His mind was reeling. Tunnels? He had called the grand network of his *Pulmonis Botanica* 'tunnels'? Not the intricate organ that would assure life for generations to come, but instead a deadly mass of weaponised stone corridors that would poison and murder the lowland people. It had not been his intent, yet his designs had created the miles and miles of pathways that were now to be converted into an instrument of death.

Cornelius tried to catch his breath. He would stop this if he could just catch his breath. They were scientists, rational people – he would explain that, with his new lungs and his seedlings, there would be no need for such a mandate. Given just a little more time, he would be able to prove his work could sustain the Empire exponentially. He had to make them understand.

Underneath the cool night sky, he swore that he would stop this most foul thing.

CHAPTER TWO
HOPE AND HELP

How long has it been now? Rin wondered, as once more her eyes searched for a hint of the sun through the thick canopy above. She felt like she had been travelling for a full day already, but as she once again picked out the few thin shards of light that cut through the dense green overhead, she could see the sun was only halfway across its arc.

Physically, she felt much better than she had even an hour before, but every step still felt as though she was trying move through thick mud. Her body cried out with each movement, pleading for rest. Not for the brief moments that they allowed themselves for water, or to catch their breath, but for the true rest and deeper restoration that comes with sleep.

Rin tried to focus on the others around her. She could see that they were still all present and, even faced with the dangers of the swamp, they were all faring better than she was. *Because none of them have felt their body break in a hundred different ways less than a day ago*, she reminded herself, a little churlishly.

Reece was ahead of her now, and she could sense that he was caught between excitement to get back to the Cove and free Tilly of the Empire's last hold on her, and concern for the damage she had sustained in the Capital to make Tilly's freedom possible. Lark did not seem to share her brother's excitement or concern. The older girl had said little to anyone since they'd left the Void behind them. Still, Rin had noticed how Lark kept glancing at her appraisingly, before darting her eyes back along the trail behind them. What remained unsaid in that look annoyed Rin, and she tried to use that anger to fuel her tired limbs a little further each time. But while Lark's glances had been irritating, it was the constant fussing from the three redheaded brothers that had been worse.

"We can stop here, Rin," Magnus offered for the third time, as he watched her eyes close tightly against the ache of fatigue. "Ieuan knows what to do if we don't make it to the first rendezvous. He'll continue to the next one. After a day's rest, we'll catch up to them easily enough."

Rin shook her head, not wanting to waste what little energy she had left on a reply. Her body might need rest, but her mind refused to allow it. She had to know. She had to stand in that place where they had agreed to meet and *know*, with complete finality, what was waiting for her. Only then could she be sure whether this feeling, which had gnawed at her since she'd left the Capital, was just the anxious imaginings of someone who had learned too many hard lessons of late, or if there was something more to the tightness in her chest.

She did want, however, to let someone else carry the oiled satchel that was pressing uncomfortably against her battered body. There was a part of her that didn't want to touch anything that had come from the Capital, and that part of her recoiled at the weight of it, yet for some reason, she couldn't bear to let it go. She couldn't simply give away this thing she had fought so hard for; its constant weight on her back reminded her of what they had accomplished, and she clung to it like a talisman – one she would not relinquish until the mission was complete. And it would not be complete for her until they reached that rendezvous and she saw Ieuan, Marta and Gibb waiting as they were supposed to be. That was the image she tried to keep at the front of her mind. Some part of her held desperately to the hope that she could will such a thing into existence if she only believed in it hard enough.

As they continued to push onward, each section of the dense swamp that passed under her feet felt like a contest between her and the once-friendly landscape, but she couldn't stop. She knew that if she allowed herself to rest for too long, her father's words would begin to bounce around inside her head again. The last thing he had said to her as he lay there, sprawled on the floor, his snide, smug voice so full of self-certainty.

"You'll be back. Incentives, my child. We all just need the right incentive."

She hadn't liked the sound of those words then, and time had only made that unease turn all the more acidic in her stomach. She shook her head, trying to clear it, trying to force the image of Ieuan and the others waiting for her to the front again, yet the confidence of his assertion echoed in her ears.

No, she thought. Nothing would make her go back there again. Nothing would let her be manipulated and used by the Empire in such a way for a second time. She shivered at the memory and the action sent a fresh wave of pain through her body. She had nearly died in that water beneath the Palace, and every inch of her ached as a prompt not to be soon forgotten. *You didn't die. You are alive and that is what matters.* Rin repeated those words to herself for the hundredth time, trying to push away the pain and her own fear at how reckless she had been. What mattered now was that they had everything they needed. They had the archives and all the information they needed to remove the Tavi chips. What else could possibly draw her back to such a treacherous place, knowing what she knew now?

But that was what made her sick inside.

Incentives.

There was only one thing in all the world that could, even now, make her turn back towards the Capital, and all she could do was hope that he was waiting for her at the next rendezvous.

The sun was lower now, and between the dragging weariness and the exhaustion in her mind, Rin had stopped paying attention to the perils of the swamp. Part of her knew she should be more careful, but her thoughts flitted from one thing to the next, quicker than she could make sense of, leaving her unable to concentrate or draw meaning from anything around her. Luck alone had allowed them to travel this far into the swamp without the need for her usual caution.

As they moved into the next clearing, a shrill squeal reminded her how foolish that complacency was.

Instantly, her head whipped from side to side as she tried to locate the thing that had made the sound. It wasn't out in the open, but she knew only one creature in this place made a noise like that.

She spotted it then: the telltale shiver in the long grass ahead, almost like a ripple in a pond. But instead of spreading outwards in placid, ever wider rings, the grasses split into two sharp lines, advancing forward.

"Climb!" she shouted, her own hands already pulling her upwards onto the closest of the branches above her head.

The creature squealed again, then grunted and snorted as it broke into the open space below.

"What *is* that thing?" Lark was panting as she hauled her lithe body up alongside Rin's. Her nose wrinkled at the ugly beast.

Rin wasn't listening, turning instead to check on the others, hoping they had some experience climbing trees. She took a deep, steadying breath, relieved. Uninjured as they were, the boys had easily pulled themselves up off the swamp floor. Rin wasn't sure if they had picked those trees on purpose, or just because they were closest, but thankfully none of them had chosen one with root rot or the white dead branches that snapped easily. The four boys would all be too heavy to gain much height in the thin, reedy branches common to the swamp, but they only needed to climb far enough to be out of the beast's reach.

She looked back at the curly-horned tusker below them. The creature was not unlike the wild boars that occasionally passed through the forest behind the Dale. It had the same short, hog-like snout and thick, dark mane of coarse hair that ran from its head to the middle of its back, but these beasts were much bigger and more heavily muscled than their forest cousins. Rin supposed they had to be to survive in a place like this, however, it wasn't their size but instead their curled horns and long, white tusks that Rin had named them for. Those were the truly dangerous parts. Looking at it again, she closed her eyes in frustration. It was a female. Of course it would be. The males were bad enough, but a fully grown female was not only bigger, but meaner and more vicious than their smaller counterparts.

Being the heaviest, Magnus was positioned lowest in the tree opposite theirs, trying to balance on a branch only just thick enough to hold him. He was forced to sit rather than stand like the others, which left his legs dangling within reach of those great curled tusks. Rin knew that at any moment the tusker would notice that, too.

Unable to reach the two girls above it, the creature turned

away in frustration and almost immediately refocused on Magnus. His eyes went wide as he saw the beast turn towards him. It paused for only a heartbeat longer, taking in the boy's precarious perch. Then it charged.

Magnus began scrabbling at the branches above, trying to pull himself higher, but the slender limbs bent under the movement, unable to bear his weight.

"Hey, over here!" Rin shouted, whistling and slapping her hands against the bark of her own tree, desperate to draw the tusker's attention back towards them.

The beast ignored her, fixed now on more attainable quarry. Magnus only just had time to draw his knees up to his chest before the beast gored the trunk below, leaving deep gouges in the wood where his legs had been only moments before. The whole tree shook violently under the impact and the sound of splintering bark mixed discordantly with the tusker's frustrated grunting. For a moment, Rin was worried that Magnus would be rattled loose, or that the tree would be felled, but both seemed to be holding.

"What's your plan for getting us out of this, then?" Lark asked, picking away the swamp grime from under her nails, as though unconcerned by their sudden change in circumstances.

Rin's brow creased and, for a moment, she thought longingly of Scratch. She'd never had to worry about tuskers when that old swamp mutt was around. He might not have risked a fight with a fully grown female like this one, but if he hadn't scared her off, his sudden absence would have warned Rin that there was trouble nearby. He wasn't here now though, and she knew such wishing was a pointless thing, especially when a much larger part of her was relieved that neither Scratch nor Tilly would have to worry about tuskers while they were safely sheltered in the Cove.

Lark was watching the creature pacing the ground underneath Magnus's perch, not with the same dread that Rin knew was etched on her own face, but instead, she seemed merely bored with having their journey delayed. Rin scrunched her eyes shut, trying to focus. The truth was, she didn't have a plan. If she wasn't so damn tired, she supposed she might have been able to think of something, but even with this new fear to fuel her, she struggled to concentrate on the problem. The haze of recent events still muted the world around her, even now.

Tentative ideas were still forming in her head when she heard a second sound – one she hadn't heard for far too long of late. A small, incredulous chuckle left her mouth. How could a sound she had been so desperate to hear earlier in the day now fill her with such dread?

"What is going on over here? I thought you were all supposed to be well practised at this business of skulking around?" the old woman scolded as she shuffled into sight. "Instead, while I am waiting like a wrung-out sheet on wash day, I come to hear you all hollering and carrying on like children at a harvest dance—"

"Marta!" Rin cried out, putting a stop to the old woman's mutterings. The moment of elation she had felt at the sight of the old woman almost instantly turned to fear for the danger she unknowingly faced. "Marta, it's a tusker. Climb!"

Rin had been imaging for days how, when she finally saw the old woman again, she would run to her and allow herself to squeeze Marta tightly and be held close in return. She had yearned for the warmth of that reunion. Now, all she felt was rising panic as she looked towards the closest trees and then back to her, trying to gauge if it was a climb the old woman could make at all, never mind in time.

She clenched her teeth. She needed to get down from this

tree. If she was on the ground, maybe she could distract the tusker for long enough and Marta would be able to climb to safety. She flexed her toes inside her boots, feeling every fibre and muscle still tender in her legs. The thought of landing on bones so newly healed made her flinch, but this was Marta, and she was in danger.

Time seemed to stretch out impossibly slowly as the beast turned towards the old woman. Then , everything was speeding back up. This prey was well within its reach and the beast thrashed its head, squealing as the thick mane of hair along its back bristled. Rin could see every line of its thick sinewy muscles as they bunched, then released for the charge. She could only watch in horror as she realised Marta still wasn't climbing.

"Marta, *climb!*" Rin shouted again, trying to rouse the woman into action.

But Marta wasn't moving at all. From where Rin was perched, it almost looked like the old woman had only set her feet more firmly in the swampy earth. Dread welled up inside Rin, finally acting as a force strong enough to overpower her deep weariness, and she began moving down through the branches, willing her heavy limbs to respond to her urgent commands. She didn't want to watch, but neither could she tear her eyes away.

When the tusker was no more than a person's length from the old woman, Marta struck out. Her familiar staff moved through the air with a striking speed and caught the beast high in the flank. The tusker reeled over in a sprawling, grunting mass, tumbling back into the long grass.

Marta's eyes flicked to Rin, and she saw the concern spread across the old woman's face as she held up her hand. The gesture didn't require any further explanation – Rin stayed still as the grass shivered for a second time. But Marta did not seem to notice, turning away from the beast to focus on something behind her. Several great towers of dried leaves and mud jutted up from the ground next to the old woman, and she tilted her ear towards each one in turn, as though straining to hear some sound. She probed her staff at the strange mounds, each one thudding solidly under examination. The last one was nearly as tall as she was, and when her staff tapped against it, it produced a hollow rattling sound. Not loud, but distinctly different to the others she had tested before. The old woman smiled in response.

Rin couldn't imagine what there was to smile about at a time like this. As the tusker reappeared, shaking its head and pawing the ground angrily, Rin distinctly felt her grandmother's time would have been better spent climbing.

She shook herself, refusing to watch this horrifying scene play out before her any longer. She had listened to the old woman long enough. Whatever Marta had thought to achieve, Rin was sure there wasn't time; she knew what was about to follow that animal's pawing. The old woman had been lucky with the first strike of her staff – the tusker had been caught off guard in mid-charge – but it was unlikely she would get away with such a move twice. Rin wouldn't wait for Marta to get herself hurt just to save her pride.

It was less of a jump and more of a controlled fall as Rin pushed her body away from the branch that held her. She wasn't that far off the ground, but she landed awkwardly and heard a snap, quickly followed by a sharp pain that she had come to associate with a newly broken bone. The gasp Rin couldn't hold in drew the beast's attention, but only for the briefest moment, as Marta yelled out again.

"Damn it, girl! I told you not to move!"

It was the last thing she had time to say before the tusker

began its next assault. Rin felt her chest tighten, knowing she would be too late to reach Marta, even if the shock of the pain, along with the disbelief at her grandmother's instruction, had not fixed her solidly to the ground.

Marta, however, was not still. The old woman was already moving into action, and this time, instead of the light tentative tapping, her gnarled staff collided hard against one of the large mounds of twigs and mud. What Rin had assumed was a solid mass of rock and debris had caved inward instantly under the blow, and a great, lazy head lifted slowly into the air.

Rin's breath caught in her throat. The slither-fang had been asleep in its den and was still a little dopey, but anyone who had ever seen a slither-fang's temper knew that this sudden destruction of its home would change its placid mood quickly enough. Its yellow, scaly head tilted from side to side, shaking off the dust from its ruined lair. The thin slits of its nose opened and closed as it took in the shock of its unexpected surroundings. Rin held her breath as she thought of how close Marta stood to this new danger, unconvinced that whatever this plan was would improve their situation in the slightest.

The giant creature's head was nearly level with Marta's when its tongue flicked out quickly, bright red in colour. Then its jaws opened wide in a savage hiss. Rin felt every inch of the threat in that sound, and she couldn't draw her eyes away from the creature's long, thin fangs that dripped menacingly. She remained frozen, trapped by fear and uncertainty, watching her grandmother as she stood between a tusker and a slither-fang. Any moment now, she was sure those hissing jaws would strike out at the old woman, who had so rudely disturbed its slumber.

Its scaly head darted around, drawn by the vibration of hooves that now shook the ground. In that instant, Rin finally saw the brilliance of Marta's plan. The tusker seemed to realise what was happening only moments after Rin did. It squealed again as it tripped, its legs flailing as it tried to change direction faster than its body could manage. The slither-fang blinked twice, a grey film sliding quickly over its black eyes as it focused on the panicking mass before it, before it left the wreckage of its den towards its prey.

The tusker regained its feet quickly and, clearly familiar with the dangers of this particular threat, it turned to sprint back into the long grass. Rin had never seen a slither-fang at hunt before, and as she watched the speed of its pursuit with horrified fascination. She hoped it was a sight she would never see again.

The others remained high in the trees, careful not to make any movement that might draw either of those things back to them, until long after the sound of hooves had grown faint and distant.

"Alright, that should do it," Marta said abruptly as though observing nothing more remarkable than the change in weather. "You can all get down now. Best we be away from here before it comes back."

Lark jumped down beside Rin, her head cocked to the side. "She sure is handy with that staff, isn't she?" she muttered, her eyes narrowing to take in the old woman's hunched form, as though only just seeing her clearly for the first time.

Rin was barely listening. Instead she found herself smiling as she forced herself to move again. It had been so long since she last saw Marta, and so much had changed, but she hadn't realised how wonderful it would feel to have the old woman tell her what to do again. Even if she hadn't exactly followed her instructions, for a moment she had felt that familiar trust in her grandmother; that unquestioning belief that the old woman knew best. That relinquishing of responsibility, even for such a brief moment, was sorely welcome amongst the chaos of the last few days and felt like a salve against the raw patches inside her. She wanted to run to Marta now and squeeze her tightly, just as she had imagined she would, but she winced as she tried her weight on her right leg.

"Goodness, girl." Marta's concern replaced what before had been certainty. "What happened to you?"

"I think it would be quicker to tell you what *hasn't* happened to me of late," Rin replied wryly, relieved that Marta was here, meaning that, soon enough, they would all be back at the first rendezvous together.

She supposed Ieuan had likely already told Marta much of their tale, and once they were reunited again, and she was done adding her part, they would share a hot meal together and then, finally, she could rest. She would hold Ieuan's hand again and close her eyes, just for a little while.

Rin felt the warmth spreading in her chest as she thought of Ieuan. When these wounds were healed, she would tell him how much he truly meant to her. She had promised herself that much. It was warm in that moment of imagining – the comfort of that feeling was more restorative than any of the short times she had rested throughout the day – and she wanted desperately to stay there.

Something was bothering her, though. An expression in the old woman's face wouldn't let her stay in that place. She could see concern – she had expected that, injured as she was – but what else was there? Pity?

Rin began to snatch short, sharp breaths from the air that suddenly felt too thick to draw in. Ieuan would never have let Marta come to them alone. He would not have heard Rin's voice cry out in alarm and then stayed away.

"Marta, where's Ieuan?" There was a coldness spreading through her now, and it echoed in the tone of her words.

"Child, I—" Marta began gently, as Rin's eyes frantically

searched for a sign of him back along the way she had come. "Where is he, Marta? And Gibb? Where are they?"

She could already feel a painful detaching from the hope she had felt only moments before, leaving only fear and disappointment in its place.

"They're not here, child." Marta put an end to her frantic searching. "He's not here, Rin."

Rin's shoulders dropped as the last of her resilience left her and she considered what that meant.

"No! Gods, no, Rin. They're still alive." The words tumbled from Marta's mouth. "Well, last I saw them, at least. I can't say for sure how they might be now." Marta glanced at the ruined den beside her. "Come, we can't stay here any longer. A slither-fang's nest is no place to build a camp. I'm not sure what you've endured since you left my care, but I know the signs of a person whose need for rest is long overdue." She gestured for Rin to follow her. "It's not far, girl. Then I'll tell you. I'll tell you all of it as best I can."

Rin felt tears pricking behind her eyes. *Ieuan might be alive, but he isn't here.* The guilt felt like a blow to her chest. She should have waited for him to come back through the fence before they left. She should have listened to her gut when she knew something was wrong. Would he think she had left him behind on purpose? That she had known he hadn't returned, and that she had left him there alone anyway? She felt like she might be sick, and pain flared fresh and sharp in every part of her misused body. It was suddenly too difficult to move – she couldn't take a single step further. It had all hurt so much, yet this was the thing that would break her.

She was reaching for *it* before she even realised what she was doing. Desperate for the strength and the detached calm it brought to her, she shivered as it rippled through her. The pain in her limbs lessened as reserves she didn't know she had bristled through the fibres of her tired body.

"Let's go," Rin said, nodding at the old woman to lead the way.

Marta paused, studying her face, eyes narrowed for the briefest of moments, suspicion replacing her concern. Then she offered the younger girl her staff.

Rin shook her head. "Keep it. You'll make better time if you hold on to it, and I *will* hear the whole of this story before nightfall."

Marta looked as though she were considering a problem, then nodded back.

"And who put you two in charge?" Lark taunted.

"*You* were supposed to keep her safe," Marta spat, her voice barely above a whisper. "That was the deal. Not this."

"She's *alive*, isn't she?"

"Barely."

"Pfft, she'll heal," Lark sneered. "Stop coddling her. She's no more a child than the rest of us anymore."

"Oh, she'll heal. That's what worries me. I raised that girl; I know how fast she heals. I can only imagine how much damage was done for her body to *still* be in such a state." Marta jabbed her finger at Lark. "I don't have time for your games at the moment, girl, but there will be an accounting for this. The Alliance is not the Empire; we don't stand for the use of our people this way."

With that, the old woman turned her back and, not waiting for a reply, moved off into the swamp. With Rin beside her, it seemed she neither cared nor felt inclined to check whether the others followed.

CHAPTER THREE
BROKEN BONDS

Marta had been right. It wasn't too much further from the slither-fang's nesting ground to the next rendezvous. If they hadn't been treed by that tusker, they would've reached it by themselves before the dusk settled in.

Rin struggled to keep hold of the feeling that centred her – the deep river of ability that always ran just at the edge of her awareness. If she wasn't careful, it would trickle away into that place inside her where it usually sat, unfulfilled but always waiting. She couldn't afford that now; if she was going to face whatever had happened to Ieuan and Gibb, she would need its strength more than ever.

As if Marta's words had not been proof enough that Ieuan hadn't made it out of the Capital, the fact that she was now standing in the place they had agreed to meet, without him, caused the pain of that loss to strike at her anew.

"Sit down, girl," Marta encouraged her gently.

Rin's jaw clenched. Somehow, standing felt like action to her, but if she were to sit for this tale, it would feel like giving up; like she had accepted that there was nothing more to be done about it, other than to sit down and hear it told.

"Oh for goodness' sake, Erin!" Marta's voice was harder now. "Stop that and sit down before you fall. I've promised you'll hear it in full , but it won't make the retelling any easier with me worrying that you're about to collapse at any moment."

Rin huffed, reluctantly acknowledging the truth of the old woman's words, and finally gave in to her body's plea for rest. She felt herself thump heavily onto the damp earth and wondered if she might not just sink through the soft ground under such a heavy weight.

Marta had already made a camp, and there was a warm tea of mint and bark steaming in a pot slung over a glowing cookfire. As she watched Marta stoking the embers, Rin guessed the old woman must have been waiting there a while before she had heard their shouting.

"Well, I suppose I'll start at the beginning of it all." Marta sighed. "You know about the Alliance now and the truth of what happened on harvest day. No point in retreading that old ground." She stopped, clearly pondering how best to begin such a vast thing, then, muttering to no one in particular, she added, "So much has happened, it's hard to know where to start."

Rin had some experience of how difficult it was to try to organise and shape momentous events into a sensible pattern for the retelling, so she didn't interrupt the woman's long pause. The others had all taken seats around the fire, and none of them broke the growing silence either.

"Perhaps I should start with what happened immediately after we left the cabin," Marta said eventually, spooning out the dark brew into cups.

Rin waited patiently as the old woman took a moment to fish a large chunk of the bark from her tea before offering it to her. Then, her story began.

At first, Marta recounted what Rin had already seen for herself: how Gibb had insisted they flee the hut together, how he had carried her on his back to the edge of the swamp and then beyond. Marta had shared her fear that they wouldn't make it, and then her relief as the mob had so suddenly seemed to give up the chase. Rin knew they hadn't just given up – they had discontinued their hunt for Marta and Gibb only when she and Lark had presented themselves as their true target. Rin decided to keep that fact to herself for the time being, not wanting to interrupt Marta, certain she was not ready for the kind of lecture sharing that truth might bring. Lark, however, had other ideas.

"Gave up? They didn't just 'give up', Marta. Rin and I drew them off. Just be certain you remember that when it comes time for this great 'accounting for' you think we owe you."

Marta's mouth pinched. She didn't reply to the girl, but looked questioningly at Rin.

"Ieuan only promised we wouldn't go back," Rin offered, shrugging a little sheepishly. "He didn't promise I wouldn't try to keep you alive, or that I wouldn't draw them off."

It had felt like a perfectly reasonable justification when she had made it to Ieuan under the moonlight. Now, with the old woman's scowl to contend with, she suddenly felt less sure. She sipped the warm tea, pleasant and soothing on her throat.

"Hmm, that so, is it? Rin felt her grandmother's eyes scrutinising her. I shall make sure to close any loopholes when I make promises with you in the future then, girl."

Rin couldn't be sure, but she thought the old woman had almost smiled.

The darkness drew in around them as Marta recounted all that she and Gibb had done since the night they fled her home in the Dale. Despite the old woman's concerns, neither of the two of them had seen any other signs of further pursuit, but they hadn't been completely out of danger, for the swamp had opened up its jaws to swallow them whole. Marta hadn't been too concerned at first, relying on her years of experience to make up for the deterioration of her reflexes. What she hadn't counted on was Gibb.

"If there was a pink pool or a purple-toothed flower within walking distance, that man seemed determined to step right into the midst of it." She shook her head in exasperation. "At first, we had to travel quickly. We weren't confident they wouldn't try to hunt us down in the daylight, and we didn't know how fast they might be moving if they did." Her face turned regretful as she went on. "By the end of that first night, Gibb was covered in more burns and scratches than I'd seen in a month and I knew then we couldn't continue in that way. A few more days like that and it would've been a tattered corpse I'd be dragging through the swamp, not a man."

They had moved much slower after that, and the journey that had taken Rin two days took them almost a week. Gibb had fared slightly better once they no longer had to rush, and Marta had tried her best to keep him safe from the worst of it. Even then, he had managed to collect more injuries than she would have liked, for a friend as dear as he was. Most of these had been minor and not a cause for any real concern, but there had been a deeper gash on his right forearm that, despite her efforts, she suspected was going to fester. That was the problem with razor-grass. The initial cuts were bad enough if you stumbled into a patch, but the real danger came from the tiny, fine hairs of the plant that hooked into the skin. They could cause even a shallow cut to turn septic within a short time. Marta had seen it at the last second: the long thin blades that were just a little too green. She had thrown out her hand to drag him back, but not before his arm had touched the first of the leaves that quivered thirstily in the breeze. Even from such a light brush, the skin had split instantly.

The first spots of red blood prickled to the surface slowly and then, as Gibb turned his arm over to inspect it, the ooze began in earnest. At first, the old woman had encouraged the bleeding, hoping to flush out anything left in the wound, and bandaged it with fresh cloth from her travel pack. She had cursed aloud then: there were any number of plants and remedies available to her in this place, but they all needed time to brew or mature into a medicine, making them all as good as useless to her in that moment. A day later, as the red tendrils had begun to snake out from under the edge of the white cotton bandage, she'd known time was not a thing they had been afforded.

Later that night, they had finally broken through the last of the foliage that marked the boundary between that treacherous swamp and the newer perils of the Void. Under the cover of darkness, and with the smell of the Clag drifting on the night's breeze, they came out at the same patch of unguarded chain-link fence that Rin had come to know so well herself. Marta knew that they had arrived too late to go tracking down friends – that kind of thing was not done in the dark – not in a place like the Void. Instead, they'd hunkered down at the back of a white liquor still, warm from its recent use and remarkably clean for a bootlegger's brewery.

Between keeping watch for new dangers and the constant urge to check on her friend for signs of a fever, she hadn't slept much that first night. The rising sun brought relief that there had been no signs of trouble overnight, but by the morning she was sure that the unnatural heat on Gibb's brow had nothing to do with the warmth of the copper still beside them. That was when Marta had decided they would once again have to sacrifice some of her usual caution for speed. If she was going to treat the infection before it got too deep into his blood, she needed to find those few friends she held in the Void, sooner rather than later.

Gibb had been leaning heavily on Marta's arm and was beginning to stumble when they finally found what she was looking for. The first boy she spotted had been too quick for her, darting away before she could catch him. The second was not prepared for the extra reach of her staff. The small child tumbled across the smooth paving stones of the alley floor, leaving deep scuff marks in the dusty remnants of the midday Clag. Marta could see that he was frightened, even though he faced only an old woman and a man who by now could barely stand. Dirt smeared his cheeks and she almost felt sorry for the little urchin as he looked up at her from under a short fringe of scruffy brown hair, with large hazel eyes that had not yet had the chance to grow hardened.

"Boy, who holds this side of the Void?" she had asked him.

The boy's face quickly turned from fear to confusion, then lastly suspicion.

"That depends on who's asking?" he replied uncertainly. Then he reached out to pick up his hat, dusting it off as best he could with a sleeve that was almost equally as grubby.

"Does it, now?" The last time Marta had made this journey, the Partisan had controlled the whole of the northeast side, and a large part of the west too. "With consideration for what a young boy tells her, how would an old woman find a *sympathetic ear*, should she be looking for one that... supports such causes as her own?" She had phrased the question with care, unsure of how the once familiar political landscape of the Void now lay, and where allegiances had settled as a result.

"The usual places," the boy replied, squinting at her slightly.

Marta nodded. This one was smart: small and too scared to refuse to reply outright, but clever enough not to say much of anything in his answers. He had told her enough. However much of the Void the Partisan still held might be under question, but there wasn't a trader, thief or panhandler that ran a racket in the Void who didn't speak to him first. She moved her cloak and the three little silver jars flashed into sight before disappearing back beneath the thick folds. She'd made sure he had seen them, though.

"Tin-Man or the Marshal?" the boy said, suddenly more sure of himself.

Marta nodded. "Tin-Man."

"Blimey," the boy muttered, his suspicion finally giving way to surprise. "You're the Old Woman, ain't you? Then what did you trip me for? Didn't need to make me fall over. I've skinned my knees, I have." Though he complained, relief had spread over his honest little face. "Could've just asked me. The Partisan will be happy to see you. Might even be a reward in it for me. They all say there ain't been nothing good on the market since your redheaded girl, the one that was here, poking around in the Book-House."

Hearing Marta recount this part, Rin felt herself flush. She had never quite gotten around to telling Marta about her trip to the 'Lib-orary' and she didn't know she had been seen by anyone on that outing. It seemed so long ago now that she hadn't expected ever to have to confess to that small omission that bordered on a lie.

"Yes, girl. I know about your little excursion," Marta chided. "It seems like a pointless thing to worry about now, and I feel we have both already had our reckonings for the secrets we decided to keep. No use flogging a dead tusker, as they say."

For a moment, Rin felt like the child she had been only a few cycles of the moon ago. One who was still perturbed by the scoldings of her grandmother.

"Still," Marta continued, "I'll have it known from now on that this habit of bending the truth between you and me will have to stop one of these days."

Rin raised her eyebrows. After all, Marta's secrets had been a little more important than her one trip to the Lib-orary. Still, if the old woman was calling a truce, and one without reprimands, then Rin was happy to take what was offered. Especially now that she had only one true concern above all others, and not when the ground seemed so soft underneath her.

Rin realised her strength was ebbing away again – no doubt the current inside her had run out of force, just like the rest of her had. She took another sip of her tea, letting its warmth restore her tired soul. Nothing was going to derail her from hearing what had stopped Ieuan and Gibb from being here now.

The old woman's eyes never left Rin's face as she waited for an outward sign of agreement. Only once Rin nodded did she continue with her tale.

Marta and Gibb had followed the small boy through the alleys of the Void for a long time, and the Clag had begun to grow thick when she finally turned on their new guide.

"Boy, if you lead me in this misshapen circle of yours for one more lap, I will tan your behind until you are unsure where the leather of your breeches ends and your backside begins!" She had been willing to play her part for a while, as was expected in this game of cloak-and-dagger, but as Gibb sagged ever heavier against her, the old woman's patience, which was thin at the best of times, had worn through.

"Hey, don't get mad at me! Rules is rules. I don't make 'em," he'd said, caught between embarrassment and petulance, "I just do as I'm told, is all. I had to check yous two had been here before. You know how it goes."

"Yes, yes, I know, but if this man dies today, the Partisan's protection will not keep me from fulfilling that promise, you understand?" She rattled her staff against the stones for emphasis as she tried to hitch Gibb a little higher onto her shoulder.

The boy chewed his lip for a moment longer, then, looking from the slumped and feverish man to the old woman, he nodded. After that, he led them in earnest, even helping Marta to half-carry Gibb across the uneven ground, as best as a small boy could.

As they had made their next few turns, Marta realised they were moving away from the more inhabitable parts of the Void and towards the rubble and ruins. This was a part of the Void that had once been the Old Town, but now they called it the Midden Stacks. It was a place that, in its mouldering, still acted as a reminder of the Empire's destruction of what were once lowland homes. While some kind of order still existed within much of the Void, this part remained in the chaos it had been left to after the Fall, and time had only eroded it further.

The longer they walked, the more the debris had seemed to build up around them. Things Marta couldn't put a name to, things broken and long ago abandoned, lay strewn everywhere. It was hard to pick out individual items – large patches were coated in the thick grime caused by decades of exposure to the Clag. But even with that covering, and after all that time, she could still recognise the odd piece of a chair or a bed, a doll long ago lost to its owner, or an instrument used to make music, although Marta had no idea how to play it. All manner of fragmented and decaying things had been piled up in this place. Such waste and ruin made Marta shiver.

They struggled on through it all, regardless, further into the Stacks, where what was left of the Old Town structures had been so badly damaged that they were unfit for even the Void dwellers to try to reclaim. Some buildings had only the one wall standing, or else the heavy upper levels of larger homes had toppled into the smaller buildings below. Roofs were caved in, or else missing altogether, and every so often, one house or another would be left with nothing more than the foundations or a single chimney stack to mark that there had ever been anything built there at all.

As they continued on through the eerie landscape of waste, she could see that ahead of them rose towering piles of bric-à-brac, higher than some of the tallest buildings in the Void. The alleys back near the trading post were made from thick slabs of stone, carefully laid to pave the ground and then hemmed in by the high building walls. There was an order to it. Here, that uniformity gave way to the haphazard tracks and passageways that cut deep into the heaped Stacks of scrap and discarded belongings. The mountainous landscape of junk began to loom over them, casting shadows onto the deep valley floors below. The air had a strange smell to it... not foul or rotting – the things left here were much too old for that – but rather a metallic tang of rust and earth.

On the steep sides of the Midden escarpments, Marta spotted flaps that opened out here or there, consisting of a flat sheet propped open on two sticks. Often the tops of these panels were disguised by an odd assortment of items selected from the debris around them. She had tried to get a good look at a few of them, but every time they turned down a new avenue, the things would snap shut, disappearing seamlessly into their surroundings. Her eyes were sharp enough to catch the flash of movement, but whenever she tried to pick out exactly where it had been, she could see nothing but an unbroken expanse of junk. Only the occasional puff of smoke hinted at a quickly smothered cookfire.

Marta tried to keep count of the turns they made – left at a bed frame, left again at some rusting container that might have once been blue, right at an old music box, left again at a collection of broken green bottles – but she soon realised there was just too much of the stuff and too many turns to keep track of.

The boy had led them through those valleys of waste and then further on still, deep into narrow warrens carved into the vast Stacks. Then they passed under a section of fallen roof, but instead of exiting that tunnel of precarious wooden beams, tin cans and broken trinkets, there had suddenly been two great oak doors before her. These were not grimy, the handles well-polished by the frequent use of people's hands. Marta tried to see where the doors might lead, but she couldn't discern more than the panels before her.

She looked around at the odd collection of discarded items that had gathered in this place, trying to decide if this had happened by coincidence or by design. Either way, the rubble and the several coats of Clag that had accumulated over the years had perfectly hidden the building from sight. Marta wondered at what might lie behind such doors that appeared so well kept and grand. It seemed unlikely that the inside of such a place could continue that contrast.

Interrupting her contemplation, the boy they had followed into this foreboding tunnel knocked a short, complex rhythm on the thick wooden doors, and a small shutter opened at the top.

"What business you got with the Partisan, Freck?" a gruff voice questioned the boy.

"Ain't your place to be asking me about my business," the boy replied, with inflated confidence. "All you're supposed to ask me is if I know the words to enter, and I do. So let me in."

"All right then, little Freck, what's the 'words to enter'," he indulged the boy.

Marta watched as the boy's shining eyes darted from side to side and his shoulders rose up to his ears.

Cupping his hand to shield his mouth, he half whispered, "May the Empire rot," and darted backwards as if suddenly unsure if it was wise to have spoken such a thing aloud.

"Hmm," the voice responded. "Now, see, if you hadn't been so rude to me, Freck, it might be that I could let you in with an old passphrase like that. Especially with me being such an understanding fellow and especially seeing as how it has only changed just this very morning. But I'd have to ask myself what I would be teaching our young Stacklings if I were to do such a thing?"

The little boy's brow had furrowed and he began to chew on his lip again. Marta rolled her eyes. Normally she would consider a lesson in manners worth the delay, but *normally* there wasn't a fully grown man who had little more than the strength to keep his feet under him at her side. The boy pulled his dirty sleeve across his nose, revealing the thick smattering of freckles for which he was surely named.

"Could be that I did that hasty speaking the Partisan warned me about, Mr Boone, sir. If you could see your way to letting me in this time, I'll make sure as to mention your kindness to my ma the next time she is asking... sir."

Marta felt perhaps the boy's second 'sir' was overdoing it slightly, but then the deep voice was chuckling and the door had promptly swung open.

"Who are your friends, Freck?" the large man said, suddenly

more suspicious at the sight of the two strangers. "Better not be trouble you're bringing home to the Stacks?"

As Gibb tried to step inside, the last of his strength deserted him and he collapsed in through the door.

"Crikey, boy!" the man exclaimed, catching Gibb. "This one's halfway to dead. Get in here quick and stop fooling around out there."

There was a cacophony of shouting and hollering, as extra hands appeared to help the old woman bear her friend into the building.

If Marta had been foolish enough to expect anything of the room beyond the door, it hadn't been this. She marvelled at the thick stone arches before her, beautifully carved from some kind of rich, red masonry in layers and layers of complex intertwining patterns. Immediately above her was a long, thin balcony and then nothing but high ceilings. The walls still held windows, which had somehow remained intact, and bathed parts of the ground in a pool of coloured light that streamed through them. Where she had expected to see only gloom and torchlight, instead she felt the welcome glow of the sun. It had seemed odd, especially with the debris of the Midden Stacks that engulfed the ornate building, until she realised how they had done it. Great golden discs, carefully placed, reflected shimmering rays of the sunlight right into the furthest corners and darkest recesses of the room. There were rows of benches not unlike the ones in the harvest hall in the Dale, except these were twice as big, with thick, plush green cushions that stretched the length of each one. At the back of the room, opposite the door through which they had entered, some stairs led up to a raised area. This was laid with beautiful, white stone that had been kept clean of any dust – no small feat in a place like this – and right in the middle sat the Partisan.

Freck had run up to the man and started speaking quietly to him, occasionally pointing to the old woman as she stood waiting at the door, flanked by Boone and some other equally large men.

Even though she had been impressed with the building, Marta couldn't help but cock her head questioningly at the odd, middle-aged man. He was a little on the thin side, but in a wiry way that spoke of a strength that was not so unusual here. Not many in the Void carried any extra weight – that was a symptom of opulence almost no one in the lowlands could afford. At best, his garb could have been described as a garish costume, a macabre parody of the original design, which Marta had instantly recognised as the grey breeches and shirt of the Capital guards. It made her skin bristle instinctively, but that was where the likeness to the uniform ended. Overlaying the drab attire was a jacket that might have been bright red at one time, but age had long since given it a darker and more ruddy hue. Its long tails reached towards the ground, and its cuffs were marked with elaborate frayed black stitching. The shoulders were fringed with golden tassels that, like the rest of the coat, had become dull and tattered with age, and it hung open over the grey shirt. Marta supposed that it couldn't truly be closed, not with every other button missing. While she wasn't sure what to make of the ensemble, there was no denying that the look was striking.

"Welcome to the Hall of the Partisan," the man's voice had made her start as it echoed out across the room. All of the faces not already fixed on the newcomer's arrival had turned to survey them. "The kingdom of the lost and discarded, the broken and abandoned, where all who wish us well are in turn warmly welcomed in our Hall." He finished with a theatrical flourish, inclining his head slightly in a gesture somewhere between a nod and a bow.

Freck had already told the man much of what he needed to know, but Marta knew there would still be the expected exchange of guarded words and carefully chosen questions before the Partisan would be satisfied with her answers. When she had finished telling him what she felt he needed to know, he gazed at her, nodding.

"Well, this is indeed an honour," he said, finally. "To have such a masterful craftswoman in our humble abode."

Marta wasn't sure if she liked this man and his taste for the dramatic. He was irritating, especially when she had no time to waste, and yet she couldn't help but be impressed by the little stronghold this community had carved out of the ruins. Discarded people amongst discarded things, and yet they had survived.

The first thing she did was to trade her vials of elixir for shelter, and the Partisan sent for a healer of his own to help tend for Gibb. She was sceptical of the young boy who turned up at Gibb's bedside with his satchel of herbs and poultices; even more so when he told her the only cure for razor-grass was to cut away the infected tissue, followed by the usual treatment for a blood fever. When the youth opened his bag of blades, Marta grabbed the front of his shirt and cursed at him. Only the small groan that escaped Gibbs's lips stopped her from chasing him from the room there and then.

"You don't have any dried eye-of-the-morning blossom then, I suppose?" Marta had asked, trying to regain her composure. "I'd even settle for stewed black bark with tiger seed?"

"No, I..." the boy wavered, smoothing out the front of his shirt nervously before tucking away some kind of token he wore on a leather string around his neck. "No. I've never heard of those."

Marta groaned inwardly. She had seen tokens similar to his before, and the last thing she needed right now was a superstitious fool for an assistant. "You have a great deal to learn, Stackling, so stay close and keep your eyes open," she grumbled. "And when I'm done, the Partisan and I need to have a conversation about what passes for a healer around here."

Without her desired ingredients, Marta had been forced to agree that there was no other choice but to turn to blades. The concession pained her greatly, but Gibb was falling in and out of consciousness, and the brief moments he was awake were plagued with delirium and rambling. Luckily, the young healer did have powdered yellow-tree fungus, so they rubbed a pea-sized amount under Gibb's tongue. He stopped struggling quickly after that, already weakened by the infection, and in a few short moments his breathing became deep and even. Marta peeled open one of his eyelids to check he was truly sedated, and then they set about their gruesome work.

Marta nearly slapped the boy as he made to press the blade to Gibb's skin, intending to make his first cut.

"Damn it, boy, might as well take his whole arm off and be done with it. Give that to me." She snatched the blade, he boy, startled, gulping as she waved him closer. "Watch."

Carefully and slowly, she traced around the wound, lifting the dead and rotting flesh from the healthy tissues underneath. The smell was foul, and Marta tried to hide her concern that they had already left it too long to begin this work.

After the excisions, she had mixed a balm of her own from the boy's limited herbal stores and then wrapped the wound once more in clean linen. Then, all they could do was wait.

For three days, they changed Gibb's dressing morning and evening, and in that time Marta had begun to make a name for herself amongst the folk of the Midden Stacks. Every day, a queue would form in the Hall of the Partisan and she would see each one in turn, always with her young apprentice, Fievel, in tow. She had to concede he wasn't entirely useless, just young. Given enough time, and the right teacher, she reasoned he would become adequate enough, and so her days were filled.

In the morning, after seeing to Gibb, they would tend to those who queued in the Hall, applying ointments for sores that festered or wept, balms for itching spots, treatments for coughs and infections, stitches for cuts and dressings for burns. Then, in the afternoons, she and the young apprentice would set out to replenish their stores. After the disaster of taking Gibb through the swamps, Marta didn't dare bring the young boy in any deeper than the very edges nearest the Void, but there was enough richness from the plants on the border for what they needed. From these, she began to teach Fievel what to gather and where, how to brew or dry something to change its potency, and what to mix it with to change its purpose altogether.

To Fievel's horror, on the morning of the third day, he removed Gibb's bandage only to see a flood of pus and bright, red blood. He yelled for the old woman, who came rushing from her breakfast, but instead of being dismayed, she sighed with relief. Taking the bandage, she sniffed it, then smiled.

"No longer rancid, boy." Turning, she showed it to him. "It would seem the old knucklehead is not ready to die just yet."

Fievel paled a little, unconvinced.

"Not all pus is a bad thing, boy. Every so often, it's just the body healing." Marta pressed down firmly on the wound, drawing out more of the thick substance before she sniffed it a second time to be sure.

When she heard the thump as Fievel hit the floor, she tried

not to smile. She would make a proper healer out of him yet, and one that didn't rely on lucky talismans or surgical knives either.

Marta had known in truth that it would take years to pass on all the wisdom that she had been taught in much the same way, and in those first few days she had felt the pressure of time, as though something was continually slipping further and further away from her for each moment she remained in this place. Then, one morning, she realised that truly, she had nowhere else to be. At any given moment, she was thinking of Rin and Ieuan, but she could only hope that by now they were safe in the Cove. She held on to the belief that eventually, through those mysterious channels that all such news travelled, word would reach her and Gibb that the pair were safe.

Marta may have found a way to keep busy – a purpose to occupy and distract her from the endless waiting – but for Gibb, it had been different. Though it took a further week for him to regain enough strength to leave his bed, he had little else to do but fret. At first, he had been too sick to concern himself with speculation about his son. The simple act of eating broth would require that he slept for the best part of the day afterwards, but once he had regained his strength, the worry began to pull at him.

Marta tried encouraging him to join her and Fievel on their foraging walks, thinking it would help to build back his strength. But, too late, she realised his worry had consumed him. Day after day, he would sit at the chain-link fence waiting for a sign, or some word of what had happened.

"When he finally accepted that no word was coming, he began asking questions in the Void." Marta winced, looking at Rin, Lark and the boys in turn. "I warned him, tried to stop him even, but he wouldn't listen. Stories had reached the Void by then of an Immutavi girl and her friend who had escaped the

Empire, and over and over he asked if anyone had heard what had happened to those two children. He thought he was being careful, but it was only a matter of time." Marta reached down to take Rin's hands in her own, glancing at her cup.

Rin looked up at her questioningly.

"You were betrayed, girl. That night you came through the fence, they knew you were coming. They knew you were heading to the Palace to recover the archives, and they knew Ieuan was supposed to come looking for us down here in the Void." Marta paused, frowning.

Rin knew that she expected a greater reaction to such a revelation, but she simply wasn't shocked. She had heard this before. Her father had all but told her as much, as he had mocked their efforts that night in the Palace.

When Rin didn't answer, Marta continued, "One afternoon, Gibb never returned to the Stacks. He was always back before nightfall, and so I was worried. I had just prepared a pack and found Freck to use as a guide when news of Ieuan's arrival in the Void reached us."

This was it. Rin could tell by Marta's tone; by the sad, sorry look in her eyes. They were getting to the bones of it now.

"I didn't go to Ieuan straight away," Marta admitted. "I'm sorry, Rin. I should have, but I couldn't face him. Not until I knew what had happened to his father. Freck and I spent most of the night looking for some hint of what had happened. I had suspicions of my own by then, and so we had to be careful. Couldn't go shouting it out like that knuckle... like Gibb had." The pauses were beginning to stretch longer as Marta looked for words that could somehow soften the pain of what was to come. "Once I knew for sure, I went to find Ieuan." She was shaking her head. "He seemed so calm. Too calm, really. I should have known then that he would do something foolish. Stiff-headedness does usually run in the male line that way." She bristled and set her face. "He led me here. Told me about the Alliance's plan; well, at least the part about the rendezvous and where Gibb and I were supposed to fit in. I hadn't expected to find you like this." Marta paused again to take in the girl and her injuries.

This time, Rin couldn't wait. "Where are they, Marta?" she asked, already knowing what the old woman would say. She knew as surely as she could feel the earth under her, but she needed Marta to say it. Needed those words to penetrate the thick numbness that had begun to settle on her. Needed to hear it said to seal her belief that the unbearable had happened.

Marta nodded once curtly, the same way she did before administering some treatment that would be foul, but for the best. As Rin took her last sip of tea, the old woman answered her.

"They must've been watching him for days, must've known who he was. They snatched him up off the streets that evening as he made his way back to the Stacks. There's only one place they take Tavi conspirators like Gibb, and Ieuan knew that as well as I did."

Rin felt her eyes grow heavy as she nodded. "The Tunnels."

"Yes, girl. That same night, after I saw Ieuan, he went back to find his father. I had tried to warn him something wasn't right, but damn me if the boy couldn't move faster than I could. By the time I reached the fence, they already had him, caught and trussed like a summer hen for roasting. He didn't even try to run or fight. Just let them take him. Let them take him to the Tunnels. I'm not proud of it, mind, but there was nothing to be done by then. So I came to the rendezvous as we'd agreed. I made this tea and I waited for you, and here we are."

Rin felt the swamp begin to spin. She needed to get up.

Needed to go after Ieuan and Gibb. At first, she thought it was the panic that she knew so well, except her heart was beating slowly and she felt more numb than she could ever recall having felt before. The empty cup slipped from her fingers as she felt the strength leave her limbs. As the cup rolled beside her feet, she knew then what the old woman had done.

"Marta, how could you? How—"

Rin's last question would remain unasked. The blackness swallowed her whole.

CHAPTER FOUR
LESSONS LEARNED

Rin was warm and comfortable as she drifted in the place between asleep and awake. She could hear Marta talking to someone, but it seemed distant and unconcerning. Someone sick must have come to visit their hut for the old woman's medicines and craft. Rin hoped they would leave soon; she didn't want to talk to any of the villagers today. She didn't want to have them smile in her grandmother's face and then whisper behind her back.

It was only as those voices became raised in argument that Rin realised something wasn't right. She rolled over, thinking to bury her face in her soft pillow, trying to muffle the angry tones that jarred against her peaceful rest.

"Was it really necessary, Marta?" a male voice asked.

"I lost the first two trying to be reasonable. I won't risk her becoming the third—"

"I don't know," another voice butted in. "It still feels wrong."

"You young ones and your feelings," Marta grumbled, shaking her head. "Flapping your gums at me like the squirming in your gut is supposed to mean something."

"Mart—"

The old woman cut the voice off. "Had much success getting her to slow down yourself? Did your *feelings* get her to listen to you when you told her she needed rest? Or listen about anything at all, for that matter?"

Silence followed.

"That's what I thought," Marta continued. "Don't confuse your 'feelings' with proper thinking. Wisdom and feelings are not the same thing, and we don't get to hide behind the latter when we know what needs to be done. She needs rest. Needs time to fix all that's been broken. So much damage – too much, all at once, even for her. The girl is still mortal, damn you all. I'll not have her life thrown away over a few reckless decisions – especially not for the sake of a good day's rest."

Their words were beginning to become clearer to Rin now, no longer empty noise that annoyed her ears, but sounds with meanings she could attach to them. She felt as if she had been asleep for a very long time, and her mouth was dry. She opened her eyes and was surprised to see that it was dark, although she couldn't yet be sure why that should shock her. At first, each blink seemed to take an age, as though the lids of her eyes had become impossibly heavy. Then, suddenly, she knew she wasn't in the hut anymore; that it was soft marsh moss beneath her body, not the stuffed straw mattress and bedding of home.

Rin tried to remember why she was here. She had a feeling there was somewhere else she was supposed to be, something else she was supposed to be doing. She shook her head gingerly, trying to clear her mind, and then realised she had expected the motion to be painful, but it wasn't. Sitting up, she stretched her neck from side to side. Pleased with the ease of that motion, she tried rolling out her shoulders and turning her wrists in circles. It felt good now, but why was that? *What happened? Have I been sick?* She couldn't remember. Everything was still so murky, like she was trying to sift the memories through the thick afternoon Clag.

It hit her all at once. The Clag. That was what it was called back in the Void. The Capital was back there, too, and the

Tunnels. *Ieuan and Gibb are in those Tunnels.*

She gasped, the haze that had been clouding her mind vanishing with her intake of breath.

Sitting up, Rin saw the old woman was watching her and she smiled, relieved that Marta, at least, was safe in this place. As her eyes fell to the empty cup still at her feet, all traces of that relief fled. Marta had betrayed her.

She was standing before she had time to think about the action, and only then did she remember that, not long ago, such a thing had been painful and difficult. Nodding to herself, she was comforted such troubles no longer seemed to limit her. That would be important now she had to go back to the Capital.

The others had noticed her rising sharply, and all conversation around the camp stopped. Rin saw the old woman take a deep breath and then set her shoulders as she stepped towards her. She knew that stubborn look all too well, and in the time she had lived with the old woman, she had learnt it was best to speak first.

Clearing the dry croaking from her throat, she asked, "How long did you keep me asleep?" and heard the cold accusation in her tone.

"Not as long as I meant to, I can tell you that much," Marta replied, pursing her lips. "But a little over a full day has passed since you finished your tea."

Rin nodded, irritated that the old woman didn't even have the grace to show regret for what she'd done.

"That's right, girl," Marta went on. "I stand by it. I'd do it again too."

Rin looked up to the sky, trying to gauge how many hours it might be until sunrise. She could hear the sounds of night creatures, and the air was cold and dewier than it would be if the dawn was near. She fixed her eyes on the thick canopy above and a strange clarity fell over her – a recognition of her purpose. The gnawing in her stomach finally eased, as she realised there was little use in contesting it anymore. She would have to go back to the Capital. She knew she should be angrier with the old woman, but there were more important things to do.

"I will be going back for them now, I think."

It was not a question so much as a statement of intent. She had already begun to turn to leave when Reece's voice made her pause.

"We can't stop you. Not even all of us together could stop you for long, if you are set on it."

Rin wanted to ignore him. Wanted to keep walking, knowing that whatever it was he intended to say was designed to keep her from returning to the Capital.

"I won't be one of the ones who tries to stop you," Reece continued, "but you should know that they're already waiting at the fence for you. Lark went to check yesterday. None of us will get back into the Void undetected that way again."

Rin had meant to keep her eyes fixed straight ahead, unwilling to draw them away from the path she intended to take, but now she glanced at Lark suspiciously. Could she trust that the girl cared what happened to Ieuan or Gibb? Would putting distance between the Empire and herself, and more importantly her brother, be enough to prompt the self-serving girl to lie? Rin felt a familiar frustration beginning to build inside her. There was something else Reece wasn't saying, and she was sure it was the thing she didn't want to hear most of all.

"Either you say it now or you let me leave," Rin said, trying to hold back the anger that bubbled not far from the surface. "I am not so naïve as to believe that there aren't other ways to enter the Void besides that damn fence."

"You could go back." It was Magnus who stepped forward now. "With our help, you could even get both of them out, although I don't know how." His face changed, suddenly as weary as her own. "But if we do, that will be it. No one else will ever come home from that place after that. They won't make the same mistakes if we try to take the Tunnels a second time. You can choose Ieuan and Gibb, but it's a choice you make at the cost of all the others still down there."

Rin stared at him, incredulous. Of all people, she would have thought Magnus would understand. Surely, he knew that she couldn't leave Ieuan in that place where he himself had once suffered so badly. She turned away from him. It didn't matter if they wouldn't help her. It didn't matter if they refused to understand. She didn't need them anyway. She tried to close her ears to their words, knowing she couldn't listen to any more of this, not when she needed to harden her heart for the task ahead.

"He knew what he was doing," Magnus went on. "Marta told us he expected to be taken; that he knew you would come back for them all once it was time. That was the choice he made."

Rin searched their faces desperately. Surely *one* of them must appreciate what she had to do?

Then she saw it.

Lark was waiting, poised, her backpack already slung over her shoulder and her face obviously impatient at the delay. Rin felt shocked as she saw her own demeanour mirrored before her. *Is that who I'm becoming? Someone who only cares about their own? Someone who will happily sacrifice all others for the sake of their own needs?* She thought of all those she'd met at the Cove: Geira's face flashed into her mind, then Alyssa's. Did her own heartache absolve her of adding to theirs?

In that moment, she knew it did not, and suddenly shame

replaced the hardened determination she had been clinging to a moment before. Looking around, she saw that not one of them could meet her eyes, except for Reece. His eyes were fixed on her and the pain in his expression spoke of a deeper sympathy.

"So what now?" Rin choked, barely able to speak the words that would take her further still from Ieuan.

"We go back to the Cove. We take back what we've found, and we plan." Magnus could see he had her attention now, and there was a feverish intensity to his tone as he added, "We make a plan for all of them. We use what you stole from the Capital to learn how to get the chips off, how to get them out of the Tunnels, how to get them clear of the Void, and finally how to take a party of that size through the Ashlands."

Rin wondered how Magnus could sound so sure of those things. When she thought about the magnitude of what lay before them, it suddenly felt impossible.

"You really think we can do it?" she asked him, pleading for any reassurance that he could give.

"I don't know. If any of those parts fail, then the whole thing collapses and a lot of people are going to get hurt, or worse. A lot will depend on what's in that pack. Maybe more of it will come down to dumb luck. The Alliance still has friends in the Void. It may be that some of them know another way into the swamps, but it's the Ashlands I'm most worried about. Taking a large party through there... I just don't know if it's possible."

"Well, I may be able to help you with that particular part," Marta said vaguely, speaking for the first time since she had answered Rin's accusations about the drugged tea.

Lark rolled her eyes. "And how is that, old woman?" The edge to her words made it clear she considered Marta just another inconvenience she would have to accommodate. "Quite honestly,

I've been wondering how we'll drag your old bones across that plain in the first place."

Marta bristled. "Perhaps I'll tell you, girl, and perhaps I won't. But beyond that I'll only warn you once not to try laying a hand on these 'old bones', let alone try dragging them anywhere."

Lark's face twisted bitterly.

"Ha!" Marta barked a short laugh. "Girl, I was old and hardened enough to scowl while you were still at your mother's teat. If you think the way you wrinkle your face has the power to move me at all, best you think again."

It was the rustling behind them that broke the tension between the two, and instinctively, Rin closed her will around that familiar focus at the centre of herself. As she did, she instantly became aware that it was a person. Her heart skipped as, for a moment, she believed Ieuan had somehow made it – that he had escaped and come back to her...

The unfamiliar scent of another young man reached her, shattering that fragile fantasy. Then she could hear the muttering and cursing of a stranger's voice where she had hoped instead for Ieuan's. Whoever he was, he was struggling hard, and she knew then that not only was this person not Ieuan, but whoever it was, they were definitely not a threat. Just an unlucky soul fighting to make their way through the savagery of the swamp.

The loss of that moment of hope was crushing.

"Someone's coming," she told the others in a flat, empty tone that echoed her defeat, watching as they all braced for the attack she already knew would not come.

The tall stranger stumbled rather than walked into the clearing, shaking his head and trying to wipe the thick web of a spindly-legged scuttler from his hair. Swatting at a creature that was no longer there, he startled as he became aware of the group around him, all but one of them poised to fight.

"Oh... eh, hello. I... I was looking for—"

"Fievel?" Marta questioned. "Boy, what fool's notion has taken you here?"

The young man looked at the old woman sheepishly. "Well... I was worried. When you didn't come back, I asked around, and Freck told me what had happened. You know Freck – at first, I thought his imagination had run wild – but then when I saw the guards at the fence, and heard about Gibb, well... I thought you might need my help." He mumbled the last few words, still swatting uselessly at the air above his head.

Marta sighed. "You did, did you?"

Clearly this was another complication the old woman didn't need, yet where Rin had expected Marta to be angry, she was surprised to see the faintest trace of fondness in the old woman's expression.

"Does the Partisan know you came here?" Marta asked.

"Yes. Oh yes, I asked him before I left, of course," the boy jabbered on. "He said he would tell everyone we'd left to replenish the stores, but that we would be back soon. Then he made me promise I would be back, and then Boone showed me how to get into the swamps from beneath the Stacks."

Fievel had an honest face, and Rin could tell he was nervous. She wondered in a detached way if he always rambled this much, or if that was just the effect of traipsing through the perils of the swamp only to be confronted by six strangers. She saw his eyes take in her red hair and she guessed that he at least suspected she was the Tavi girl the guards were searching for.

"Well, at least you got one thing right," Marta muttered, "but I'm afraid we won't be heading back there anytime soon."

Rin noticed that Fievel's face perked up at Marta's thin

approval. She guessed then that he knew praise from the old woman was scarce, but meaningful, on the odd occasion she conceded to give some.

"It's not really all that far back to the Stacks, and I'm sure your friends would be welcome too?" Fievel continued, hesitantly. Evidently, he had already begun to regret his decision to follow after the old woman.

"No, boy. We can't go back there. Not now, and I don't see any choice but to take you with us, at least some of the way." Marta was clearly still considering the problem aloud. "Can't send you back on your own. It's a mercy you've made it this far without getting yourself hurt." Her face hardened. "I don't know what you were thinking... Just step where I tell you to step and try to keep up. Remember Gibb's arm? Well, he got that by stepping where he ought not to, so let that sharpen your focus should you get tired of following my instructions."

Rin saw the gulp the boy took and, by the fear in his expression, she knew he would do as Marta told him.

"He'll need to wash, too," Rin added dryly.

The boy flushed visibly. "The audacity, madam! I can assure you I bathe quite regularly," he said indignantly. "The idea that all of us who live in the Stacks stink is just unfounded Void slander."

Rin didn't know what 'audacity' meant, but she could tell by his face that it wasn't something good. She couldn't help but grin bemusedly at the disgruntled boy. "And *I* can assure you I have never heard anything of the sort," she said, mimicking his words, "but unless you want every spindly-legged scuttler within a mile of us following you, you had better wash off *all* of that webbing. They're none too pleased when someone destroys their home, and they'll come looking for the cause. The scent of that webbing will draw every one of them to you like bees to a hive. But it's your choice, of course," she added, shrugging.

Fievel's eyes widened in horror and he was already taking strides towards the nearest pool, which glistened with a pink sheen, when Marta shouted after him.

"For goodness' sake, boy, do you have wool between your ears? Not *that* pool. Not unless you want to take off every hair on your head alongside those cobwebs." Marta shot Rin a scowl. "Best you take better care of that boy. Right now, he's the only one of us who knows for sure how to get out of these godforsaken swamps without bringing down every Capital guard on our heads."

Rin's heart sank. Marta was right; she shouldn't have teased Fievel like that. None of this was his fault, but something inside her hurt so badly, and in some strange way, it felt better to see someone else hurting a little, too.

It didn't take long for the boy to strip down and wash himself and his clothing. She had thought he would have to travel in his wet garments, as she had done often enough, but she was wrong. Instantly the three brothers pulled a mismatched bundle of spare clothing from their packs and offered them to Fievel. The odd collection was not exactly flattering, but they didn't fit him too badly, and they would be much more comfortable than his wet clothes after a few hours' travel. Soon enough, they were re-ordering their packs and getting ready to move on.

"So, do we continue towards the Ashlands?" Ivor asked tentatively, as though trying to avoid causing yet another argument.

Marta gave Lark a hard look and the pair held the tension of their gaze for a long moment. Finally, Lark shrugged, indicating she didn't care which way they went, as long as it was far from here.

"No," Marta said finally, "not east towards the Ashlands. We need to go a little further north first."

"Why?" Torsten asked. "What's in the north of these swamps?"

"The answer to how we're going to get those people home," Marta replied ambiguously. "He'll take some convincing, mind, but we'll remind him just what he owes us if we have to."

"Well, fall in behind the old woman," Lark sighed dramatically, making it abundantly clear that she considered Marta's decision a terrible waste of time.

Rin knew that coming back here at all was something Lark had only reluctantly agreed to for the sake of her brother.

Torsten looked as though he had more questions, but Lark was already shoving them all into a line.

"It's time we get moving!" Lark continued to bustle everyone along. "We've been here too long already, and if *that one* can catch up to us" – she pointed at Fievel – "it's only chance that's saved us from a full guard doing the same."

Although they were deep in the swamp, and she could see nothing but thick foliage in every direction, Rin took one last look westward, back towards the Capital. She knew it wasn't luck that had kept the guards away; they were simply waiting for her to come back, sure that she was the kind of person who wouldn't leave a friend behind. The knowledge only added to her shame. This first step might be the hardest she had ever taken; the final admission that she was going to leave Ieuan behind.

Rin closed her eyes as his face flooded her mind. She could still feel what his chest felt like under her cheek and could almost smell his skin, the way it was when it was warmed under the sun. Still, she knew what he would want her to do. Since the moment she heard he had gone back, she knew what he would have expected of her. Ieuan would never accept her returning to the Capital for him and Gibb alone; that wasn't who he was.

Was it who *she* was, though? It felt to Rin like it could be. The thought of losing him now was unbearable. If she went back – if she just appeared down there in those Tunnels – would he really refuse to go with her? He might just be stubborn enough. She knew him. Ieuan would choose to protect others he did not even know if he thought that was the right thing to do.

Rin paused as she considered the idea that she could force him. Perhaps it didn't matter what he wanted – she could drag him out if she had to. Suddenly, the image of Reece struggling with Tilly surfaced in her memories, and she cringed away from it sharply. She knew then that if she chose to cross that line with Ieuan, his forgiveness was not guaranteed to her.

"We'll come back for him." It was Reece's voice that pulled her from her thoughts. "When it's time, whatever else happens, I'll come with you and we'll get him back."

Rin turned to look at him, gratitude in her eyes.

"Maybe we really can get all of them out," he added, holding her pack out to her.

Inside that pack was the oiled leather roll that held everything he still needed to help Tilly. She could tell by the way he offered it to her that this was a last request for help – to complete this thing they had started together – and beneath that gesture was the offer of a pact.

Rin reached out to grab the bag and for a moment they both held it. Then, he inclined his head to her in acknowledgement, and she found herself nodding back in agreement of their unspoken terms.

As she turned her back on the Capital, she saw Lark watching the exchange. The slim girl rolled her eyes again and sighed, and

Rin knew then she had not only secured Reece's promise of help but, however reluctantly, Lark would come back with them too.

CHAPTER FIVE
ACTIONS AND INTENTIONS

They had been travelling northwards for the last two days. During that time, Rin had kept to herself, unwilling to be drawn out of her dark thoughts and the misery they brought. She walked apart from the others as much as she could, and it still grated on her to see how they had all so quickly accepted Ieuan's absence. It felt wrong that they should resume their normal ways when everything was so lost or broken for her.

She watched on in irritation as the three brothers tried to recount all that had happened since she and the old woman had parted ways. Occasionally, they asked Rin to add in some piece of her own story; at other times, Marta tried asking Rin questions directly, but Rin only replied in short, one-word answers where she could, or else grudgingly gave remarks when pressed. Sometimes Rin wondered if Marta was trying to share something important with her, but the conversation faltered every time. She wasn't ready to speak to her yet. She had not forgiven her for the drugged tea. Part of her knew she was being unfair, but it was easier to be angry with the old woman for letting Ieuan go back for his father alone than it was to blame the boy whose life hung so precariously in the balance.

It was only as they made camp on the third night, while they sat around the fire chewing fresh rabbit and the hard ration biscuits they had brought, that Rin's curiosity finally overcame her despair.

"Where are we going, Marta?" she asked quietly. Though she had no appetite, she forced down each bite mechanically, knowing she would need sustenance later.

"Not much further now," Marta replied, maintaining that same vagueness she had adopted when first asked.

It didn't make any sense to Rin. The old woman had implied that she knew a way to avoid the dangers of the Ashlands, but Rin couldn't see how three days' travel north would change anything. Magnus had told her once that people had tried to find other ways to make the crossing before now, but the treacherous terrain stretched on endlessly, only getting more unstable the further a person went. Looking sideways at Marta, Rin felt a growing resentment building in her chest. *Why did we risk our lives crossing such a treacherous place if there was another, safer route all along?* She was about to voice that thought when a rustling behind them caused them all to startle. The old woman was on her feet with her staff raised only moments after the others.

"Blimey, Lark," Torsten muttered peevishly as the girl skulked out of the darkness, smiling smugly. "Is now really the time to be sneaking around in the dark? As if the last few days haven't been bad enough—"

"Oh Torsten, always so twitchy," Lark replied in a light-hearted tone that did not match the tension of the moment.

As she spoke, her eyes never left Marta's, almost as though she was examining a puzzle that she didn't yet have all the pieces to. The old woman muttered something under her breath as Lark casually slinked back towards the glow of the fire.

As she passed Rin, she gave a conspiratorial smile and whispered, "Just how *old* is that 'old woman'?"

Rin knew then that the girl had spooked them all on purpose.

Was she trying to test Marta? To see if she was too old or frail for such an undertaking? The old woman had been an 'old woman' for as long as Rin could remember, and she knew that was a little unusual. People in the lowlands rarely grew to be old. In fact, she knew none who spoke of tending babes who were now fully grown, with children of their own. Few in the Dale had ever held the title of grandmother for long, even if Marta's own appointment to that office had been a fiction of their own design.

She watched a moment longer as Lark stretched out on the fur of her bedroll, and that familiar feeling washed over her: an inclination that, once again, there was more going on that she didn't understand. She shook her head, trying to clear the nagging feeling. It was the swamp air that kept Marta healthy; that was all. Her house was free from the dust and ash that settled on the villagers' homes. Rin paused then, uneasy. That was the same lie she had believed once before. Her brow creased as she tried to make sense of why this should bother her now. Then she shook her head, dismissing the trouble. She had enough problems to concern herself with already, without worrying that Marta might not see another winter moon or slip away from her before they even reached the Cove.

It was this realisation that finally thawed the impenetrably cold wall she had built between herself and the old woman. Marta had always seemed so formidable to Rin that it just didn't seem possible that she might succumb to anything at all, never mind something as insidious as time. Rin suddenly wanted to be held, the way Marta had held her as a child, with her face pressed into the old woman's apron. She wanted to feel safe within the strength of those arms that had always been so capable of protection and forgiveness. But she was no longer a child, so instead, she turned to Marta, only to realise the old woman had been watching her, face full of concern. Rin paused, worried that her anger might return, but instead she only felt a longing for the closeness that they had shared before.

Quietly enough that the others wouldn't hear, Rin spoke. "Good night, dear one, and go to sleep."

It was part of a rhyme the old woman used to say to her as she'd tucked the covers under her chin. Rin had been plagued by that recurring nightmare as a child – the one that gave her flashes of her life before the swamp – which had so often left her shaking and afraid. One night, when Rin had been too scared to sleep, Marta had followed the sounds of sniffling and squeaking to her bedroom. Thus began a little ritual between the two of them. Marta had promised her that the song was a spell given to her by a fairy queen, designed to keep away dark dreams. Marta had told her if she closed her eyes and believed in those words hard enough, the nightmares would stop, and for the most part, they had. It was only once she had gotten too old to believe in fairy queens and magic songs that the nightmares had returned. But even then, they had continued the tradition, and not a single night had passed under the same roof without Rin and Marta saying those words to one another before they turned in for the night.

It was the first thing Rin had said to her grandmother that had not been tinged with frustration or anger since she had drunk the tea. The meaning of it was not lost on Marta.

"May the dreams you dream be well and sweet," she whispered back, her eyes glistening. "Good night, little one."

Although Rin had not expected it, for the first night in a long time, she found restful sleep.

When the sun rose the next morning, they continued their trek northward, and with the growing distance, Rin felt something inside her shift. Now that she was too far away to change her mind and turn back for Ieuan, the importance of getting back to the Cove with the stolen archives began to pull at her, knowing that they could only return for her friend once they had formed a plan. This created a new urgency in her and, whenever they had to stop for too long or found themselves pushed off course by the swamp itself, the time wasted grated on her.

It was around noon when Marta called them to a halt once more. At first, Rin thought it was just another water break; there seemed nothing unusual about the spot. They'd had to stop more often than Rin would have liked, and always for Fievel to catch his breath or to remedy some problem he had unknowingly floundered into. Still, she had to admit that after his initial hesitations, the boy was beginning to grow in confidence. Torsten, Magnus and Ivor seemed to have taken to the gangly youth, welcoming him into their group as though he were just another brother. Where the tall boy had been nervous and unsure before, he now seemed to be thriving amongst their friendly jostling. It was only the ungainly way he moved his limbs – sharp, angular jerks that cut across his own purpose – that revealed he was not accustomed to physical activity the way the others were.

Rin wondered how a boy raised in the Void, who could speak so finely, had so quickly befriended a group of Tavi. There was something odd about the way he had not seemed surprised by their tales of trouble and adventure that made Rin hesitant to trust him.

If Fievel had become more comfortable with the three brothers, the same could not be said about Lark. At times, she seemed to stalk the awkward boy, always waiting for just the right moment to sway past him, or to catch his eye and smile ever-so-slightly too knowingly. Then the girl would watch – Rin would not have been surprised to hear her purring – as Fievel jumped as though scalded or else flushed red and stammer his apologies, clutching absentmindedly at the token that hung around his neck.

"What's the holdup?" Ivor asked.

"This is it." Marta held up her hand, looking pleased with herself.

"This is *what* exactly?" Lark sneered, drawing her eyes away from the game she was playing with Fievel. "Your favourite picnic spot?"

"This is how we're going to cross the Ashlands," Marta snapped back.

Rin had to admit that Lark's assumption seemed more likely, but she held her tongue, knowing better than to voice her doubts before she had heard all Marta had to say.

"There's nothing here but more swamp," Lark sighed, as though she had known all along that this senile old woman would lead them to nought. "Well, unless you count us and what looks surprisingly similar to a patch of razor-grass about to shred us to pieces."

"Oh, it's razor-grass alright," Marta agreed, nodding to Fievel as though to emphasise its dangers. She shuffled closer to the patch of shivering green. "I should know. I planted the stuff."

That surprised Rin: after lumpsuckers, razor-grass had to be her second-least favourite thing in the swamps. She supposed it was all just nature's way, but she hated how razor-grass survived on the death of living things. The only way it could spread its seeds was by hooking those hair-fine spores into the skin of passing animals lured to it by the promise of its rich, green sustenance. When an unfortunate creature eventually succumbed to the infection caused by its festering wounds, a new patch of the stuff would take root within the corpse. This provided a wealth of nutrients for the young plant and, in the otherwise harsh marshland arena, the seedlings would thrive where other species struggled to compete. The idea that anyone would spread the growth of such a dangerous thing on purpose was inconceivable.

"Now, where did we put those damned chains?" Marta had begun prodding her long staff into the grass, careful to stay just out of reach of the vicious plant, which quivered at her closeness.

That was another thing Rin hated about razor-grass. It looked like the stuff was alive, almost as though it could think for itself. Which, in a way, she supposed it could. Razor-grass could sense the heat of living things in the air and, regardless of the breeze, it would sway closer, ever hopeful of snaring a host.

"What are you up to, old woman?" Lark questioned, seeming almost amused.

Marta ignored her and continued with her methodical probing, muttering to herself, "They'd better not be rusted through or it'll take a week to weave enough leaves to do the thing right."

"Listen," Lark continued, her irritation showing now, "we've wasted enough time on this scheme of yours. Everyone knows there is only one way to cross the Ashlands. Stop stalling. There is no need to be so proud; my offer to drag you across it is still val—"

They all heard it at the same time. Instead of the dull thump of her staff on the damp earth, a tinny ring of wood on metal filled the air. Now it was Marta's turn to smile.

"Young ones, always so sure they know all there is to know;

never stopping to remember who it was that taught them in the first place." She passed the staff through the long grass. "It wasn't for you to know that we all agreed, long ago, that no one would use this way anymore."

"Wasn't for us to *know*?" Lark hissed.

"It was for the best – we couldn't take the risk that an Empire guard would follow someone here. If they found this place, the safety of the Cove was over." Marta took a deep breath. "The Empire might think the Ashlands keep the lowlanders within their reach, but for years beyond counting the opposite has been true for the Cove. The Ashlands keep the Empire wolves from their door."

Lark's eyes flashed dangerously and Rin knew she was considering the idea that Marta and her secrets were to blame for her risking her brother's life each time they had been forced to make the Ashlands crossing.

"Yes," Marta confirmed, acknowledging Lark's thoughts with a hardness in her voice. "I knew what dangers we left you to face. I know how bad it can get up there on the surface. That there could be trouble if you weren't careful. That all of you might get hurt, or worse, if you made too many mistakes." She looked at each of the young Tavi in turn, lingering on Rin a moment longer. "It is not a forgiving place, but I knew you could make it, and I would face it with you too if circumstances weren't different now."

Rin thought she heard an edge of doubt in Marta's voice, and she knew the old woman was thinking about what the three brothers had told her of their last crossing. That had been the first time Rin had seen the Gen1, and they had all almost been killed inside a rusty iron cage while she fought for their lives atop it.

"But things *have* changed," Marta continued, "and, like it or not, there is only one way to get all the Tavi from the Tunnels back to the Cove alive. So, I will show you the way, and you'd best learn it well. When the time comes, you won't need to take them across the Ashlands – you will take them underneath." She tapped the iron links with her staff before adding, "Cornelius is not going to like this one bit, but he still owes me a favour."

"*Cornelius* is involved in this?" Ivor asked, his face suddenly ashen.

Marta looked with concern at the three brothers for a moment. "I think you three will like it even less than he will. Still, we'll have to use this route this one last time. When we evacuate the Tunnels, we'll destroy it behind us."

Silence followed, as each one in turn tried to make sense of what they were hearing.

Rin felt as though her wits had been rattled from her head. It was too much to think that Marta knew the cantankerous old man they had met deep below the Ashlands, never mind that they had built a maze of secret passageways that linked her world and his together.

"I don't mean to doubt you, Marta," Magnus said uncertainly, "but are you sure it's safe down there?"

Rin had to admit his question echoed her own apprehension. She had seen how deep some of the rifts ran and how angry and hot the earth was underneath that thin crust. It was not a comforting thought to have to return to those depths. Marta paused just long enough to let Rin know she must have had concerns of her own. When she spoke, it was as though she were recalling a memory from long ago that had faded with time.

"Am I sure? No, not sure. Cornelius was sure, though. He was always convinced that this passage runs within a seam of old rock. He had other words for it, of course, but he knew it was a kind of old rock that had been pressed hard by the earth for thousands of years." She seemed to become surer of herself as she went on. "He said *that* was why the splits and rifts never tore it apart. Not when there was softer rock to break all around it. I suppose that has been true for a long time, but it will only remain true until it is not." She shrugged, the gesture inviting anyone to propose another course. "We could attempt to follow it along the surface if anyone knew the route, but even if you *could* follow it, parts of it run deep into canyons and the Gen1 seem to have an uncanny knack for settling in those. I don't think I need to tell any one of you why that makes it a place best avoided."

That sealed it for Rin. If she had been considering trying to lead them along more solid ground on the surface, the idea of running into another pack of those things was enough to change her mind.

"Erm, sorry to be the one to ask," Fievel spoke timidly, "especially as this seems to be... well, awkward, but... does anyone else have absolutely no idea what's going on?"

"She's talking about taking us under the ground, to a place that makes the Void look like a welcoming, hospitable kind of place," Lark answered, her cold eyes never leaving Marta's face. "Don't worry, Fievel, I'll hold your hand." She glanced at him now, raising her eyebrows suggestively.

Ivor and Torsten were exchanging looks that quite clearly said they would rather take their chances on the surface, but not so Magnus. He was looking at Lark, a mixture of intrigue and longing in his gaze. Then, quickly, he wiped his face clean of expression.

"Cornelius is going to take some convincing," Marta spoke again, before anyone else could raise an objection, "but he owes no small debt to the Alliance after what we did for him. Never mind that now, though – we will deal with that wretch when the time comes. For now, I need young bones and strong backs." She gestured towards the three brothers and, using her staff, scraped a large link of the chain free of the grass and motioned for them to pick it up. "Keep the pressure steady, and don't go jerking it around. That thing was made of old parts when we built it and that was long before any of you took your first breath. The last thing I need is you lot yanking it apart now."

The boys looked at each other curiously and, instead of refusing, reluctantly stepped forward.

"Well, come on then." Marta motioned to them again. "Get going!"

The squealing of metal filled the air as the chain went taught under their straining. It was a sound that set Rin's hair on end as she remembered the mechanical squeal of the upper-downer and the following fight for her life. She couldn't help looking from side to side, almost expecting to see the snarling of Gen1 teeth, but instead the grass before them quivered and rippled as something hidden stirred from beneath its roots. Great metal teeth appeared as the grass began to part in the middle. Rin heard the creak of cogs long-rusted complaining loudly as patches of dirt and loose stones fell into the opening before them. Rin could see that, instead of the grass being dragged out by the roots, it seemed to spread outwards, drifting atop huge, metal sheets and gliding smoothly over the mossy floor around it. She realised that, when the two halves were reunited once more, there would be little sign they had ever been there at all.

"Alright now, that's plenty," said Marta, shaking her head as though still questioning the wisdom of this decision. "It just needs to be wide enough for one person at a time. We mustn't disturb the ground any more than we have to. It's risky enough using this place – we don't need to be going around waving a flag and inviting every guard that wanders this way in after us."

Rin walked to the edge and looked down. She couldn't see the bottom, only a rusty iron ladder with a thick safety rail running along one side, stretching endlessly into the darkness. There was a staleness to the air that seemed to warn against entry for living things. She wasn't sure if she was imagining it, but her ears seemed to be picking up a hint of something echoing down there, like something far away was ringing out against the hollow metal.

"Who's first, then?" Lark asked, as she joined Rin to stare down into the foreboding black expanse.

Rin felt her shoulders sag a little as the meaning behind Lark's question resonated, knowing Lark's tone implied she ought to be the first.

"Will you both move out of the way?" Marta bristled as she waited for the two girls to move. "The climb down is hard enough – you won't enjoy speeding up your journey with a fall."

"Marta," Rin started, "maybe it should be me. I—"

"Nonsense." Marta cut her off. "Only one of us has been here before and it's not you. God knows you'll only stumble into some mess or another if things have shifted down there."

Rin was stunned into silence, watching on as the old woman sank creakily to the edge, placed her staff on the grass and swung her legs over the side, into the nothingness.

"Once I'm down, I'll tap three times and then the next one comes," Marta continued giving orders. "No more than one on the ladder at a time. Who knows what condition that thing is in anymore... and one of you best bring my staff. We'll have a long walk once we're down there."

Marta rolled onto her stomach and Rin's heart stopped for a moment as she watched her grandmother's legs flailing in the empty space before her foot settled on the first step. They all watched in silence as she slowly descended, rung by rung, and within a short time, the blackness engulfed her. Then the only sign of her progress became the scuffing of soft leather shoes on the iron underfoot, and the occasional grunt of effort that echoed from deep below the ground.

Rin did not like this waiting; all manner of ill thoughts flitted through her mind. In each new scenario, the distance between herself and the old woman only seemed to grow larger and larger. Rin couldn't help but think that if Marta ran into trouble, the old woman may already be too far away for her to reach in time to help. She was just starting to doubt the wisdom of waiting any longer when the shrill ringing of Marta's signal caused them all to jump.

Rin looked to Lark, who smiled and shook her head, begrudgingly impressed by the old woman's feat. "You next, Killer, then the boys. I'll bring up the rear."

Rin strode forwards, thinking the initial crawl over the edge would be the most disconcerting part. She hadn't accounted for the vulnerable feeling of stepping downwards into the complete darkness of the pit. She was sweating by the time her foot hit the solid floor at the bottom of the shaft, and it had nothing to do with the exertion of the climb.

"Marta?" she called out. The cacophony of noise that reverberated around in an echo made her wince.

"Hush, girl," Marta whispered back, only a few feet away, making her startle again.

Reece came down next, and Rin whispered for him to join them. Soon after, Torsten appeared, followed by Magnus and Ivor.

Fievel stood at the top, looking down. Watching each of them disappear into the dark, one after the other, he gulped hard, trying to force the panic in his chest to ease.

"You next, Stacks," Lark said, nudging him forward.

"I, eh..." he spluttered, "eh, perhaps you'd rather..."

"Nope, I wouldn't. Don't worry, I'll be right behind you." She winked at him. "Just holler if you need my help; I'll even come to rescue you if you ask nicely."

If the thought of the climb had flustered Fievel, Lark's teasing nearly unseated the tall boy's nerve entirely. He wiped his palms on his shirt, trying to remove the clammy sweat that had begun to slick his hands. He swung onto his stomach and searched desperately for the thick handrail on the right. As his fingers touched the rusty, cold iron, he tried to settle himself. Pulling every ounce of his will to the task, he forced his foot to move down.

"Both hands on the rungs, Stacks," Lark called jovially after him. "Better grip that way, if your foot slips."

After the first few steps, Fievel found a rhythm. Left foot down, right hand down, right foot down, left hand down. He was glad he had settled into the climb before the darkness swallowed him, and concentrated hard on maintaining the rhythmic movements he had established in the daylight. It felt like time had stopped as he moved through the black space, and he longed to reach the safety of the ground below.

He had lost perspective of how far or how long he'd been climbing for, but as soon as he lowered his weight onto the next rung, he knew something was wrong. The metal creaked and groaned and Fievel felt the sickening sensation of a drop as his stomach rose up into his throat. His hands tightened instinctively, but it didn't stop them from wrenching free, and then, he knew he was falling.

His scream echoed around the metal-clad shaft, the fear seeming to intensify with each reverberation.

Lark rolled her eyes in exasperation. "One time, could things not be simple?"

Hesitating for a moment, she considered her options. Then, shrugging, she leapt for the handrail. Locking her legs around the thick circular safety rail as a guide, she loosened the tight grip of her hands and slid down after the boy.

CHAPTER SIX
TUNNELS, SHAFTS AND TRACKS

Rin heard Fievel cry out before a body hit the ground hard, followed seconds later by a grunt that Rin knew for certain belonged to Lark.

"Alive?" the snarky girl shouted out, and Rin winced as her voice rattled around them.

"Alive," several voices whispered back, once the ringing reverberations had lessened.

Then, lastly, a more shaken, "A... alive." The tremor in Fievel's announced his astonishment.

Rin's ears picked out each voice and, more notably, the one who did not respond.

"Marta?" she hissed urgently. When no one answered, she raised her voice a little and called again. "*Marta?*"

"Over here," the old woman replied from somewhere off to the side.

"Oh, this is a fine mess," Lark hissed. "We're *definitely* a lot safer scraping about in the dark like this than we were up there!"

Rin could tell that Lark was reaching for the offhand contempt she so often used alongside such remarks, but this time, the girl hadn't quite been able to hide the edge of irritation that only concern for Reece had brought out in her before now.

"Rin, come over here," Marta cut in, halting Lark's complaining. "Step towards my voice until you reach the wall, then follow it round and down the slope."

Rin moved cautiously towards her. The surface was hard and uneven underfoot, and the fear of tripping into such nothingness was difficult to ignore, but Marta kept up a steady stream of words to guide her and, before long, Rin felt the old woman's outstretched arms in front of her.

"Here, girl," Marta said, placing Rin's hands at shoulder height and pressing them against something smooth and cold. "It's here."

"What is this?" Rin asked, trying to make sense of the shape under her fingers.

"That's the lever," Marta whispered back. "When I say so, pull it down, then don't move or touch anything else until I tell you to." Raising her voice slightly so the others could hear, she added, "All of you, make sure you're not touching anything other than the ground under your feet. You hear me?"

A small, echoing chorus of agreeable hisses indicated they had.

"Now heed me and touch nothing until I tell you," Marta reiterated one last time. "Okay, go ahead, Rin. *Pull.*"

The metal handle of the lever fitted easily into Rin's palm, which was just as well – it needed a fair amount of force before Rin heard the telltale crunch that signalled the long-since rusted iron had consented to move once more. Ticking and clicking filled the air, and the sounds of rattling chains tinkled from somewhere higher up. Tilting her head back, she watched as the tiny spot of distant sunlight vanished above them and she knew the entrance had resealed itself.

A loud cracking sound followed somewhere behind them, and Rin turned sharply towards the sound. Expecting to see only the black of more darkness, she was surprised to be met by a glowing, orange speck. It almost made Rin feel dizzy, this sudden appearance of light without the context of the space around her. At first, it was just a dot, but as her eyes held onto the abstract illumination, she watched as it slowly stretched into a drip. Then, as the moments passed, she realised the glowing fluid was turning into a steady trickle.

She wanted to step towards it, the way all living things seek out light in the dark, but kept her feet firmly in place, heeding the old woman's words. It moved painfully slowly at first, but soon enough the light became a thin stream of liquid orange that ran along the edge of the slightly inclined trench. It occurred to Rin that this could only have been carved for just such a purpose, and she was reminded of the molten rock that flowed along the back of Cornelius's home. That was where the similarity ended, though. While Cornelius's home was a place that had made use of the natural cave-like structures within the rock, this place had the straight edges and smooth finish of forced industry. The very walls marked it as a place that could only have been created by the work of machines, in a time before the Fall.

It was still dim, but after the total darkness they had known before, the soft glow of orange light seemed to fill the space adequately enough. Now, for the first time, Rin could see the framework of metal struts and grey concrete walls that surrounded her and, above that, just how intricate the system of cogs and levers truly was. At least four wheels of different shapes and sizes had been mounted firmly onto the smooth walls, with streamers of chains draped across each one. The whole thing was linked together to feed down to this one handle. Rin didn't know what she would have called such a mechanism that both closed the trapdoor above and released the glowing liquid. Whatever it was, she could see now that the loud crack had been made when a large spike had punched a long, thin hole through the wall and into the rough rock face underneath, letting the glowing earth spill out.

"Alright." Marta exhaled loudly with relief, "You can all move now. Stay away from the trenches, though. That stuff will strip the flesh off you in seconds if it gets anywhere near your skin."

Lark didn't need to be told twice. At the old woman's signal, she had already turned further away from the others and begun to stride back towards the ladder. No more than six rungs up, she placed her hand on the remains of the rusted bar that had given way under Fievel's foot, and her eyes fell on him reproachfully.

"Really?" she sighed, gleefully unimpressed at the magnitude of his fall.

"Ah yes, sorry about that." Fievel looked up from under his heavy brows sheepishly. "I eh... I... I thought at the time that it was... well, in the dark I thought it was... higher."

Lark did not try to suppress her enjoyment at his discomfort.

There was a moment's silence before Magnus took pity on the boy and leaned forward, close to her ear. "Play nice, Lark."

"Oh, *always*," she whispered back, savouring the moment.

Magnus took one last look at Fievel, and even in this light, the red flush that spread blotchily up his neck and face to the very tips of his ears was clear to see.

Then, he added, "It did seem to me, Lark, that you got down here awfully quickly after you heard that boy's hollering?" His considering tone hinted at some deeper meaning, though Rin had no idea what it might be.

Lark narrowed her eyes, squinting calculatedly into his. "No point hanging around up there when the rest of you were having so much fun down here, was there? Besides, I wanted to make sure Stacks over there hadn't squashed my little brother with his *great fall*."

"Is that so?" Magnus said, nodding, but his raised eyebrow cast doubt on her words.

Rin noticed the muscle ripple in the other girl's cheek as she clenched her teeth.

"So, eh, which way do we go now?" Fievel asked, keen to divert the focus from an increasingly uncomfortable situation.

"We follow these." Marta rattled her staff against the iron beams that striped the ground. Parallel rows of the thick metal adorned the otherwise empty passage, disappearing off into the distant smouldering light.

Something was bothering Rin, though. It was hard to tell with the others moving around so much, their noises ricocheting off the mass of hammered iron and hollow concrete that encased this place. She closed her eyes, straining to focus her ears on that nagging sound. For the briefest moment, she thought she could pick it out again. A shuffling and grunting that was too far away to be their own. Then it was gone, and once more she doubted whether she had truly heard anything at all.

"What is it, girl?" Marta asked, her eyes poring over Rin's face, trying to read what was behind her concern.

"I don't know. I thought I heard something. Maybe." Rin closed her eyes again, trying to sift through the sounds to find it once more. When she opened them, she saw apprehension on Marta's face.

"Hmm." Marta inclined her head. "Could be we're not as alone down here as I would like. Or it could just be the rifts and splits on the surface. Sound travels strangely down here and the earth is not silent above us."

"Let's get moving," Rin said, cautiously peering into the dimly lit shaft in front of them.

She wasn't sure it was safe. She wasn't sure who or what might have made that sound, but she *was* sure that every moment they lingered here was another moment Ieuan's life was at risk. Every moment would mean another lungful of that polluted air that permeated the Capital Tunnels. Marta looked as though she was on the verge of reconsidering the wisdom of this plan, but as she saw the determination on Rin's face, she faltered.

"Alright, then. Get in a line: each one puts their hand on the shoulder of the one in front. If you lose grip on the person ahead, you say something; if the hand on your shoulder loses grip of you, you say something," Marta instructed. "Don't go wandering off. I don't have time to be searching around down here, looking for young ones who can't do as they're told."

For a moment, Rin was reminded of Cornelius and the similarly brusque warning he had given them. Something about that niggled at her, and she was just about to ask when Lark was pushing in front of her. The deliberate angling of that action shifted her focus: Marta would be first, with Lark now behind her, making Rin third. The three brothers came next, and they purposefully pinned Fievel in the middle of their pack, leaving a friendly shoulder in front and behind him. Reece would bring up the rear.

Rin saw her do it, but the action was so unexpected she didn't have time to stop it. Instead of putting her fingers on the old woman's shoulder as instructed, Lark placed her hand between the woman's shoulder blades and pressed her fingers deep into Marta's hunched and crooked spine. The old woman gasped in pain, her neck and left shoulder spasming forward.

Rin was still trying to process what she had just witnessed when Marta's staff flashed out behind her, catching the girl's elbow with a loud crack.

"Ow!" Lark howled through gritted teeth as her probing

fingers fell limp and useless at her side. "That hurt!"

Rin watched incredulously. Lark's words seemed entirely out of place alongside the satisfied crease of the girl's lips and the way she nodded her head, as though finally making sense of a thing that had long troubled her. Then, Rin was moving, stepping between Lark and Marta.

"What did you do?" Rin accused, looking contemptuously at Lark.

"What did *I* do? She's the one who damn near broke my arm," Lark complained, trying to rub the tingling from her numbed fingers. At the sight of Rin's furious expression, she added, "Just a small misunderstanding. I couldn't see where I'd put my hands in this dim light. Just an accident. Wasn't it, Marta?" she added, slyly.

Rin knew Lark was lying. She had seen for herself that whatever cruel thing the girl had done, she had done it on purpose. So why was the old woman nodding?

"Mm, a misunderstanding," Marta agreed, still a little breathless.

Rin had never seen Marta look so vulnerable before, and the wrongness of it rattled her. She struggled to keep down the part of her that was already reaching within, seeking that reserve of strength, that inner torrent of ability that would make Lark pay in kind for what she had just done. Only the concern in the old woman's eyes stayed her. Consciously, she let the feeling ebb away before she spoke.

"If there are any more 'misunderstandings', Lark, it will be you and me who go to the task of straightening them out." The strain in her voice added more threat to the words than any amount of shouting could have.

"Oh, I think Marta is more than capable of looking after

herself," Lark replied. There was an air of caution about her now, but still that smugness remained.

"Maybe so..." Rin reached out, turning the slender girl's shoulders squarely towards her. "But, capable or not, it will be *me* you find at the other end of that problem should you go looking for trouble again." The pressure in her grip and the barely controlled anger left no doubt as to her meaning.

"No need to tell me twice, Killer. Besides, there's nothing left to misunderstand now," Lark said, slipping out of her position in the line and tucking herself back in, just in front of Fievel. "Don't be afraid to hold on tight if you get scared, Stacks." She grinned as she placed his hand on her shoulder, shimmying slightly as she moved into place.

Magnus looked behind him at the change in order and shook his head. "You alright back there, Fievel?" he called behind him, the forced joviality in his voice making Rin wonder whether it was a mask for something. She guessed that it was to hide his own fears about being back under the ground yet again.

"Oh eh... yes," the boy stammered. "Yes, I think so."

Even though Rin couldn't see Fievel from where she stood, she knew those blotches of red would be back.

Marta had been right to ask for her staff, as once again they took up their long march. Mostly the passageways contained only one set of what Marta had called 'tracks', but every so often, a second line would branch off and present them with a choice of two directions. Each time this happened, they stopped so Marta could show them where the next lever could be found, and then she would make them all recite the turns they had taken so far. It took a lot of concentration, and each time they added a new one, Rin was sure she would not be able to remember the last. She stopped engaging in conversation with the others and took to reciting the turns over and over until they reached the next one.

"Won't we just be able to follow the light trenches down here when we come back?" Magnus asked.

"Yes, but not unless you remember where each of the levers are," Marta muttered. "Each time you pull the next one, the one behind us will seal back up. He might be a wretch, but there's no denying he was damn near a genius." She was a little out of breath, grunting with the effort of each step now.

For the first time, Rin realised how much this pace must be taking out of the old woman. She knew she was letting Marta push herself beyond what was right for one of her age.

Around the next turn the tunnel opened out a little and, once more, the tracks broke off in two directions. Here, the sides of the tunnel were raised to about head height, making high platforms with the iron lattice cutting a path through the middle. There were steps leading upwards away from the tracks on one side, but these were piled high with rock and rubble that had tumbled down from the roof above. Rin wondered where they would have led, once upon a time.

She shook her head. It was a pointless thing to think about. Besides, it was better the route was barred now. Nothing could get down here onto the tracks from that direction.

"We should stop here for a while," Rin said, lifting her hand off the old woman's shoulder.

As the old woman felt the lightening of Rin's touch, she stopped. "I can manage a little further," she wheezed.

"I know," Rin agreed, without offering anything that would allow the old woman the chance to dispute the call to rest.

It was odd to make camp without laying a fire or setting snares, but they had enough food and water for a few more days, and the glowing trenches provided all the light and warmth they needed.

Rin knew the others felt strange, too. The break in tradition, plus the eerie way sounds rippled through this unnatural place, caused every hair on the back of her neck to rise.

As before, being down under the ground had wrought a change in Torsten and his brothers. In this place, the horrors of the Capital's Tunnels came alive again, and they were forced to confront the demons they had tried to leave buried under the earth. Unfortunately, their preoccupation with the past meant Lark was free to enjoy her game once more, without the periodic interruption of uninvited players.

"Where's that accent from then, Stacks?"

Fievel choked on the water he had been drinking, and had no time to respond before Lark continued her interrogation.

"Sounds more like that Capital jabber than anything I've heard in the Void."

"Oh, I eh," he muttered between coughs, trying to clear his lungs of the miss-timed gulp. "Well, I spent some time in the Capital when I was younger."

"And just how is it that a Stackling finds themselves 'spending time' in a place like that?" Lark's previously mischievous tone took on a more suspicious edge.

"Well, the Partisan arranged it, actually. Arranged for me to get some schooling there. I'm not too sure about the details of it all. But, eh, yes. For a while... or for a time at least, I learned some at the Educatorium up there."

"Rubbing shoulders with the uptown folk," she sneered, then sniffed as though the air had suddenly been filled with some foul smell. It was clear from the way she said it that the girl thought nothing could be more disgusting. "Your mother must be *so* proud."

"Well, I'm not sure. I suppose she might have been," Fievel

mused, as if it wasn't something he had considered before now. "The Partisan said she left money with him, so I could learn the medical arts. So, I suppose she might have been, yes. At least, I hope so." He was squinting now, his eyes looking upwards, seeking out a memory inside his own head. "I don't know that she had the Educatorium in mind when she said it, though," he finished, doubtfully.

"Why didn't you ask her?" Lark countered, her tone already softening.

Rin realised then that, just as she did, Lark knew what his answer would be.

"She died when I was very young." Although Fievel's words told of something that had happened long ago, the hurt still sounded fresh and full of a deep and terrible sadness.

"I'm sure she would be proud of you, Fievel," Rin said gently, unable to bear Lark's silence at the boy's pain.

"I don't know," he said, a flush of red filling his cheeks. "The whole thing didn't exactly go to plan for me. I... well, I suppose the word is 'fled', in the end."

All of them were looking at him now, but when no one spoke, he went on.

"I don't remember much about those the first few days after she was gone. I know I was alone for a number of nights. It felt like a lot of nights back then, but I think now it was no more than three or four. They seemed to stretch on forever though, and all of them felt too long to bear. I remember that my heart did not stop hurting in all that time. My eyes and nose were sore from rubbing at them." He swallowed hard, the memory still threatening to let tears come, even now. "I tried to find the money to have her buried. To do it properly, like she'd talked about. Like how they did it in the time before the Fall." He paused to finger the token tucked away against his skin. "I found a man who said he could do it, and I got all the money together just like he asked, but when it was time, well."

Rin felt her chest tighten, her anger flaring as she imagined what the younger version of this boy had endured. It had all happened so long ago, and she could not change nor help it now, but that helplessness clawed at her. As though her inaction now somehow made her no different to those countless others who must have turned their back on him then.

"He just took the money, then he told me to dump her body in the river and let the rats take care of it." His brow furrowed and he looked down, unable to make his eyes meet any of theirs. "I'd never been in a fight before that – but I did try to stop him." Fievel's voice had risen; it seemed as though it was important to him that they believed that part. "Once I was down, he started kicking me. Kicked me a fair few times, I think. I don't know for sure how many, but I split my head on the ground, or under his boot; either way, I was unconscious for a while."

Rin had never seen someone talk like this. To admit so earnestly to losing everything. She knew from her own experience that it took a certain type of strength to say such things out loud to others without conceit or shame.

"When I woke up, I was in the Hall of the Partisan, and my mother's body was there too. They'd washed her and wrapped her in a white sheet. I'd never seen such a white sheet as that one. I told him right there and then that I didn't have anything left to pay him with, but he told me it didn't matter. He said she had left money for me there, with him, and that she must have forgotten to tell me before she died. At the time I just accepted it – not that I had much choice." His pause spoke of a doubt he now held. "They let me say goodbye to her, and then they sang a few songs. Old songs that I didn't know the words to, but they sounded familiar. I felt like she would have liked them. She liked to sing old songs too." He sniffed, trying to clear the thickness in his voice.

All of them had stopped speaking and were fixed on Fievel as he spoke. Much of his tale was not uncommon: there were as many orphans in the Void as there were children with parents. Perhaps, because of that, something about the way he spoke resonated within them all.

Now he'd started, it seemed hard for him to stop. He told them how, after the singing, they had fed him and asked him to stay. With nowhere else to go, he had just kept on staying. The Partisan had asked others to find out if the boy had kin in the Void, but as the days turned to weeks, it became clear that he was on his own. That was when the Partisan arranged for him to go to the Educatorium. The man had explained to him that there was a woman in the Capital who needed money badly enough to take in a 'long-lost nephew' for the right price, so he would have somewhere safe to stay. The Partisan had told the young boy about the role he was to play, and together they had practised the flowery enunciation of the uplanders' lilt until he had mastered a passable imitation.

"I didn't want to leave the Stacks," Fievel said quietly. "Not really. I'd never had someone look out for me the way they did there. My mother had always been sick – it wasn't her fault that she didn't make it – but I wanted to stay there, not with some stranger in the Capital."

When he had arrived at the uptown home, the lady of the house had wrinkled her nose at him and he had been worried. Once he'd showered and dressed in the finer clothes that had been acquired for him, they had sat down to eat together and she had seemed mollified. Fievel had used the metal dinner tools the way the Partisan had shown him, and he had conversed with her on the polite and benign topics exactly as he had been instructed. Day by day and meal by meal, the lady warmed up to his presence and, while they had never become as close as a true family would be, he felt she enjoyed his presence in her home and had been nice enough to him.

"For a while after that, things went well," he said, titling his head from side to side as though still appraising that part of his life.

He told them how he had even made friends among his peers at the Educatorium. The best of those was a girl his age called Carmela. She would tease him and they would laugh together, both of them working hard as they studied the science of medicine and the art of healing.

"I think after a while I almost forgot that I was merely playing at being an uplander," Fievel said, uncomfortable with the admission that he had begun to believe in the lie of his new life. "It never ceases to amaze me how seemingly small decisions can have such a momentous impact on the course of one's life."

He explained that Carmela was a good friend, but, while she worked hard, she did not have the natural talent he had displayed. Often, she needed his help to complete the work the school asked of them, and he was happy to give it. They would spend hours closeted away in the Educatorium library, or in some empty classroom, but even with his tutorage, it was Fievel who would win awards for his grades or academic papers. Achievements the lady of the house had taken great pleasure in sharing with her neighbours. Carmela never seemed to mind; while she enjoyed her studies, she had other interests outside of the classroom that kept her amused. She was inquisitive in a way that often led her into mischief, and one day, the main focus of her curiosity became a fascination with the illicit activities of the Void.

"She begged me to go there with her. At first it wasn't hard to say no – no decent upland boy is supposed to be interested in that place – but she begged and pleaded with me. In the end, she said she would go alone, and I couldn't let her do that. The Void is no place for the unwary, and Carmela had no idea what she was walking into." The detached tone he had held a moment before faded into embarrassed mumbling. "She was so happy she kissed me. My first kiss from someone who wasn't my mother."

Rin felt the impact that moment had made on him, and she thought immediately of her own first kiss with Ieuan.

Fievel told them that he and Carmela had gone once or twice a month to the Void after that... but that regularity had been his greatest mistake. On that last day, they had been waiting for them. A group of boys from the Void, who had been watching the repeated returns of the young man they had once known. A boy who once had nothing, just as they had nothing, but who now walked in fine clothes, with a fine girl, and who lived in a splendid upland home. They had called out to him, and he had tried to ignore them, moving Carmela along in the other direction. If they hadn't remembered his name, perhaps she wouldn't have believed it, but the louder they shouted, the more suspicious she had become.

Things had changed quickly for him after that. Carmela became distant and would often ask about the boys who knew him by name in the Void.

"I should have been smarter. I should have made up some elaborate tale of mischief and scandal, but love makes fools of us all, and young love doubly so," Fievel said, the words sounding like an old adage he had repeated many times. "I told her everything. I thought, if I told her the truth, she would forgive me. Maybe even love me anyway, but alas, she did not. By the next day, I realised things had started to unravel: not just with us, but within the Educatorium as well. It started with whispering behind hands; looks that said nothing and too much at the same time. Then they called me out of class to tell me that allegations had been made."

Fievel's brow creased and, for the first time since he had started his tale, he seemed embarrassed.

"She told them I had 'made advances under false pretences', which I suppose perhaps I had, but not intentionally, and certainly not in the way she had convinced them of, either. Carmela might not have had my talents in academia, but she knew what that trip to the Void had meant before I did." He shook his head regretfully. "Everyone knew how much time we had spent together and she understood that she had to get her version of events out before the taint of my past rubbed off on her, too." He paused again. "That was perhaps forgivable – at times the Educatorium was even more cutthroat than the Void."

Like the others, Rin was gripped by the boy's tale of love and betrayal, and as Fievel's eyes dropped to the floor, she knew that whatever was coming next was the thing that had cut him deep enough to scar.

"Carmela also told the head of the department that my grades had been achieved through deception, and that my papers had been no more than theft or plagiary of her own work. She said that, until now, she had been too scared to contest it, due to my unpredictable Void temperament." He sighed, his gaze fixed on his feet, unable to meet the eyes equally fixed on him. "They suspended me, pending investigation. Of course, I knew what they would find once they went looking for it. No more than two days after that, someone had spread the word, and everyone knew that I was not in fact an uplander but a Void charlatan who had panhandled my way into the Capital. The lady of the house heard it first – you have to admire the network of gossip she had access to – but she still cared enough about me to help me escape when I did. It was only because of her that I made it back over the wall before the guard kicked down her door looking for me." He sighed. "Later, I heard that she had denounced me as a murderous villain who had slain her true nephew and heir, but I don't begrudge her that. Truly, what else could she have done?"

Silence followed that last question, punctuated by the occasional hiss as a drip of condensation hit the lava trenches below.

"Worst of all was having to tell the Partisan what had happened. By then, I was old enough to understand what he had done for me. I think I always knew my mother had nothing of anything to leave me – that it had all been his kindness, and I had squandered it. I thought he would be angry or disappointed, but instead, he laughed, slapped me on the back and told me they hadn't had a healer with half my education in the Stacks in living memory."

Rin saw the brothers nodding in approval. All three of them were making the same strained and serious gesture that said they approved of the man who had offered their new friend such a kindness.

"That's where I was when Marta and Gibb arrived, and I am ashamed to say that only then did I realise just how poor my Capital education had been."

Rin saw her own concern for Fievel mirrored in the features around her, in all but one of the faces. Lark's jaw was clenched tight and the anger in her eyes verged on murderous. When Fievel finally looked up, he was startled at the intensity of it. Their eyes met for only a moment, before the girl spat and turned aside, walking away from them all.

"Oh, dear. I didn't... I eh..." Fievel stammered. "I didn't mean to upset her. Perhaps I should apologise?"

"No, Fievel." Magnus looked at him sadly. "It's not you Lark is angry with. Just give her some time."

CHAPTER SEVEN
WRETCHES, MONSTERS AND MISTAKES

"Carmela had better hope she never meets our Lark," Ivor muttered under his breath, and Torsten winced in silent agreement.

Rin closed her eyes. She didn't expect sleep to come, but if they had to stop here, she would console herself with the idea of trying to be as well-rested as possible. At first, she was all too aware of the others' whispers, the rhythmic dripping and hissing within the damp tunnels, and the eerie repetition of those sounds as they echoed off the strange, man-made stone encasing them. Soon enough, though, it became nothing more than background noise, easy to ignore in its irrelevance. But it was in these quiet times that it became more difficult to stop her mind from seeking out Ieuan. She tried not to, but each time she stopped consciously pushing them away, her thoughts returned to him.

Where is he now? Is he okay? Then, if she let it, her imagination would take her towards darker notions. *Do they know what he did? Will they hurt him to get to the Alliance? To get to me?* Ever since she had made the choice to leave him behind, she had been constantly fighting to contain such thoughts, to force those terrible images back into the dark recesses of her mind, where she had always kept the things too difficult or painful to examine. It wasn't a deliberate decision to allow them out of those confines now, but rather a weakening in resilience that accompanied those in need of rest. With each new horror she imagined, she was unconsciously reaching closer and closer towards the dormant place inside herself: the place that offered her its strength and protection.

When a sudden shriek split the expected pattern of pattering, the others jumped to their feet in a panic, but Rin didn't flinch. She was too close to the torrent flowing inside of her for that. Instead, she found herself ready and almost eager for the fight this shrieking promised her. Strangely, this new threat did more to restore her than anything else could have. Purpose rippled through her, washing away her apathy and pleasantly replacing all other concerns with only this immediate one.

It was almost a relief.

"Form up together," she called softly to the others. "Here we go again."

She could hear Lark's light steps now, and Rin could tell by the frequency of each thump that the girl was running just about as fast as she could. It wasn't Lark's footfalls that she was concentrating on, though, but the heavier tread in pursuit. She could hear it stumbling a little, with an uneven gait and, where the girl's stride seemed to skip lightly over the ground, this larger thing was landing awkwardly and scuffing the floor with each cumbersome bound. Rin looked behind her and saw that the others had assembled into a tight group at her back. That was good, but like always, it seemed they were waiting for her to decide on their plan, and quickly.

There wasn't as much room down here as she would have liked, and she knew that at any moment, two more bodies were about to appear at the far-away entrance, only crowding the space further. Rin looked into the dark mouth of the passageway before them. She didn't know what other dangers might be hidden in the depths of that darkness, and she wouldn't risk making an attack on unknown ground. She took one last look over her shoulder at the small group that had formed up at her command, and she knew she couldn't allow whatever this thing was to reach them. That left her with very few options and even less time.

Darting towards the same passageway that the shriek had rippled out from only moments ago, she stopped short of the entrance, throwing herself flush against the wall. Then she counted. For every step of Lark's, the thing behind her was taking two of its own. Rin knew that if the girl didn't emerge from the dark soon, she wasn't going to.

Rin's skin felt as though it was tingling as she sensed how close they were now. She shut her eyes, concentrating, and let her strength flood her. Instantly, she could read the tremors of the ground more clearly. Where the tunnel beyond her had been eerily motionless only seconds before, now she could feel the way the air was moving inside it, the currents stirred by the forms within. Without instruction, her body wound itself tighter and tighter, readying her for the moment she would need it to burst into action.

Lark shot from the entrance of the passage, her eyes wide with fear, her lungs lacking the breath to spare for cries of fear or warning.

Rin's eyes snapped open. She strained to focus, still counting, and in the next instant, the creature emerged from the dark behind Lark. Rin's legs were already thrusting her forwards, leaning hard into the motion, and she took the creature high in the chest with striking precision. Colliding hard with the Gen1, Rin felt as though she had hit a solid wall of rock rather than the soft skin and tissue of a living thing. That didn't stop her, though, and together they tumbled across the hard floor, the momentum of her strike carrying them away from the others and towards the far wall. She saw Lark's surprise as the girl risked a glance back over her shoulder, clearly expecting to see her pursuer closing in on her.

Rin could hear the others shouting something, but she ignored them. This would be between her and this Gen1, and she didn't need any distractions now. Bringing her knees up, Rin pushed out hard with her feet in an attempt to separate herself from the Gen1's sprawling limbs and grappling arms. As she rolled free and into a crouch, she got her first real look at it. The creature's greyish skin seemed papery and thin in the orange glow of the tunnel, and its cheeks had the hollow look of something that had hungered for a while. Its left arm looked normal, but the one on the right seemed to be crippled from an injury long since healed and set at a crooked angle. One of its ears looked as though, sometime in the past, something had bitten away at least half of it.

Rin looked at it in a detached way. Part of her was aware enough to understand that, without a grasp on the storm inside her, she would have been terrified of such a sight. Instead, she was perfectly calm and centred, already analysing which of its injuries she could use to her own advantage. A movement to her left prompted her to shift her focus, and irritation flashed hotly through her as she realised some of the group were attempting to come to her aid. That was a problem.

The creature saw them too, and the instinctual knowledge of an animal that has spent its whole existence hunting drew its focus towards them hungrily. It shrieked again as it scrambled to regain its feet and then it turned towards Ivor, the closest of the group.

Rin didn't need to say anything: she could see that the smallest of the three brothers knew in that moment he had made a mistake.

The creature broke the tension as it charged towards him with blistering speed. Rin paused only a second longer, incredulous, as she realised Ivor wasn't going to move. He was stuck solidly in place with the anticipation of a person who expected to die. The look in the boy's eyes was enough to snap her back into motion.

Before she even had time to consider the wisdom of her actions, she chased after it once more. Catching up to it in two strides, she pushed hard against the solid ground and, with a last powerful leap, launched herself high up into the air. The moment she collided with its gristly, muscular back, she wrapped her legs around its waist and wrenched her body backwards. The jerking motion caused the creature to stumble, and together they crashed into the group, scattering a few of them to the ground. The Gen1 kept its feet, but Rin had succeeded in halting its charge and, as she had hoped, its crooked, injured arm was unable to reach her. Instead, it could only claw at her with its one working limb on its left side, and she had positioned herself slightly over to the right to limit the damage of that attack.

Unexpectedly, its elbow shot backwards, catching her in the ribs, and she felt all the air leave her lungs as she fought down the wave of nausea that followed that impact. Doubling over, she clutched at her side, watching as the others spread out in a half circle, none of them knowing if an approach might do more harm than good. She was still unable to catch enough breath to call out to them, but she waved her hand, trying to motion them backwards. They were still too close – one of them could get hurt, and she needed space and time to think.

Sensing a threat from their gathering, the creature began flailing wildly, and it was all Rin could do to hold on, every muscle tightening to keep her seated on its back. The hard rock of the tunnel's walls and ground flashed past her and she lost all sense of where they were moving. Then the light began to dim, and Rin realised it was trying to pull her back into the darkness of the passage beyond. Rin had no way of knowing what lay further down this track – all she knew was that she needed to finish the fight quickly, before the last of the light was lost to her.

As the Gen1's wild thrashing continued, she caught a glimpse of it: the next of Cornelius' light-making contraptions. It was hard to look for anything, as the world spun around her with each twist and turn of the monstrous form, and the dimming light only exacerbated the problem. *Is that it?* She was sure she could see the deep groove of a trench running before her. Maybe, just maybe, she could end this before anyone got hurt.

"Get to the next lever!" she shouted to the others, no longer caring that the sound rang out around them.

The creature screamed back some kind of incomprehensible answer. She could only hope its blood was up enough to ignore the others moving beyond the passageway.

Before that moment, they had all stood fixed in the same half circle they had formed after the creature had briefly scattered them. Rin's intention had been clear when she had waved them back. Every one of their faces had held the same expression: a desperate hopelessness as each of them felt the wrongness of their inaction, but no-one knew how to help. So far, their presence had only hindered her. When Rin had taken an elbow to the ribs, Magnus had broken the line and tried to move closer, but that movement had only caused Rin to release part of her grip to stop them. He knew she would need both hands to keep her hold on that thrashing thing, and he didn't know how she could disentangle herself safely either. He hadn't needed to hear Lark's desperate hiss to stop him – he already knew there was nothing he could do.

"Magnus, don't!" she had spat in the hushed tone they had all adopted along the tracks, the fear and anger in her voice competing for dominance.

So, they had all watched, tense and horrified, but unable to look away as the entwined forms disappeared into the darkness of the next tunnel.

It had felt like an eternity to each of them, standing there, still and breathless, trying to decipher the fate of their friend from the disorienting sounds that magnified in their reverberating chorus. When at last Rin's cry had echoed out, breaking through the sounds of struggle, it had been the bugle call to action they had all been hungering for. Each foot was moving before the second ripple of the cry had echoed around them, and they almost tripped over one another as they rushed to find the next lever.

Rin could see the point on the far wall now, where the trench met the gritty grey of man-made stone. Just another few steps would be enough. She furrowed her brow, knowing there wasn't much room for error. If she misjudged it by even a hand's breadth on either side, it would all be pointless. She was still trying to work out how to position the thing when she realised that her chance was happening now. The Gen1 began to jerk more wildly, this new ferocity not only threatening to shake her loose but causing the creature to stumble under its own frantic movement. She shifted her weight, pushing it more off balance, and the creature pitched forward onto its knees.

Before it hit the ground, she sprang free, kicking out and rolling as far from it as she could. When she came to a stop, Rin was pleased to see that she had managed to put some distance between them.

It didn't take the Gen1 long to realise that it had rid itself of its unwelcome load. It was already trying to regain its feet for another attack, but Rin was faster and more agile. It had only just come to standing when she rammed her shoulder into its guts, half pushing, half lifting, driving the thing backwards towards the far wall. She felt the full force of a heavy blow strike at her back, causing her to cough, stumble and choke. Unable to defend herself properly, she mustered every ounce of her strength to push the Gen1 further still.

She felt, rather than saw, when they reached the wall, their combined weight slamming hard into the immovable stone, causing them both to grunt under the impact.

Rin looked up hopefully, relieved to see that she had hit her mark perfectly. As long as it didn't move, this was the spot.

She realised the folly of her plan in that moment. *If it didn't move?* The creature was thrashing as wildly as ever, and Rin recoiled in disgust as she heard its teeth snapping in the open air and felt its hot, rancid breath on her cheek. She wanted to draw back, to put as much distance between those teeth and her own flesh as she could, but this was it. This was their best chance.

Rin felt her knees buckle slightly as another heavy blow landed across her back. She would have to hope the others had found the lever; she knew she could not endure many more of these strikes. She felt the air swirl away from her, signalling an upswing of the Gen1's arm as it prepared for another attack, but her own body had already begun to move in response. Releasing her grip from around its waist, which had been keeping it pinned to the wall, she stepped back. Now she had the space to swing, she let loose blow after blow into the creature's midsection. They were blows that would have felled a normal person, but the beast only grunted and hunched slightly, absorbing each one.

"*Now!*" she shouted and she tried to concentrate, listening for the clicking sounds that filled the air seconds later.

She had to focus on the timing of those sounds; this next part was going to hurt. She heard the crunching of rusty brackets, followed by the slight whoosh as they released. With one final burst of speed, Rin ducked under a blow from the Gen1 that would have knocked her witless, then reached out to slam its lumpy grey head against the rock. Holding it there, Rin screwed her eyes tightly shut and took a deep, sharp breath. Every inch of her skin tingled in anticipation as the fibres inside her screamed at her to move. Instead, she pushed harder against the creature's face. Holding its head firmly in place, she waited for the impact.

Then there was only noise. The creature shrieked long and high, and Rin was screaming too, but the crack that followed was louder than them both. The spike punched down, through her hand, through the creature's skull, and deep into the wall behind.

In Rin's mind, it all seemed to happen both too fast to make any sense of, and yet impossibly slowly at the same time. There was blinding pain coupled with absurd clarity as she watched the long metal point wrench clear of her flesh and retract back into the mechanism above them. She pulled her hand back towards her body protectively, letting the lifeless Gen1 drop to the ground.

Remembering Marta's warning, she stepped back from the little orange dot that had appeared where its head had been only a moment before. Disorientated by its increasing brightness, she watched as it began to spill into the trench below. Soon, this dark place would be lit with a warm, orange glow.

Knowing it was a bad idea, she glanced down at the torn flesh and shattered bones of her ruined hand. She shut her eyes, trying to fight down another wave of nausea that followed as her body tried to purge the image from inside her. Taking a deep breath, she understood that watching her body's ability to knit its skin and sinew back together, and re-form and re-fuse her bones, would neither make it hurt less nor happen more quickly. Steeling herself, she pulled a dirty handkerchief from her pocket and shakily wrapped the offending wound tightly. Pausing for a moment, she looked down at the fabric. It was as dirty as she was. She knew Marta would have scolded a villager who took such poor care of such a serious wound, but Rin wasn't a villager. It wouldn't matter if she didn't clean and dress it with ointments or salves to fight infection. As long as her heart continued to beat, the damage would heal.

Not wanting to look at what lay on the ground beneath her, she turned away and walked back towards the others. She realised that those waiting on the tracks beyond still didn't know whether beast or girl would be returning to them.

As Rin emerged from the darkness, Marta came rushing towards her, the old woman's desperate eyes scanning every inch of her bruised body.

"Oh, child. You didn't—" Marta's eyes fell to the blood-soaked handkerchief at her side.

Rin wasn't sure if the old woman could tell what had happened in there, and for a moment she was worried about being held accountable for such self-harm. She shook her head: she had done what she had to, and it was nobody's choice but hers.

Shifting her gaze to the others, she realised Reece was still peering into the darkness behind her, as though he was not yet sure if the danger had truly passed.

"It's dead, Reece. The spike went straight through its head," she said, holding up her hand to her face and indicating where the metal had gone through hand and head alike. "It'll heal," she added quietly, seeing the old woman's concern. Her voice still held its controlled edge, making the words sound flat and emotionless.

"Well done," Magnus said with a grin, clapping her on the shoulder. "That was nothing short of insane, but well done."

His brothers' faces mirrored his own.

"I thought I was a goner for sure," Ivor half laughed, half choked, still in disbelief. "But then you clambered onto its back like a rat up a Void drainpipe and rode that thing like a bucking horse!"

Rin chuckled at his choice of words.

"Not a ride I'd like to take again anytime soon," Rin replied, feeling the throbbing in her hand intensify at the movement. "Is Lark okay?" she asked, noticing the girl's absence from the group.

"Hard to say," Ivor said, screwing up his face curiously. Then, seeing Rin's concern, he added, "Oh, the Gen1 never touched her, don't worry – never got the chance, thanks to you – but something *is* wrong with her." He pointed back towards the place where they had made their camp earlier.

Rin turned, finding Lark sitting close to Fievel's unconscious body. She had laid him out carefully, with her own pack propped under his head. Now she simply stared at him, a mixture of anger and concern on her face.

"What happened to him?" Rin asked, suddenly concerned.

"Not sure." Ivor grimaced. "But somewhere in it he must've taken a blow to the head."

Rin was about to dismiss Fievel's injury when she remembered the boy wasn't Tavi. Blood could settle on the brain after an injury like that.

She was concerned for the boy, but she also didn't want to be in this place any longer. Even with the Gen1 dead, it didn't feel safe for them to stay. They needed to push on, to get off these tracks and into open space.

She was about to suggest they carry the unconscious boy when she saw Magnus's face. Where before he had been smiling, for the briefest moment she saw something else in his expression, as he watched Lark staring at Fievel. There was pain there.

His eyes flicked to Rin's as he became aware of her watching him, and he shrugged, trying to dispel the honesty of the moment. Rin wondered at the meaning of a look like that, but she didn't have time to consider it further. Marta was already speaking.

"If there was one down here, there could be others. I'll examine Fievel – if I can wake him, we should keep moving. I don't like it, mind. It'd be better for him to rest, but it is what it is."

Marta hadn't needed to do anything, however, as they all heard a quiet groan spill from the boy's lips. Slowly, he pushed himself up to sitting and placed a hand against his head.

"What happened?" he said thickly, his hand propping up his aching head. "Did you kill it?"

They all waited, expecting Lark to answer, but she continued to stare at the boy, unmoved by his change in condition.

"It's dead," Magnus answered reassuringly, when the silence had grown too awkward to bear.

"What happened to you?"

Reece's question caused the boy to blink quickly, as though trying to remember a night's dream that had faded with the dawn.

"Oh, I... I'm not sure. I saw that thing come out of the darkness after Lark." He paused then, flinching under the glare of the simmering girl. "Then I felt too hot, and more than a little dizzy, and then I just wasn't standing anymore..." He trailed off.

Each one of the others looked away uncomfortably, knowing that it sounded as though the boy had simply fainted. Only Lark seemed pleased by the news, as the coldness and anger in her demeanour seemed to melt away at this revelation.

"It happens, Stacks," she replied in an offhand way that both dismissed the thing and dared anyone else to say otherwise.

Fievel looked at her for a moment, confused by the sincerity of her kindness.

Then, just as quickly, the moment passed.

Marta shuffled closer to examine the bruise that was spreading across his brow. What followed were her usual questions. Rin had heard them so many times she could have asked him herself. Did he feel sick? Was he dizzy? How many fingers was she holding up? It took a while to run through the list but, finally, Marta seemed satisfied that no real harm had been done.

"Best we get moving, then," the old woman said at last.

Magnus reached down a hand to help Fievel up, holding onto his shoulder a moment longer to make sure the boy remained standing on his own. Satisfied he would keep his feet, Magnus then offered a hand to Lark, who looked up at him from beneath disdainful brows, her mouth set in a forced grin that did not speak of a person well pleased.

Rin thought that if it were her in Magnus's place, she would have pulled that hand back faster than if had she offered it to a biting dog, but Magnus just left it there.

Lark rolled her eyes, the gesture full of its usual condescension.

Then, without taking his hand, she pushed herself lithely to her feet and winked at him. Rin wondered at the meaning of that exchange, trying to decide if Magnus was supposed to be hurt or offended by her abrasive manner. He appeared to feel neither emotion, chuckling and shaking his head instead, as if it was a thing he should have expected all along.

CHAPTER EIGHT
WRETCHED MISTAKES

With the way forward already lit, they wasted little time packing up their few possessions and moving on. Rin fell into her usual spot behind Marta, and noticed that the others had all taken their former positions in the line as well. It was just as she was about to turn and place her hand on the old woman's shoulder that she remembered it. For a second, her heart seemed to thump hollow in her chest, as though it had forgotten how to beat its usual rhythm. The way Magnus had looked at Lark... for the briefest moment, she had seen something of the way Ieuan used to look at her.

Pain immediately followed the recognition of her friend's absence, and the magnitude of such loss threatened to break her anew. If it hadn't been for the challenge that Lark's hard eyes had offered to Magnus in reply, she wondered if the girl might have cried. The red-headed boy's look had mirrored her own loss too closely, yet the tension the pair held between them now made Rin uncomfortable. Something inside her squirmed against Lark's simmering anger and the way she offered it to Magnus in return for his kindness. The feeling seemed so misplaced that Rin could neither understand nor easily dismiss it.

"Is everyone ready?" Marta croaked. "If we walk through the night, we should reach the old wretch by morning."

How Marta could tell how much time had passed, Rin didn't know. She only knew she had slept little down here, but was not yet tired. From that, she could assume that not much more than a full day had passed above them.

"No reason to hang around that I can think of, unless you want to admire the view?" Lark remarked dryly, her eyes flashing to where they all knew the body lay, unburied.

They continued to walk on in silence for what felt like a long time. All the while, Rin strained her ears to pick out any sound that might indicate something amiss on the tracks ahead, but only the sounds of their own movement echoed back at her, cold and deafening in the nothingness.

Regrettably, that left a lot of time for thinking, and once more Rin began to question what twist of fate had led Marta down onto these tracks in the life she had lived before. The only information she had to draw from was what Marta had muttered to them all at the opening to the tracks. Namely, that Marta knew Cornelius from a long time ago, that she had always known these tracks existed, and that the cantankerous old man owed her a favour. Rin hoped it was a big one. It would need to be in order to balance the cost of what they were asking for.

Rin knew for sure now that if they succeeded in getting the others out of the Tunnels, their only hope of getting everyone all back to the Cove alive lay down here on these tracks. If there had been any doubt in her mind before, her fight with that Gen1 had made that clearer than ever. While the odd one might make it down here, the Ashlands above were teeming with them. She set her teeth in frustration. They only had one shot at this: they would have no choice but to destroy this place behind them. It would be difficult enough to take such a large group safely through the swamp, but to do it quickly? She knew they would end up carving a trail that even a blind man could follow, right to the hidden opening of these tracks. The thought of leaving such a direct passage to the Cove open to every guard in the Empire made her insides twitch.

She shook her head, not wanting to think such thoughts right now; it was too close to thinking about Ieuan. Getting the others out had become irrevocably linked with getting him back. Trying to refocus, she considered instead what she remembered about Cornelius and tried to imagine in what possible life Marta could have crossed paths with such a person. An old man, hermitted away and obsessed with his work, oddly fixated on seeds and studying the Gen1 creatures. What would drive someone like that into such isolation, deep under the ground? Rin felt a prickle of unease, a sensation that told her surely nothing good could have shaped such a life that way.

Marta came so suddenly to a stop that Rin nearly walked into her. The light and tracks ended together in this spot. Only a smooth, stone wall, punctuated by thick wooden pegs, marked that this was the end of the track.

"Now what?" Lark drawled from the back, unable to see what Marta and Rin were looking at.

"Water skins," Marta replied, not offering further explanation and reaching out towards Rin.

Without hesitation, Rin handed hers over and turned to collect the others that were already being passed up the line.

"What has that kook built now?" Ivor said, the jibe clearly trying to mask his trepidation. "Not more explosions, Marta?"

"Pfft, men," Marta huffed. "All that noise and smoke and for what? The same outcome but double the problems. No, nothing quite as dramatic as that. He wanted to, mind you, but no. When it comes right down to it, you just can't trust all those powders and grits. When they get old, sometimes they just start banging and cracking all on their own, and then at other times the damned stuff just fizzles like wet leaves on a fire. No. *This* is more reliable. It'll take a while longer mind, but it's reliable."

While she was mumbling her thoughts to no one in particular, she had begun sloshing water onto the wooden pegs. The dry timber took up the water thirstily, and soon she had used all but the last of their water rations.

"Now we wait," she said authoritatively, stepping back.

At first, they all watched the pegs keenly, like they were waiting for some spectacular magician's trick. But nothing seemed to happen, and as the time stretched out, Rin became less and less convinced. She was starting to wonder as to the wisdom of using almost all of their water when the cracking began. Each noise was deafening and magnified by its own echo, as crack after crack appeared in the wall before them. Each jagged line soon joined with the next, all of them meeting at the wooden pegs. That was when she realised the simplicity of it: the dry wooden pegs had greedily gulped down the water they were offered and had begun to swell with each drop. One or two alone might not have been enough to do it, but so many of them, spaced as they were, acted like a dozen little wedges driven deep into the stone. Even Rin understood that two things could not occupy the same space at the same time, and with no ability to accommodate the swelling wooden wedges, the man-made stone had simply split and cracked.

With the last crack ringing in her ears, Rin felt a rush of moving air as the dusty stone toppled away from them and into the space behind.

"Ahh!" The old man's voice rang out, startled and creaky from lack of use.

At first, they could see nothing through the thick dust, but as it began to settle, Rin saw him. The falling stone had knocked him to the floor, and a heavy covering of powdery white dust coated him from head to toe, filing the lenses of his glasses.

"Who's there? Who is causing all this mess?" Cornelius called out, dismayed.

Unfortunately for the youngest brother, it was Ivor who stepped through the haze of stony dust first, just as the old man had wiped his coated glasses.

"You! Oh, a fine mess! The clumsy one is back and is bringing down Cornelius's house on Cornelius's head. A fine mess!" He coughed slightly as the particles hit the back of his throat. "Not enough that they break his upper-downer, now they have come back to break his home as well!" He continued coughing and spitting little flecks of debris from his mouth. "Well, not this time. This time Cornelius will not be running around helping the brats. He doesn't care how many seeds they have this time. This time the brats can—"

But what the 'brats' could do Rin would never find out, as the man suddenly stopped speaking. He was looking up from his spot amongst the rubble, straight into the Marta's face.

"Well, I'll be damned."

"Oh, you are already damned, Cornelius. You and I both know that," Marta replied coldly, and the man flinched back from her as though struck.

"That one is older – much older – but it is still her." He was peering up at the old woman more closely. "Not my fault, Marta. You know it wasn't my fault. I..."

Rin thought he was going to start rambling again, but he abruptly changed course.

"You're not supposed to come that way! It was agreed. Agreed not to come down here and agreed it was not Cornelius's fault." He added the last part as though reminding himself of something important.

"And yet, is there anything more wicked than the righteous intentions of misguided men?" Marta said, keeping her eyes fixed on him.

It was a saying Rin had heard her utter in different variations many times, but never had she felt such a weight of sincerity behind those words until now.

The old man blinked hard and shook his head determinedly. "Not Cornelius's fault. Nope."

"Yet your designs still remain in place," Marta retorted. "Don't they, Cornelius?"

The dust was still swirling around the room, creating an ominous atmosphere of smoke and mystery. The others stood unmoving, watching Cornelius and Marta exchange unfinished thoughts that made no sense to anyone. Rin wondered if Marta's tactic was wise. Clearly, she wanted to remind the old man of whatever it was that had happened in the past, but it seemed like an odd way to go about asking for help, even if help was owed.

"Cornelius is sorry. Not my designs, not truly. Well, perhaps they were my designs once, yes. But not my ideas. Not their purpose. Not my fault." His shoulders slumped forwards and the usually terse man looked almost pathetic, sitting defeated and dusty on the cave floor. "Why are they coming here and reminding Cornelius of these things? Terrible things they want him to remember." He bristled again. "They are not supposed to be here, so he asks again, *why* are they coming here now?"

Marta let the silence build as her scowl deepened and her eyes narrowed. Every inch of her made it clear that she did not care what his intentions had been. When she finally spoke, her mouth was pinched as if her lips begrudged the words slipping free.

"Well, you are in luck. I have come to give you a chance to set it right.”

The old man’s face hardened and took on a suspicious edge but he said nothing.

“We are going to tear it down, Cornelius. All of it. And you’re going to help us.”

For a few seconds, the man continued cleaning his glasses on his shirt and then, as if suddenly the words had landed on him all at once, he quickly placed them on.

“Ha ha!” Cornelius laughed, clapping his hands together gleefully, his eyes large and round under the magnification of his lenses.

Rin was not the only one shocked by his suddenly change in demeanour.

“I have waited a long time for this. I have not been idle. I have plans, Marta. I know how to do this thing now. Not like before. I know how to make splits where I want them now. I... oh, but Cornelius is stuck again.” Concern replaced what a moment before had been jubilation in his voice.

The speed at which the man jumped from idea to idea was almost dizzying.

“The people? They filled his place with people, Marta. Cornelius asks himself, how do we take them out? Cornelius doesn’t hurt them. I don’t do that, Marta.”

“Will you two stop speaking in riddles?” Lark snapped, and Rin realised for the first time that the girl seemed jealous to be sharing her usually prickly friend with the old woman. “It’s very tiresome.”

“Not riddles, he says to the smart one. Old stories. Bad stories. Cornelius doesn’t like to remember those stories.” He shook his head again, as though trying to dislodge the memories.

Lark glared first at him, then at Marta, raising her eyebrows dubiously, and Rin thought she knew why. It was one thing to trust Cornelius down here – they had no other choice, as his knowledge of the shafts and the Ashlands was unmatched – but it was a different thing entirely to consider him an ally against the Empire. Lark's face mirrored Rin's thoughts – Cornelius was a liability.

Walking over to Marta, Lark leaned in closer, whispering, "Are you sure about this?"

"Oh, I'm sure." Marta didn't bother to whisper her reply. When the pause had grown long enough to be uncomfortable, she added, "After all, Cornelius built the Capital Tunnels."

Every head turned to fix on the man, who winced, shrinking smaller and closing his eyes, only further confirming the truth of her words. Marta's face was hard, as though she had known it was the right time to deliver this bitter thing. The rigid tension in her stance declared that it was better said now than later, when such an admission might harm the group more fatefully. It seemed, however, that she had still underestimated the effect it would have at this moment. Magnus moved first, seizing the old man by the front of his shirt and lifting him off his feet.

"You loathsome excuse for—"

He didn't get to finish. Lark had kicked the back of his left knee, buckling the boy half to the ground. The old man's feet touched the floor once more and Lark's hands wrapped over Magnus's.

"Let him go," she said, the warning clear in her voice.

"Do you have any idea what it was like down there?" Magnus panted, barely able to catch his breath through his anger.

"No, I don't." She stared hard into his eyes. "Let go of his shirt, Magnus."

Her tone lacked its usual patronising edge. Instead, it held both pity and calm, yet there was no compromise in it.

When he didn't let go, she went on. "Are you going to kill him? Or maybe just hurt him some? Will that make you feel better?"

Magnus's hands tightened, the cloth of Cornelius's shirt bunching closer around the man's neck.

"It won't change anything that happened to you, Magnus. Besides, *look at him*. You heard what he said, same as I did. Whatever it was he did, he deserves the chance to explain." Lark looked from the boy's eyes to the old man and felt Magnus's hands relax a little. "This better be good, old man," she added, her eyes flashing quickly to the other two brothers, then back to Cornelius, "or I'll kill you myself." The last she said in a chillingly calm voice that spoke of the honesty of the threat.

Cornelius gulped as he loosened the material that had bunched around his neck. "That brat is a brute, coming into Cornelius's home and roughing him up like a..."

Lark shot him a warning look and the old man trailed off, though still managed to hold onto his air of disgruntlement. Rin found herself stepping closer when he finally spoke again. His voice was more defensive now than it had been, and quieter.

"Cornelius was just a young man then. With all the hairs still on his head," he said, patting the bald spot in the centre as though that was an explanation in itself.

The silence stretched out behind the words and each of them continued to stare at him. Eventually, he seemed to realise that this would not be a sufficient answer, and Rin watched as his face creased in concentration.

He winced, tapping his brow. "Young one's heads, so full of nonsense. Cornelius's young head was full of nonsense too."

Rin felt her intrigue growing with every word he spoke. She

was eager to finally find out what had happened all those years ago, and how it had led them to this place now.

Cornelius began by explaining how, as a younger man, he had believed in the goodness of the Senate. That, back then, he had loved his work and was convinced that the restoration of the Empire would be built on the back of scientists like himself.

"They did not understand the greatness of Cornelius's work. How I could set things right. They were not smart like *that* one." Cornelius looked out from the corner of his eye at Lark, clearly trying to regain his ally with the thin complement he had used before.

The girl's eyes only narrowed further in reply but, even though she clearly saw his duplicity, the corners of her mouth twitched, threatening a grin.

His next words were softer and less jumbled than they had been before. Rin could see that he was choosing them carefully, seeming to understand that he would only get one chance to share his tale. With great care he explained how, at the time, it hadn't mattered to him who was receiving the most praise or funding. With the exuberance of youth, he had been certain that if he could perfect his work, they would all understand. Then he would have all the funding and resources he could dream of and the need for the Military Division would be obsolete.

Rin could see a glimmer of that younger man he had once been as he detailed the work he had been engaged in. He seemed to become more focused when describing how, in those early years, adapting the seedlings hadn't been that hard. How, back then, he had spliced and grafted until whole new varieties of grains learned to thrive in his test environments. She could sense his pride when he explained that, in the following year, several of his species had been shipped out to villages and had begun to thrive equally well in the fields out there.

That had been the year he had been ready to start his new research, but it would be this next project that would really test him, and there was a feverish light behind his eyes as he recounted it.

"Oh yes, they laughed at young Cornelius. Laughed at my ideas when I first proposed them to the funding committee. But I knew I could do this thing. I thought many times that I would enjoy showing those old professors that I was not foolish."

Using a great many words that were not known to Rin, he explained the botanicals he needed to graft, and the technical difficulty of designing the structure. With something bordering on theatrical flourish, he announced to them that he had called the project '*Pulmonis Botanica*'.

Seeing their blank faces at his grand reveal, he shook his head. "See? You see! They would do the *breathing*." He took deep, demonstrative breaths. "Cornelius's botanical lungs would be breathing in the waste of the world and then sighing out clean air. They would have changed everything. They could have *fixed* everything," he said, with the air of a performer unveiling the final twist.

Looking at the confusion on the faces around him, he rolled his eyes. Then he started speaking more slowly, as though addressing a group of small children.

"They doubted him. Always, they were convinced I was going to fail, but their short sight was not Cornelius's problem. I was always knowing I could make it work."

Even after a year's work, when he still hadn't completed even one full working system, he told them that had remained sure. He had dreamt that it would only be a matter of time before they could rebuild the entire Empire. That they could reach, and even surpass, the heights other generations had known in the Age of Greatness.

The three brothers were beginning to lose patience with the tale and Rin could see that the old man's enthusiasm for what had eventually become their prison was only increasing the wounds it had inflicted.

Cornelius seemed oblivious as he went on, telling them just what had happened during those fateful years in the Capital. "But they were not smart. Old thinking. Tired and foolish. It wouldn't fix anything, that thinking," he grumbled. Looking down, his tone suddenly took on a sad and regretful edge. "Cornelius didn't know they would use his work like that. My nephew is not a good boy. Too much caring about the accolades and not enough caring about the work. Too much caring about the funding and what the military men were asking for."

Then, Cornelius described how he had found out their true intentions that fateful night he was taken down by his nephew into the Lab.

"Cornelius did not like what he was seeing down there. So he tells his nephew these things are wrong and he wants no part in them. But Theodore was not listening to me though."

Rin felt the others' eyes flash towards her, as her own stomach turned over. She didn't know if Theodore was a common name in the Capital, but it certainly seemed an unlikely coincidence that two named such might work in the Labs at the same time. She fought to keep her face neutral as she considered with an intense horror that this may be another dark legacy her father had created.

Cornelius was now in full flow, unaware of the ripple that had washed over the others as he continued to tell them how he had protested.

"Such terrible ideas I heard down there – they made Cornelius sick. Many times sick." He wiped at his mouth as though he could still taste the bile. "But in the days that came after, they were not seeing sense. They were not seeing anything Cornelius was showing them. I tried to stop them with all the different words I knew, but they were not hearing."

He groaned again as he explained how it had seemed to him that he was the only one who could see the despicable nature of what they were proposing. When they wouldn't listen, his only option had become clear to him. He knew he must tell the people. He had been sure that only collective outrage over such vileness could unite a population against the Empire. He was convinced that if they all knew the truth about the Generation Project, and the Abatement Mandate that would limit the life cycle of the lowland population, they would rally together and end this for sure.

"Cornelius still doesn't know how the Senate found out. Perhaps I was betrayed by someone I was telling, or maybe they were just seeing it on my face."

Either way, they had come for him. He told them how he wondered if perhaps they had intended for it to look like a fall down the stairs in the night, or some other ill-fated accident at home, but by chance, he had been awake at that late hour, desperately penning missives to any he thought may still listen to reason. It was then he had heard them, sneaking down the corridor to his room. He had hidden and listened as they searched his quarters, all the while plotting and scheming about how they might dispose of him; laughing as they read his letters and his desperate pleas for the abandonment of Theodore's plans.

"Cornelius was a long time inside his trunk. I was wishing then that my shoes were not in there with me, or at the very least that they did not smell so bad. Inside his own trunk, inside his own cupboard!" He repeated it, making clear the indignity he had felt at such a thing. "I stayed there until long after their voices had faded, still thinking it was not safe to be moving."

With downcast eyes, he told them how he had found the courage to flee just as the sun was starting to rise; how he had spent almost a week hiding in the Void. That was when the Alliance had found him, and he considered himself lucky that it had been them and not the guards.

In exchange for certain information, the Alliance had helped him into hiding. "So, now I am here. I learn what there is to be learned about the mutations they created – the ones they didn't expect to live, just like they did not expect Cornelius to live – and I continue my work on the plants. Only my work can fix things. Only that can clean up all this corruption in the air."

"How did the Alliance get you here?" Lark asked, squinting at him and then at the old woman.

He nodded before answering. "Marta was already a part of the resistance by then and—"

Marta sniffed loudly and Cornelius looked at her. Rin could have sworn she saw the almost imperceptible shake of the old woman's head.

"Yes, well, probably right," Cornelius continued. "That is a story for another day. Not Cornelius's story either, that one. Not really."

Rin had a familiar feeling that the old woman was once again keeping secrets from her, and more than ever she felt irritated at the deception. She was just about to voice her objection when Torsten spoke.

"The Clag. That's what they're using to 'limit the life cycle', isn't it?"

Cornelius didn't answer, but nodded his head again .

As the enormity of his revelation fell on Rin, she was momentarily staggered. If all that he had said was true, the Tunnels must stretch on for miles and miles under the earth. Miles and miles of darkness, pumping out that thick and deadly foulness. She felt a lurch inside her: the Clag wasn't some unavoidable legacy left behind by the Fall. It was a foulness created by her own father and scientists like him. Not an ill-fated inheritance, but a weapon that even now, day after day, people were breathing in by the lungful. It was poisoning them all...

No, that wasn't right. Not *everyone*, she realised, recalling how clear the air in the Capital had been that night she had gone after the archives. A fresh wave of anger surged within her. She had seen for herself how the Clag was thickest in the Void, but she knew it carried far into the villages too. Wave after wave of horror intensified inside her as she considered the dust and grime that settled on people's homes in the Dale was not merely a consequence of the uptown industry, as they had all been told, but rather a cruel mandate of a corrupt Empire.

Ieuan's mother flashed into her thoughts. A young woman who had sickened and died of lung fever. She had not just died, though. She had been *murdered*. How many others like her had met the same fate?

She was still trying to understand what she was hearing when she remembered that Gibb and Ieuan were down in those tunnels, where the air was most concentrated and deadly.

"How long can someone survive down there, in the Tunnels?" she asked frantically, unable to stop herself.

"Depends," Cornelius replied, shrugging.

"Depends on what?" She was barely holding her anger in check.

"Tavi don't sicken." It was Torsten who spoke. "In theory, we could survive down there indefinitely. That's right, isn't it, old man?"

A collective shudder ran through the three brothers.

"From what we saw of the others," continued Torsten, "if they were healthy enough before they came in, perhaps a year. Less, if they were susceptible to it."

Rin frowned. *Susceptible to it?* That was the second time someone had said that. What did that even mean? Everyone was susceptible to death. She might not understand about botanicals and ventricles, but she knew about death as well as the next person.

She wracked her memories, desperately trying to remember if Ieuan had been ill much as a child. Aside from the odd winter fever, she couldn't think of anything that stood out. Not like his mother. Was *she* what was meant by susceptible? The woman had been plagued by one sickness or another for as long as Rin had known her.

"Why hasn't anyone stopped this?" she asked, outraged and confused in equal measure.

"You think we didn't try?"

The indignity of Marta's tone let Rin know that this would not be the first time the Alliance had tried to bring down the Tunnels.

"We lost good people, time after time, in our attempts. Even after we realised we couldn't hope to do it alone, we tried to warn the people, just like Cornelius thought to do. But if you think they were keen to join arms with Tavi and Tavi collaborators, you can think again. We lost almost as many people that way, too, and the few of them that didn't mark us as liars and traitors were soon put off when the fighting started."

Lark snorted at Marta's words, clearly disgusted by the kind of people whose silence had participated in the genocide of her kind; whose ignorance was killing their own kind now too. Rin wondered then whether Lark might be happy to leave the Tunnel system standing, once they had got their people out. Perhaps she would see it as a fitting justice to let it continue to spill out the deadly smog for people like them. Maybe Lark would not see the crimes of the Empire like she did, but instead as a fitting punishment for the lowland sheep.

Rin frowned, fear and defeat rising in equal measure. "If you've tried before, what's going to be different this time?"

"Well – you, Rin. *You* are what's going to be different," Marta said, almost sadly.

Rin looked up from under her eyebrows. She didn't know yet what that was supposed to mean, but she could tell from the way the old woman said it that it wasn't something Marta wanted her to do.

She thought of Ieuan's mother, gasping for a breath she could never quite catch. She thought of the little bit of light that had left Ieuan's eyes forever on the day that she had died. That alone would have been enough, but the horror still on Magnus's face, the anxious sweat that Ivor had often wiped away while they had been down here, and the dead emptiness behind Torsten's eyes since they had descended into the earth would have persuaded her too. Just as quickly, her thoughts flicked to Fievel, who had watched all of this with grave attention. His mother, was she just another of the thousands whose lives had been cut short by the Empire's design?

All those terrible things would have made her agree to just about anything in that moment. Anything that would bring an end to such despicable foulness. Yet, in her heart, she knew none of these horrors would be the true reason she would go back. Her father had known it, and she knew it too.

No matter who tried to stop her, no matter the risk or the cost, whatever it was they asked of her, she would do it to get Ieuan back.

The others were still talking, but she had not been listening.

"When Cornelius was just a young boy," the old man was rambling again, "he did not know how to make his own splits or rifts. He knows now, though. Still won't be enough. Not unless we can get the chips off. Not unless someone goes in and takes them off. Otherwise, he won't. Won't kill the ones already down there, Marta. *Won't.*"

He seemed almost feverish now as he scrabbled through his papers. Rin didn't know how to read the blue-lined drawings or any of the words scrawled onto them, but she did recognise the piece of tattered paper that he was currently pulling out. The familiar design of the chip stared back at her, and she instantly recalled Tilly's horror when Cornelius had thrust it under her eyes. He was tapping it hard now, as if worried they would all overlook such a thing of importance.

"Have to find out how to take them off," he went on. "All of them. Have to."

"Rin, show him," Marta said calmly.

Rin wasn't sure she wanted to. The old man's intensity unnerved her. He seemed so scattered. What if he lost the papers she had gone to such trouble to recover amongst all the other pages scattered here, or damaged them somehow? She looked at Marta questioningly.

"It's alright, girl. Show him."

Rin still wasn't sure she trusted him, but if they needed his help, she knew she had no other choice. Reluctantly, she removed the oiled leather cloth from within her travel pack, carefully untying the strands that held it tightly rolled. Cornelius quickly cleared a space on the table for her, as though hungering for a meal long overdue. His eyes widened as they feasted on the pages.

"Oh my. Yes. Why, yes, this..." There was utter amazement in his voice. "How are the brats getting these papers?" He began to turn them over, faster and faster. As his eyes raked over each new sheet, his smile grew wider and wider, almost disconcerting in its glee. "They will need keys, but he sees that it is all here. Quite simple, really. He can make these keys. Hundreds of them, if they need them. They will have to practice. Need to learn to read the codes. That's harder. Learn how to match them up – some of them can learn this, though. *That one*, yes, and her too." Cornelius pointed first to Lark, then Rin.

Closing one eye, he squinted at the others, appearing less convinced about their prospects. Then he shrugged and went back to examining the archives.

"This time, Marta. This time we'll stop them."

CHAPTER NINE
RESILIENCE AND RESISTANCE

Rin had stopped paying attention. Their talk had shifted to the matter of planning, as they weighed each idea and every obstacle in turn, always circling back to the same problem they could not solve. It had felt as though all of them seemed to have something of value to add to the task apart from her, and she had grown frustrated and tired, listening to their ideas building in momentum, only to end up stuck at the same complication each time.

They had already considered and dismissed several of the ways they could gain entry to the Tunnels. One plan had seemed the most promising: a small group dressed in Empire uniform could be enough to overwhelm the guards at the entrance. This plan, while obvious, had seemed to offer an immediate solution, until Torsten pointed out that once inside there were several more checkpoints, and all more heavily manned than the outer one.

"Sooner or later, we'd run into a group too large to fight our way past," Torsten had argued, his mouth pinched at the words. "The problem is getting through all the checkpoints without alerting the guards. Once we're through the last one, no one will care enough about us to check if we're alive or dead."

After that, they had considered the ventilation hatches that were unguarded but alarmed, then a number of different forms of subterfuge, designed to draw out the Tunnel guards. Cornelius had proposed another option, landing firmly in favour of creating an entrance of their very own. He had felt strongly that it would be quicker if they used a carefully placed split to punch a hole from the adjacent Capital sewers into what he called the 'left lobe' of the Tunnels.

Unfortunately, the problem with all of these plans, which they kept returning to, was time. Rin understood before they had started planning that the tunnels were vast, and now she knew they were complex and intertwined too. That alone would make finding Ieuan and Gibb problematic, let alone the hundreds of chipped Tavi. Not the kind programmed for guard duty or defence of the Empire, but the dulled and dead-eyed drones that would labour away unquestioningly, their sole purpose to expand and maintain the Empire's most insidious weapon. Added to these numbers would be who knew how many lowland prisoners. Those citizens accused of helping her kind, or some other treasonous act against the Empire. Without proper records, they had no way to accurately guess how many bodies might be stuck down there, or what kind of fluctuation they could expect on any given day.

Despite Cornelius expounding on the subject for quite some time, Rin still didn't truly understand how they were going to remove the chips. What he *had* been able to impress upon them all was that each removal would take time. Each one would require some kind of unique code as well as the use of the key. So far, this obstacle seemed to be the most complicated part of the plan; a part that would need to be repeated over and over if and when they found their way down into that evil place. Rin had to accept that, for this test, her strength and speed may not be enough to ensure their success. She could feel their options narrowing the longer the endless debating went on, although all of them had agreed on one thing; they had to get into those

Tunnels undetected. Fighting empire guards, setting off alarms, or blowing holes in the infrastructure wasn't going to give them the kind of head start they needed.

Feeling the sudden need to be alone, Rin drifted away from the others. *How am I ever going to find Ieuan and Gibb down there?* Closing her eyes, she sighed deeply. They would be lucky if any of them survived this foolishness. It was such a complicated plan, scrappy and incomplete, and it all felt so hopeless. For a second time, she considered the idea that she might only be able to save Ieuan and Gibb. Of course, she would help those others if she could, but part of her knew now that if she left the Capital for a second time without her friends beside her, some part of her would not survive that loss intact.

Something inside her settled into place, then. A surety that she would leave that place with Ieuan and Gibb or she would not leave it at all.

Sinking to the floor and stretching out her hand to touch the empty space beside her, she felt oddly calm. It wasn't that long ago that she and Ieuan had sat here together. It had always been her who was supposed to risk the danger of the Capital, not him, and with that thought the guilt inside her grew. The sensation was nauseating and hot as she realised that she hadn't truly considered that he might be the one who did not make it back – not until it was too late.

She could still hear the others continuing their debate.

"Well, the Alliance might have found some way around that." Marta's voice grated with exasperation. "You saying the same thing to me in all manner of different words is making my damn head hurt."

"Not Cornelius's fault that the woman asks him the same question but wants a different answer," he replied, lifting his chin and pursing his lips indignantly.

"So, what now?" Magnus interrupted, before Marta could voice whatever scathing response had been forming on her tongue.

The old woman huffed, letting her insult pass unsaid. "Cornelius will make the keys. At least one for each of you, more if he has time. Then we'll need enough of his powders to collapse the Capital Tunnels." She looked at Cornelius meaningfully and pointed back towards the collapsed wall, indicating the tracks beyond. "Of course, Cornelius will have to collapse the tracks down here as well."

"Should have done that years ago," the old man piped in. "Before these ones arrived and made a mess of Cornelius's home..." He trailed off as he noticed them all staring at him.

Marta was scowling fiercest of all before she went on. "You six," she said, pointing to Reece, Lark, Rin and the three brothers, "will go back to the Cove. Learn how it is done and then take that contemptible thing off Tilly's back."

"How are we—"

"No, Torsten, don't ask me how. I've no head for the chicken scratches on that parchment." She pointed at the lines and markings on the papers that Cornelius had laid out into piles on the desk. "Just find a way to get it done. Fischer is a practical man and he's taught ones younger than you a great deal more. He'll be able to make sense of it." She nodded, as though reinforcing her own confidence in the man. "If by some miracle the Alliance can work out how to get you into the Tunnels, you'll need to be able to work quickly, so find a way to practise until you can repeat it blindfolded."

Rin was nodding back now, finding that the squirming ache inside her was lessening with this semblance of a plan. Then she noticed Lark staring at Marta with a cold fury that made Rin stand up and move protectively towards the old woman without thinking.

"And you two?" Lark said through clenched teeth, her darting eyes focusing on Marta, then Fievel. "What is it that you'll be doing?"

Marta looked at the girl for a moment, her own eyes narrowing at the challenge in her tone. "We'll be going back to the Void. We'll need the Partisan's help if we want to take a group that large through his Stacks—"

"You really would take him back there, wouldn't you?" Lark cut her off. "Even now, you'd take him back into that Clag?" She all but spat the words at Marta and the old woman's lips thinned as she tried to quell her irritation at the interruption.

"He's the only one who knows the way out of the swamp to the Stacks, and he promised the Partisan he'd be back. I don't intend to start my negotiations by telling the Partisan that was a lie—"

For the second time, Lark did not let her finish. "I shouldn't be surprised. You've known about the Clag all this time. You've always known. Why not let him marinate in it some more?"

"Fievel and I will go back to the Void," Marta tried to continue, as though completely oblivious to the girl's outrage.

"Except it's not a risk for you, is it, *old woman*?" Lark's voice was twisting with disgust. "Not dangerous for *you* like it is for *him*."

"Watch yourself, girl. I've indulged you for about as long as I'm going to on this."

Rin had never heard so much threat in the old woman's tone, but Lark didn't stop, and she was walking towards Marta.

"Torsten already told us, didn't he. Already told us who is

and who isn't 'susceptible'. That's what he said, wasn't it?" Lark pushed the old woman back, hard.

Rin made to catch Marta's arm, intending to steady her, but the old woman didn't need the help. Marta flicked her staff out behind her, bracing herself against the shove, and then swirled it forward, hooking one of Lark's feet off the ground and causing the usually agile girl to fall. For a brief second, Rin was reminded of the beetroot-faced man who had been in the crowd the day Marta had first claimed her as kin. Rin had been so surprised by the speed and strength that the old woman could still muster.

Lark made to rise, but Rin stepped between them and the girl faltered.

Rin's voice was lower than usual. "I told you it would be me you'd find."

Lark snorted a disdainful laugh. "That one doesn't need your help, Rin. She knows how to take care of herself just fine." She pushed herself up to sitting, but stayed on the ground, dusting the powdery remnants of cracked stone from her hands. "When are you going to wake up, dummy? How many times do you have to dance the same dance with her before you can recognise a barefaced liar when you see one?"

Rin's brow creased as she looked back at Marta, as though unable to see how such a comment could relate to anything between the two of them.

Lark's mouth drew upwards into a sly smile. "Last chance, old woman."

Rin turned away from the girl on the ground and was looking at the old woman now, confused. She hadn't expected Lark's taunts to carry any weight. After everything they had been through, what possible secret did Marta have left to keep? As she saw the concern and sadness etched on the old woman's features, though, she knew that Lark's threat had not been an empty one.

"Rin, I..." Marta started, but she didn't finish, seeming to run out of words before she had even begun.

"I guess you'd rather I tell her, then?" Lark said slowly. "You see, Killer, your dear 'grandmother' over there is—"

"Stop," Rin said flatly, turning back towards the girl, trying to halt whatever it was that was about to happen.

Lark looked as though she was starting to enjoy herself now, and she chuckled. "Oh, you are going to want to hear this, Erin."

There was a pause as no one spoke. Each one of them was waiting for Marta to be the one to say whatever it was that had been held back.

"Really, Marta? Still nothing?" Lark scoffed in disbelief. "Well, time's up, old woman. You know her secret; I think it's about time she knew yours. After all, there's no need for secrets between *Tavi*." Lark paused, savouring the surprise that seeped through the group as some worked it out more quickly than others. Then, seeing the blank look on Rin's face, she added, "Your grandmother is one of us, Rin. Or at least, she was, before they made whatever mess is left of her under there." She pointed at Marta's hunched back.

The others turned to look at the old woman, as the recognition of what Lark had said became clear to each one of them. Rin, however, kept her eyes fixed on the girl on the ground, unwilling to turn; to risk seeing the truth of the old woman's lie on her face.

None of this made sense. *Marta isn't Tavi... she would have told me... why wouldn't she have told me?* Then Rin was shaking her head as she choked out her breath in contempt of her own stupidity. Marta hadn't ever told Rin about herself, hadn't really ever told Rin *anything*, not outside what she absolutely *had* to know. She tried to swallow the tightness in her throat that rose with the realisation of that betrayal. Lark was right – she was stupid to believe that this woman, who had been a stranger on the day she had crawled out of the swamp, had become her family. Stupid to believe Marta had ever really cared anything for her at all.

As Rin looked at Lark's smug face, she found herself still hoping it was a lie. Yet the longer she stared at the girl, the more things began to filter into place. Marta was old – much too old, really – and stronger than she should be. Hunched, yes, but still faster than many who were much younger. Rin remembered that night by the campfire. Lark hadn't been testing to see if the old woman was capable of the journey... she was testing her. Seeing just how fast one who was already too old for this world could be.

Turning to face the old woman, Rin's eyes swept over that twisted spine. *Had they done that to her? Had someone crippled her like that, trying to remove her spurs?* For a moment, she felt a wave of pity and then pushed it away. She wanted to be angry; pity had no place in her heart right now.

No one else would meet Rin's eyes as she looked at the small group around her. She shook her head; she needed space. This place was too crowded and she longed to be alone. *No, not alone,* she thought. *With Ieuan.* He would know what to say to make it hurt less. But he wasn't here, and she couldn't think straight with so much tension hanging in the air.

Marta stepped forward. "Girl, I—"

"Don't." Rin cut her off. "I don't want to hear any more of your lies." She spat out the words, an ice-hard edge to her voice.

Marta flinched as Rin turned her back on all of them. The entrance to the shafts stretched out in front of her and the solitude it offered was too comforting to resist.

"You shouldn't go alone," Magnus called after her, but she

didn't stop.

Picking up her pace, she hoped none of them would follow her.

Rin walked for a while through the rough-cut stone. Not the smooth stone of the tracks, but the same shafts they had traversed with Cornelius all those nights ago. The blue glow from the moss dimly lighting the path both ahead and behind.

She realised then that the ringing in her ears would usually have started by now – that old familiar precursor to her violent tremors. But it had ceased to make an appearance. Now that she thought back, she hadn't truly felt that flooding panic since the night inside the Palace. Nowadays, the nightmares that haunted her were not flashbacks from her past, but entirely new, unknown terrors. Fear of the present and for the future. Fears for Ieuan, who could be alone and hurt in the tunnels. Fear that he was being tortured in the labs like Tilly had been, or worst of all, fear that Ieuan was already dead. Just simply gone, far beyond her reach to ever get back. She thought her head might burst with each new horror that flitted through her mind, and she fought to pull herself back into the now.

Marta was Tavi. After all the two of them had been through together, Marta had still kept so many secrets from her. Rin felt like she didn't know her grandmother at all, and somehow this one lie tainted every sincere moment they had shared. That hurt, but what hurt more was trying to reconcile the woman she thought she had known – who had cared for Gibb's wife, befriended her widower husband, looked out for his son – with the one who had allowed them to remain in the dusty remnants of a Clag that she knew would eventually kill them. That was the thing that was too awful to forgive.

Rin had been vaguely aware of footsteps following behind her since she left the others, but she still wanted to be alone. While the person had stayed far enough away not to be seen, their presence still encroached on her solitude.

"What?" Rin finally asked in frustration, turning around.

"Don't be mad at me, Killer. I'm not the one who lied to you," Lark replied cheerfully as she stepped into view. "Oh, and don't look so pathetic."

Rin felt her hackles rise.

"Ah, that's better." Lark nodded in satisfaction. "Angry is much better than pathetic."

"Just leave me alone," Rin muttered, the defeat in her voice leaching all the power from her words, making them sound hollow and flat. The girl made no sense to her at all.

"Ah I see, you want me to feel sorry for you, do you? You want me to feel bad, or else helpless like you do? And now you're upset because I don't?" Lark shook her head, as though dismissing the frivolous wishes of a child. "It's time you understood a few things, *Rin*. This world doesn't care how good you are; in fact, it doesn't care about people like us at all, not outside of making sure it can control us. All that matters is how strong you are, because if you can learn to be strong enough, you can force them to care." Lark waited, but when Rin said nothing, she sighed as though the task at hand was even more mammoth than she had feared. "It's easier for the Empire to convince us that we are the rabbits than it is for us to remember how to be the wolf." She paused, looking Rin up and down. "I for one would prefer not to be chewed up and spat out."

"What you did back there was cruel," Rin hissed through

clenched teeth.

"What I did was tell the truth." Lark laughed harshly. "You all want to hear the truth, right up until you can't stomach any more of it." She lazed against the wall, letting her head rest on the stone as though exhausted by the lesson. "Come on now, how long are you going to keep cowering and beating yourself up over rules no-one else is playing by before you realise what's going on here? They're all waiting to use us any way they can. Any way that suits them. The Empire is more direct about it, but the Alliance will use you too, if you let them. You must have heard them say it? That the Alliance has 'friends' all over the place, and yet Cornelius will tell you they never forget the 'favours' those friends seem to owe. Sooner or later, they find a way to get you mixed up their grand schemes, and it seems to me that it's never those doing the scheming who end up risking their necks over it."

"But not you, right?" Rin said, trying to mirror the girl's snide tone. "You're too smart to let anyone use you, I suppose?"

"Yes and no," Lark said, wrinkling her face and shrugging slightly. "If it was just me, then you could bet I wouldn't find myself caught up in this mess. But *him*?"

Although Lark hadn't said it, Rin knew she was talking about her brother.

"He's still foolish enough to join in with this nonsense. Still thinks there is some value in doing what's right, even in a world as corrupted as this one." The girl chuckled as though it was a charming but ridiculous notion.

"Someone needs to stop this," Rin argued, her voice rising with the anger she was struggling to hold back.

Her tone had made it sound like an accusation, and partly, it was. She knew the girl across from her understood better than anyone what fate awaited those currently trapped in the tunnels.

How could anyone just turn their back and ignore all those terrible things? There were children down there, the ones too small to fight on their own. Children like Lark had been, all those years ago, taken from their parents and expected to live lives of pain and suffering. Rin couldn't see how anyone could ignore that, but Lark didn't back down.

"You going to stop them, are you?" Lark asked, as though she did not expect an answer to such a ridiculous notion.

"I'm going to try." Rin knew how weak that sounded.

"How noble of you. Well, I didn't make the world this way, Rin, and if it was up to me, I'd take my brother and get as far away from here as possible. I'd let the whole sorry lot of them rot in it."

Rin failed to blink back her shock, then her face fell.

"You think that's cruel?" Lark went on, answering the look. "Do you think you could never be so awful as that, or is it the truth that, deep down, you crave a little piece of such freedom?"

"I would *never* be like you." Rin was relieved that her voice, at least, sounded certain of that.

"Oh, you think not? Tell me you don't feel it when that power is rushing inside you? The pull to let go of all the pain; to silence all the rules and forget about anything outside of fighting those who would see you hurt instead? A little part of that self-righteous, greater good that you could have traded to keep safe what you've lost? Or perhaps you think it's better to be here now, without your *friend*? Moping around, alone, wishing you had done more?"

For a moment, Lark left the question hanging in the air, but when Rin didn't answer, she went on.

"Well, I'm here, and Reece is here, and until you realise that you hold the potential to be the wolf and not the rabbit, then you're just waiting to lose to anyone who's already worked out that they have teeth."

The sting of her words caught in Rin's chest. It was true that Lark had kept her brother safe and that was more than she had managed to do for Ieuan. The pain of that admission galled her and she slumped back against the rock. It was too much when her heart already hurt this badly. She was tired and nothing about this was right, and yet some of it was too close to the truth for her to unpick what of it had merit anymore.

"No," Lark said firmly, noting the edge of defeat creeping back across Rin's face. "We don't have time for that, not if you want that boy of yours back in one piece." There was a pause before she added, "It's time you realised what you're capable of. *We're* the wolves, Rin, not them."

Rin was unsure what was rebuke and what was advice, and of the latter she wasn't convinced she could separate out what she once would've instantly known to be wrong. She did know what Lark meant. She had felt the draw of her abilities before, but, while the absence of emotion had liberated her, it had also scared her. The remorseless focusing of her senses had been a welcome tool when she had needed it, and there was little doubt it had saved all of their lives, but some of the things she had done while in that state had been savage.

"Wolves run in packs," Rin said half-heartedly, that part of the lecture making the least sense to her.

If Lark was suggesting that Rin should forget the others and care only about herself, that was not how wolves behaved. She had seen enough wolf packs hunting in the forest behind the Dale for that fact to cut through her confusion.

"Correct, and that's why I'm here," Lark replied, looking back the way they had come. "If that's what it takes to keep them safe, then it seems that you and I have something in common at last.”

Rin kept her head pressed against the cool rock as her eyes focused on the girl’s face. This was the first time Lark had said ‘them’, not just ‘him’. Was she talking about keeping *all* of them safe, instead of just her brother?

Even as she thought it, Rin knew that couldn’t be true. Maybe she was referring to Fievel... yes, that made sense. *That* was why Lark had come after her, and she had warned Rin of it, too. Right at the start, she had warned her that everyone was waiting to use her – and Lark was no different.

The older girl was smiling at her. “Looks like you’re finally getting it.”

“So what should I do?” Rin asked sullenly. “Say no? Refuse to let myself be used?”

Part of her already knew that she would not. Even though it would make her task harder, she was relieved to find she had not so easily given up on her friends.

“Just when I thought we were making progress,” Lark sighed, rolling her eyes dramatically again. “Don’t you feel it? That thing that’s eating away at you? The buzzing like angry bees inside your head? The way it nags at you and refuses to leave you alone?”

Rin felt a lurch at the girl’s words. Lark was the last person she would have thought might understand anything about those feelings that gnawed at her.

“How do you make it stop?” Rin asked quietly, suddenly desperate to learn how to silence such noise.

“We all have a monster inside of us. You keep yours trapped, shackled by the misguided sense that the world is good and fair. It doesn’t matter what you tell yourself though: it knows you’ve made the wrong choice. It tries to talk to you, to make sure you learn your lesson so you don’t let these things happen to you both again. You didn't let it out to fight for you when you should have; you kept it chained by that tiresome self-sacrificing act. You let them convince you to leave Ieuan behind, so now it's turned against you. It's trying to take up more space; make itself louder because it knows that until you learn to listen to it, to use it, there is a part of you that will always be tethered to repeating those mistakes again and again. You have to embrace it; understand what it's trying to tell you. Then go ahead and become whatever it is you need to become so that you don't let those mistakes happen again." Lark nodded at her, as though it was obvious and she should start doing this thing right now.

Rin stared at her in disbelief. "You make it sound easy."

"It's not." Lark shrugged. "But it gets easier. You'll see. When it stops eating away at you and starts chewing up your enemies instead, then you'll see what I mean."

Rin was surprised at the momentary sincerity the girl offered her, then her eyes narrowed suspiciously.

"I don't think I trust you."

"You shouldn't." That overly-pleasant smile was back on Lark's face. "You already know it, but I'll say it again so there is no confusion. Whatever happens, if you start to fall apart out there, I *will* leave you behind. If it comes to the moment where either you die or we both die, know that I won't risk my life for yours. But, with that said, you don't have to do all of this alone. If we work together, we might be able to avoid that moment – or at least delay it for a while longer."

Something inside Rin clicked into place at her words. This might not be the way she'd treat a friend, but Lark *was* being more honest than anyone else had been of late, and that honesty was not something she took lightly.

Lark held out her hand and Rin nodded as she reached out

to clasp the girl's wrist, sealing their pact. Looking down at the dirty bandage that still covered the place where her wound had probably already healed, she tried not to shiver at the memory.

It would take time, but perhaps there was something to be said for learning how to fight as a pack.

CHAPTER TEN
KEYS AND COOKPOTS

Lark had left her to her thoughts, though Rin suspected the girl had not gone all that far away. She knew she would have to face the others sooner or later. There was no option to just keep running this time, though. If she wanted Ieuan back, she was going to need them, and no amount of ground passing under her feet would change that – but she couldn't yet will herself towards that confrontation.

Closing her eyes, she sought inside for that familiar current, and was pleased to discover that the more often she reached for that part of herself, the easier it became to find. She didn't immediately grasp it, not wanting to let it drown her this time, but instead simply stroked the edges of that awareness, letting other sensations replace the concerns she had felt before. She wasn't seeking that kind of focus or the complete absence of fear or pain; she only wanted to quieten the noise just enough to be able to set it aside for a time.

As her senses sharpened, the damp cave seemed to burst into life around her, filling her nose with the earthy smell of mushrooms and her mind with the sudden certainty that not far from her were the furry bodies of little whiskered creatures that called this place home. The blue light that emanated from the moss had been dim before, but now it was bright enough to cast shadows. It was peaceful, in a strange way, at least compared to the last few days.

She took a deep breath of the damp air, trying to capture the moment of quiet in a way she could hold on to, then pushed herself up.

The walk back seemed to take longer than the time it had taken her to walk away from them, but when she finally stepped into the warmth cast by the molten rock, she found it comforting. Whatever was in the pot Torsten was stirring awoke a hunger in her that she hadn't realised was there, and her stomach rumbled its anticipation.

A hush fell over the room as she stepped into the light, but only Lark met her eyes. Cornelius seemed oblivious to her entrance, fixated as he was on the thick black cauldron hanging above the place where the lava pooled, not far from the cook pot. Rin didn't know what was in that larger kettle, but she could guess it wasn't stew.

Marta was sitting apart from the others, sorting through the small bottles from her pack, checking the stopper of each one before placing it carefully back inside.

She did not look up.

Rin didn't know what she had expected from the old woman, but it wasn't this. Perhaps if there had been an apology offered in that moment, it would've made a difference. Perhaps the right words said at the right time, or even an attempt at such a thing, would have softened the hard, calloused thing between them. Rin would never know, for neither of them extended such a kindness to the other. Instead, Rin found this extended silence was only making her more angry, but before she had time to react, Lark broke the tension.

"If you're finished sulking in the dark, I'll catch you up on what you've missed."

Rin felt so exposed, standing there without the veil of a

purpose to hide behind, and so, though Lark's insult irked her, she was grateful for the offer. She walked to where Lark stood at the table and nodded for her to continue.

"We'll be here for the night. Maybe another day depending on when Cornelius finishes the keys." Lark motioned her head towards the man at the kettle. "He thinks he's almost completed a test model, and if that first one works, he can make the others more quickly." She paused, looking up at Fievel, then frowned.

"Are they still going back?" Rin asked quietly, unwilling to say Marta's name.

Lark's jaw tightened as her teeth ground together. "So they say."

Rin nodded again. It would be better once they were gone. She would no longer have to look at the woman who had lied to her, and she could already imagine the relief that absence would bring.

They were interrupted by Torsten, bringing them some stew in two of the same random containers they had been given the last time they had eaten here. Rin didn't examine hers too closely, knowing it was best not to wonder what such a thing had previously been used to store. Instead, the two girls took them gratefully and followed Torsten back to where the others were waiting. They were all sitting in a half circle around the cook pot, aside from Marta, who had not moved from the spot she had been in when Rin first arrived. Cornelius also stayed beside his kettle, watching it intently.

"If there are no more delays," Magnus was saying to Fievel, "we could be back in the Cove two days from now."

Reece put his hands to his face, covering his mouth, and almost whispered, "Two days."

Rin knew he was thinking of Tilly – Reece had felt for years what she herself had only experienced these last few days. But even though he had rescued Tilly from the Tunnels some time ago, her pain would not be over until he did this last thing for her. Rin smiled sadly, torn between her happiness for Reece and the way his relief made her own loss feel sharper.

She lifted the makeshift bowl to her lips, relishing in the warmth of the stew. It tasted better than anything she had eaten in a long time, though given their increasingly stale travel rations, that was hardly a surprise. Lark didn't seem to notice; she barely took her eyes off Fievel now. Rin thought she looked hungry, but evidently not for the meal in her hands.

"Once you're finished with supper, you and I should take a walk, Stacks," Lark finally spoke. "There are some things I want you to hear before you let *that one* take you back to the Void." She tilted her head towards the old woman.

Magnus's eyes flicked quickly to Lark's face, then back to his bowl, and though Lark didn't seem to notice, Rin did.

"Oh... okay," Fievel stammered. "Certainly, yes."

Rin didn't envy the boy. There was a strange glint in Lark's eye and Rin didn't like to guess what kind of menace a look like that might mean. Certainly not when she had already heard about as much as she could tolerate from Lark's sharp tongue today.

"Move out of the way," Cornelius broke the silence. "Out of the way. All of the time when they are here, they are all in his way." He was using a blackened metal stick to push the thick arm that was holding the kettle, which swung away from the heat and towards the group.

Ivor lunged to the floor, not trusting that the kettle's molten contents weren't about to splash all over him.

"Good." Cornelius nodded approvingly. "The clumsy one is

moving away the fastest. Good."

Ivor's jaw dropped open in disbelief before he mouthed, "*He's* the clumsy one."

"Nope," the old man replied without turning around. "Cornelius has made many mistakes, but he is never clumsy."

Setting the kettle down on the cave floor, he moved aside as the dust hissed and plumed up from the scorched ground beneath.

Rin looked across at the table, where Cornelius had placed an intricately carved wooden mould. It was a complex design; when they had spoken of keys, she had imaged the toothed kind she had seen used on fancy doors, but this was not that. The carving looked like it would produce something much smaller than she had expected, which made sense when she thought about the size of the chips. Instead of the usual pattern of steps and grooves, it was more ornate, like a picture set inside a rectangular frame. Some of the lines were curved, whereas others were sharper and more angular. It was a delicate piece of work and would have taken time to carve.

The realisation made Rin squirm. While she had been out there, concerned only with her own anger and pain, he had been here creating this tangible thing that would bring them closer to success. She found herself reaching a little deeper into the current, using it to push aside the feelings of guilt that would only distract and hinder her. She refused to fall into that same self-pitying indulgence again.

"Where is it?" Cornelius stood on the other side of the room now, rifling through a cupboard built into the wall. "Where has it gone? Cornelius has not used it for a long time, a great long time. It should be here, where he leaves it, and he always leaves it here."

"What have you lost, old man?" Magnus asked.

"My smelting scooper," Cornelius huffed. "And I have not lost it. Someone has moved it."

Ivor grinned. "Seems more likely that you've lost it, old man."

Cornelius stopped in his search and looked up, considering the problem. "*Seems more likely*," he mimicked. "Does the clumsy one think that he will be the scientist now, hm? Is that how he will write his theories? '*Seems more likely*, and so it must be'? No doubt that one must be losing his things all the time..." His muttering trailed off as he went back to checking through the same cupboard.

"I'm just saying, you know, since you live down here *alone*, that it's more likely you've misplaced it," Ivor replied indignantly, trying to add an air of being above such rebuke. "That's all."

"Mm, except Cornelius knows that correlation and causation are not the same, even if the clumsy one doesn't know such things." The old man was flustered now. "More likely that someone has been sneaking around in Cornelius's cupboards and moving his things."

"Why would any of us—"

"What does it look like?" Reece asked, cutting Ivor off.

"It looks like a smelting scooper," Cornelius answered, his head still inside the cupboard.

"And what does a smelting scooper look like, Cornelius?" Lark added dryly, as though it were a well-rehearsed line in a performance she had grown tired of acting.

"It's a *metal pot* with a *long handle* and a *little crevice lip for pouring*," the old man explained in an exasperated tone, as though talking to someone he considered unable of comprehending such things.

Rin saw Ivor tense before his shoulders sagged forward. He raised his fingers to rub at the spot between his eyes.

"It's over by the cook pot," he groaned.

"No, Cornelius does not keep his smelting scooper by the cook pot," the old man went on, still rattling the items he had already searched. "He keeps it here, in this cupboard."

"I had my stew from it," Ivor muttered under his breath.

The rattling stopped.

"He had his *stew* from it?" Cornelius repeated incredulously, his red face popping out from inside the cupboard. "He puts his *stew* in it! His *stew* in Cornelius's good smelting scooper!" He shook his head slowly as though he had never heard a more outrageous admission, then straightened up, looking down his nose with all the superiority he could muster. "Cornelius *knew* that he was not the one who was losing his smelting scooper."

Rin knew she was not the only one trying not to smile as the old man shuffled off to retrieve it.

After Cornelius had washed and inspected the iron pot several times, muttering curses under his breath all the while, he set about his work. Taking a scoop of the molten metal, he trickled it slowly into the mould, careful not to spill a drop. It smoked as it hit the wooden cast, flowing out to fill every gap, and giving a faint burning smell to the air.

He began to tap the sides of the mould repeatedly. "No bubbles. Bubbles could ruin the whole thing," he explained to no one in particular. "Bubbles... *or* old stew."

Ivor's nose twitched, but he didn't respond to the taunt.

The metal had glowed red and hot when first poured, but already it seemed to be cooling. Cornelius picked up a long strand of metal – about the length of his finger but thin as a reed sapling – and pressed it onto the still glowing creation, sending up another, smaller puff of smoke. With blackened tongs that looked too cumbersome for such fine work, Cornelius lifted the finished metal key from its cast and placed it into a bucket of water. There was one last short hiss as the small piece of hot metal hit the cold liquid, followed by silence.

Cornelius slowly dipped his hand into the bucket to lift it out. "Hmm," he mused.

Rin felt the tension rising.

"Will it work?" Reece asked, unable to hide the worry in his voice.

"Should do," Cornelius answered, still studying the thing. "Why they have chosen this key, I don't know."

"What's wrong with it?" Reece asked, still concerned.

"Nothing is wrong with Cornelius's work," he replied disdainfully, "he just doesn't like this type of key. The old symbol for strength and protection, and they are using it for such dark work. Rotten and foul to do such a thing."

The old man held the small object closer to the light, running his fingers over its pattern. Rin wondered if the key reminded Cornelius all too keenly of the Capital's corruption of his own projects. She watched as he dried off the small key and took it over to the table, laying it atop one of the pieces of parchment that Rin had taken from her father's office. As the metal covered every line on the paper exactly, they could all see it was a precise match.

"If the work they bring him is right, then the key is right too," Cornelius said, finally satisfied.

Reece was staring at the old man's face, blinking heavily as though he hadn't dared believe until this moment that such a thing was possible. Cornelius met his gaze, confused by the boy's emotion over such a simple thing as the creation of a key. Then the older man's brow furrowed and he nodded.

"The quiet one is your friend. She is a friend to all of you, maybe, but she is his friend most of all." Cornelius slid the cooled key onto a thin strip of leather and handed it to Reece. "You still need the code, but it is all there in the papers. If she was here now, Cornelius would show you how to take it off, but without the thing in front of him, Cornelius doesn't know its code. Each one will have a different code."

Reece's hand was shaking as he reached out to take the key. "Thank you," was all he was able to say, before he clamped his mouth shut tightly, trying to stop the tears that threatened to spill from his eyes.

Lark shifted uncomfortably. "Well, now that my brother has a pretty new necklace, and all seems well with the production line, I think it's time you and I have that talk, Stacks." She took one last glance at Reece, then moved towards the exit for the shafts, without waiting to see if Fievel would follow her.

The awkward boy looked stunned in the silence that lingered after her. "I suppose I should follow her... unless anyone needs me for anything?"

Rin wasn't sure if he was looking for permission to go or a reason to stay. Either way, no one answered him. He looked nervously after Lark, then, taking a deep breath, he wiped his hands on his shirt and strode off after her. Rin supposed those long strides were an attempt to look confident, but alongside the jerking way he moved his arms and the anxious twitching of his hands, he reminded her of a much younger child, steeling themselves for some terrifying adventure.

Magnus watched them both leave, then quickly forced his face back to an unreadable expression before turning to Cornelius. "And you and I need to have a talk about those codes, and exactly what is written on each of those papers, before we leave."

There was an air of conspiracy in his words that made Rin

curious. She thought about following them, but she had some questions of her own, and they were ones better asked when Magnus was somewhere else.

She turned to Ivor, who was still watching Fievel leave. "Did they... were they..." Rin trailed off, unsure how to ask, or even why it much mattered.

Ivor shrugged at her un-asked question. "Who? Magnus and Lark? No, but I think he's always been a little bit in love with her. Well, with part of her anyway." The smallest of the brothers screwed up his face in consideration. "Perhaps it's a thing best left alone?"

"But why is she so angry at him?" Rin could tell Ivor was uncomfortable, but she couldn't seem to let it go now she had started. Now she had said it out loud, she knew the truth *did* matter.

Ivor didn't answer her right away. Instead, he looked over at Magnus, who was sifting through the papers with Cornelius. There was pity in his eyes.

He lowered his voice. "He's in love with a part of her, the best part; that part that sneaks out now and again when she forgets to stop it. He's in love with the potential in her, and the idea of who she could be."

"That doesn't sound so awful," Rin replied, a little bit more sceptically than she had intended.

"No? You don't think so? To have someone love who you *could* be, but not who you *choose* to be?" He shook his head as though he knew the words weren't coming out the way he wanted them to. "For the first few years, he couldn't stop himself. Couldn't stop being Magnus and couldn't stop trying to save her. He nearly got himself killed half a dozen times, trying to help her when he should have been worrying about his own skin."

Rin looked at Ivor, still confused.

The boy sighed sadly. "They would never work. You saw how angry she was when she thought Fievel had hurt himself trying to fight the Gen1?"

Rin thought back to the moment they had all realised that he had fainted rather than fought, and how instantly Lark had softened.

"You saw it then, right? That girl doesn't want someone who would risk their life for hers. After everything she's been through – what we've all been through, I guess – sometimes it feels better to be the one who gets hurt than live with the regret of failing to keep the people you care about safe."

Rin swallowed hard. That was a thing she already understood all too keenly.

"I don't know why," Ivor continued, "but part of her seems to hate that he will always run into the fire to try to save her – when what she wants is someone smart enough not to get themselves burned."

Rin was shocked. She hadn't expected those words from Ivor; not from the light-hearted boy who always seemed so quick to laugh or joke. Rin tried to consider what Lark saw in those two boys. Magnus was so strong and capable and, by comparison, Fievel seemed so nervous and awkward, someone who likely avoided problems before they happened. *No, that's not quite true*, Rin corrected herself, thinking about his mother; his time in the Capital. It made her uncomfortable, and she realised it wasn't fair to judge him so unfavourably. Whether he had fainted at the sight of the Gen1 or not, Fievel had still gone into the swamp alone when he thought Marta needed his help. She had to admit that had taken its own kind of bravery.

She looked at Magnus, then towards the exit to the shafts.

"What do you think she's saying to him out there?" she asked, her mouth dropping into a mocking grimace.

"With Lark, it's hard to say anything for certain. I wouldn't like to guess at how she'll go about persuading him, but if I had to put a wager on it, I'd say she'll be trying to convince him to come back to the Cove." Ivor's eyes flashed to Magnus and his face fell a little before he shook his head. "I don't think Fievel will go with her, though. She might want to wrap him up in soft wool and leave him on the shore while she finishes this, but he doesn't seem like the type to me. I think there's more fight in that one than she's bargained for." He shrugged in an exasperated way that suggested the working of women's minds was something he'd never understand. "Who knows – when she finally sees it, that might be the end of her fascination with our new friend."

In the silence that followed, Rin could tell they were both considering whether it might be better for all of them if that were the case.

CHAPTER ELEVEN
PARTING GIFTS

The torches burned down low in their brackets, occasionally sputtering and wavering for a moment before resuming their usual steady burn that bathed the cave in its warm glow. Rin had lost track of whether it was day or night in the world above them; time moved so strangely down here. The hours they had spent walking seemed to drag out in an eternity both in front and behind them, yet when she had fought the Gen 1, and when she had heard the revelations from Marta and Cornelius, time had unravelled so quickly, she had felt as though she couldn't keep up with it.

She blinked long and slow, and found herself struggling to will her heavy eyelids back open against their desire to remain closed. The dimming light was calling to her sweetly, trying to convince her mind of the need to rest. She supposed she could sleep – after all, there was nothing else she needed to do right now – but with a determination not to let the exhaustion overwhelm her just yet, she forced herself to consider the others. Magnus and Cornelius had spoken at length before rearranging the papers into two separate piles on the table, after which Magnus had busied himself with his pack and Cornelius had set about turning out more of the oddly ornate metal keys.

Rin studied the strange little man as he hunched over his work, quickly flitting from task to task in an intricate tangle of motion. She watched him closely and saw the manic pattern repeat itself twice more. Slightly surprised, she had to admit to herself that while his movements might seem jarring to anyone watching, in truth he was methodical and always in control. For the first time, she tried to reconcile the idea that this man was her father's uncle, and what that meant he was to her. Large families that stretched across generations were just another thing the Empire had taken from the lowlanders, so whatever the word for your father's uncle had once been had long ago fallen out of use.

She wondered if she was supposed to feel differently about the abrasive little man now? As she watched him scurrying from place to place, she had to admit she did not. In another time, or perhaps if things were different, she thought it might be possible to feel some joy at meeting someone who was truly her kin. But as she considered her father, who had treated her like an experiment, and the woman she had thought of as a grandmother, who had lied to her repeatedly, she only felt hollow. She did not need another person to call family, who would no doubt expect something from her and offer only disappointment in return.

Time stretched on, with the crafting of Cornelius's additional keys progressing more and more quickly. Before long, he would have enough to give at least one to each of them. Ivor and Torsten had been sitting apart for a while now, speaking quietly, though not secretively, and Reece was sitting alone, turning that first key over and over in his hands. None of these things required anything from Rin, but she still couldn't shake the feeling that there was something left undone that she should be attending to.

When Fievel and Lark eventually returned, Rin found herself relieved that the boy did not look too much the worse for wear. He was a little more dishevelled than he had been when he'd first left to follow Lark, but other than that, there were no obvious signs that their conversation had come to blows. Rin realised too late that Fievel had noticed her studying him, but instead of looking away, she held his gaze for a moment and tilted her head to the side. Every gesture of her body asked if he was okay, even if no words left her lips.

The boy's mouth lifted upwards into a slightly confused and dopey grin. He looked as though he had taken one too many sips of one of the old woman's calming tonics and was ready to float away on its blissful current. Rin smiled back before she knew what her face was doing, suddenly understanding why his hair looked so ruffled and what had caused the honest joy on his face.

Her eyes flicked to Lark curiously, but if she had expected to see a similar expression, she could not have been more mistaken. Lark's face held only the faintest trace of a smile, over which sat an expression of cold challenge.

Rin had reached for the steady current of power inside her before she had time to consider what she was doing. As she brushed against the raw strength within her, she pulled back, trying to let it fade just as quickly as it had risen. The unspoken threat was not directed at her; it was just a face Lark wore for the whole world, and Rin knew what it meant. It was a look that said *you will not take what is mine*, and however strong Rin might be, she knew she wouldn't risk testing the truth of it.

Marta stood up, the motion drawing Rin's gaze. Angry at herself for allowing her focus to be pulled towards the old woman, she huffed loudly, prompting a few of the others to turn towards her. She felt a flush of embarrassment at having voiced her displeasure so childishly. She didn't know how to make it better now the sound was out, so instead she swiftly turned her back on all of them, moving towards her bedroll. Clenching her teeth, she decided the morning could not come quickly enough. The memory of Marta's pained face flitted through Rin's mind.

She could still see the way the old woman's mouth had creased with hurt as Lark exposed her.

For a second, Rin felt a flash of pity so sad it was almost unbearable, then there it was again. She didn't know if she was imagining it or not, but for a moment, just as Lark had said back on the tracks, Rin was sure she could feel something inside clawing at her. This time, instead of shrinking away from it, she leaned towards it, and felt something within her harden.

Even though she was sure sleep would elude her, Rin closed her eyes again, no longer wanting a reminder of the truth of this day.

Rin sat up with a start as Lark's foot nudged her awake.

"Rise and shine, Killer. The sooner we get out of this place, the sooner we can be done with this whole mess."

"I didn't know you were in such a rush," Rin replied, trying to clear the thick, sleepy grit from her throat and focus on the girl standing over her.

For a moment, she wondered if Lark was on her side, keen to get moving so they could complete their mission at get Ieuan back. But as she followed her gaze, she saw Lark staring at Fievel again. Rin scowled up at the older girl from under her brow, wondering how many times she would have to be shown a thing before she had the wit to believe it.

Most of her belongings had been packed the night before; now she only had her bedroll and the papers from the Capital to add to it. As she walked over to collect them from Cornelius's desk, she noticed again that he and Magnus had divided them into two separate piles. One was much bigger than the other, with the smaller of the two stacks containing only a few sheets. She stood looking at them, reluctant to mix the two sets together without knowing the reason they had been split in the first place.

"Good morning," Magnus said as he approached her, setting his pack down beside hers.

Rin paused for a moment, wondering if it was truly morning, or if it was just habit to say such a greeting to someone who had just awoken. Deciding it didn't matter, she returned the pleasantry, then watched his eyes flick upwards to the stone canopy, as if now wondering the same thing himself.

"I was going to finish packing," she added, gesturing to the two piles on the table.

Magnus nodded, drawing his eyes back down to the papers. "I thought so." He lowered his voice. "Do you trust me, Rin?"

The turn in conversation was sharp and the suddenly serious tone in his voice let Rin know that this was not a question asked without good reason. She kept her head fixed, looking down at the table, but turned her eyes towards the boy, trying to subtly read something on his face. Pausing, she considered his question. *Did* she trust him? The ill-used part of her squirmed as she thought of Marta, then Lark. Did she trust *anyone* anymore? Magnus had never done anything to deserve her doubt, but was he just another person about to use her? To make her believe in him now, only to leave her feeling foolish and betrayed at some time in the future?

His eyes searched hers and she could read his confusion. Still unsure of the truth, but deciding she had nothing to lose by saying the words, she answered him.

"Yes, I trust you, Magnus."

She watched his eyes narrow for a second, the doubt on his face surely mirroring her own lack of faith in what she had said.

At last, he nodded. It was clear to Rin then that, regardless of her trust in him, he was too invested in his own plans to let an opportunity pass him by now. He glanced around at the others and Rin wondered for a moment why it should matter who here overheard them, but she said nothing. If there was some part of the plan to be kept secret, she wanted to be the one to know what was going on first for once.

"Here." Magnus picked up the smaller of the two piles of paper and handed it to her, before quickly slipping the larger bundle into his own pack. "Don't mention these to anyone. Not yet. You'll know when it's time, the same way I will." With a final nod, he turned away from her, slinging his pack up onto his shoulders.

Rin's mouth twitched in irritation. Was this the way it was always done? Even when she was supposed to be in on the plan, she still didn't understand half of what was going on. There was no time for clarification, though; the way Magnus had swung his pack onto his back seemed to have caused a ripple effect through the group, each of them sensing it was time to go. The different paths they were to take had instinctively split them into two groups, an odd tension rippling between them: Fievel and Marta on one side of the room, the rest on the other.

Rin wasn't sure why the others seemed so uncomfortable, but she knew why she was. Silently, she waited for the moment in which either Marta or she would have one last opportunity to try and breach the gap between them. She had thought about this moment often during the previous evening, and every time she had considered telling Marta that she forgave her, she felt something twist inside her uncomfortably. Now the moment had come, she knew she would not be the one to make the attempt, though she had not fully resolved within herself what she would do if Marta tried in earnest to make things right between them.

It didn't take long for Rin to realise that she need not have worried: the old woman kept her chin up and her eyes fixed determinedly ahead of her. There was no offer of apology in that stern face. When she finally spoke, it was with the militant precision of someone relaying orders rather than the soft affection of a grandmother. Rin bristled when she realised some part of her had been hoping for the latter.

"We'll wait three days, then after that, someone will check the fence every evening at dusk. Not the place where you entered last time; that's no longer safe." Marta looked at the tall boy standing beside her. "Fievel tells me the best place would be two hours north of there. Travel in the swamp for the most part, but every now and again, get your bearings at the fence." She gestured at Fievel, to see if he would add anything.

"Eh... yes," he stammered. "If you have a keen eye, you will see the tallest of the Midden Stacks above the skyline. Keep going until you see the rubble of the first house, where all that's left standing is three chimney stacks."

"Take a line out eastward from there and wait," Marta cut in again. "One of us will come for you."

No one spoke after that, but several of them nodded their agreement. Rin could feel they were all waiting for the same thing, hoping for the moment when there would be some kind of resolution between the old woman and herself, but only painful silence followed Marta's final instruction.

It was Fievel who ultimately broke the unnatural hush. Clearing his throat, he stepped forward towards Lark. Rin was surprised to see the slender girl's eyes narrow at him in response.

"Lark, I..." the boy started, the hesitation in his voice showing his apprehension.

"Are you coming with me?" Lark asked, with coldness in her voice. When Fievel took another step towards her, she moved backwards, keeping the distance between them. "I asked you if you are coming back to the Cove with me?"

"I... I can't. You know I can't," he said, his voice pained but certain. "Not until this is done."

"Then we have nothing else to say to each other," she replied, shrugging, and suddenly as flippant as always. She turned her back on him, but Fievel took two quick steps towards her and caught her hand. "I want you to have this," he said, forcing the token he usually wore around his neck into Lark's hand, "until we see each other again." Those last words sounded more like a promise than the tenuous hope it really was in these dangerous times.

Lark turned the token over in her hand and, for a moment, Rin thought she saw a flicker of emotion cross the girl's otherwise indifferent expression.

She paused for only a second longer, then looked Fievel straight in the eye. "You made your choice. I have no use for the tokens of a boy who's as good as dead." With that, she tossed the talisman back at him as though it meant no more to her than a stale ration biscuit.

Fievel struggled to catch it, both clumsy and shocked by the rejection.

Rin looked away quickly, unable to witness his pain at the refusal of such an honest gift. Her fleeing gaze found Ivor's, who looked back at her, sad and knowing.

Then, the small space was filled with the commotion of moving bodies as they all made their final preparations to leave. The three brothers took a moment to hug Fievel and slap him on the back, telling him to be careful and to stay away from spindly-legged scuttlers and poorly made ladders. Rin saw how hard the three of them were working to take the sting out of Lark's rejection and leave him bolstered for his journey ahead. Ivor pulled the boy in close and whispered something into his ear, then there was a quick flash of hands and the shorter red-headed brother was tucking something into his pocket and nodding. Before she had time to guess at what might have been exchanged between the boys, Cornelius was in front of her, busying himself with securing her onto that same connecting line they had used before.

With all this going on, Rin barely had time to notice Marta disappearing into the stone passageway that led westwards, without so much as a goodbye. Fievel turned to face them and, with one last tentative wave, followed after the old woman. Rin was staring at the now empty space where the old woman had stood only moments ago, feeling both immeasurable loss and the familiar prickle of irritation. The line in front of her jerked tight and she realised that their procession had begun its march, back under the mountain and towards the Cove.

Rin's place along the line was somewhere in the middle of the others, which suited her fine. She was glad to be on the move again, with something to distract her from wondering how long it had been since Ieuan was taken by the Empire.

After a while, she realised they were moving slower this time, and Rin observed that this was because every time the shafts split or joined another section, Cornelius would take time to stop and build a small stone mound.

"Cairns," he explained, answering a question no one had asked. "Cornelius will leave the stones and then the brats will not need him to show them again which way to go."

Rin was a little hesitant at this, knowing that if they could follow these little piles of rock, so could any other person who stumbled across them. Then she reminded herself that only the Alliance could enter the shafts from this side of the Ashlands. Even then, this way would soon lead to nought, once the tracks beyond Cornelius's home were collapsed.

The shafts were narrower than she remembered, and after the more open space of the tracks, Rin felt like the rock here was pressing in at her from all sides. Even though there was space for her to stand upright, something about it caused her to duck her head and hunch her shoulders in a way that she hadn't felt she needed to before. They were also stopping more often, not just for Cornelius to lay the marker stones, but also because the path ahead had sometimes been blocked by heavy rubble.

"I thought you said the stone down here was safe?" Magnus muttered through gritted teeth, when they had to stop a third time.

"It is. You don't see any of it falling on your head, do you?" Cornelius answered indignantly. "A few pebbles here and there is all. Cornelius will move them again and we will be on our way soon enough. Unless that brute knows a better way?" The old man paused, waiting for Magnus to answer. "That's right, Cornelius thought not."

The time it took for Cornelius to lay down his powders and fuses with careful precision had slowed them down much more than Rin had realised, and when they finally reached the dragon pools, she knew Cornelius could not continue. With the rising air warm with steam and the cool false rain falling down on them from the cold stone above, the others all seemed ready to take a break from their march too. Only Reece appeared to share Rin's urgent need to press on. If either one of them had known which way to go, they both would probably have continued on together, leaving the others behind to trail after them the next morning. But there was no way of knowing how to navigate the labyrinth of rocky corridors without their cantankerous guide, so they were forced to accept their need to make camp, perhaps not for the whole night, but for a few hours – certainly long enough for Cornelius to rest.

Grudgingly, Rin admitted to herself that they could all benefit from the chance to fill their bellies again. Choosing a place where a large rock jutted out far enough overhead to keep the constant mizzle from splashing on them, they all laid out their bedrolls. With nothing else to do but wait, Rin looked out longingly over the pools of water, remembering how she and Ieuan had longed for a restful dip in those warm craters not so very long ago. Maybe once she got him out of the Tunnels, there would be time for them to come here again.

She enjoyed the warmth of that thought as she looked out across the splashing cascade of rain. The constant pattering of the drips on the rock above them was soothing; a sheet of noise drowning out the need for conversation or companionship. It reminded Rin of being safe and warm at home while a summer storm washed over the Dale. That kind of weather always left the ground feeling washed clean and the air rich with the smell of new earth.

Rin stretched out on her blanket, letting her back rest against the pack she had propped against a pile of stones near one wall. Idly, she watched Lark opening her rucksack, expecting the girl to bring out her bed roll or one of the hard ration biscuits to eat. Instead, Lark blinked back her shock and drew Fievel's token from her pack. For a moment, Lark held it high in front of her face, and Rin could have sworn she saw the girl's breath catch in her chest. Then Lark's head whipped around dangerously, her eyes darting from person to person, seeking out the perpetrator.

The moment Rin had seen the girl's reaction to the stowaway token, she had busied herself, suddenly becoming very concerned with the state of the leather on the sole of her left boot. She neither wanted to be suspected, nor did she wish to get caught in the crossfire when Lark started apportioning blame. It was only when she heard a boy's cry, followed by splashing sounds, that Rin realised all three brothers were not in the cave anymore.

"Ivor!" Magnus shouted across the splattering din. "Quit fooling around!"

"I've got one!" Ivor's voice echoed back through the downpour. "One of the lizard things!"

Rin was on her feet as quickly as the others, but none looked more excited than Cornelius. Ivor was soaked through and grinning from ear to ear as he squelched into the shelter, carrying something by the tail. The reptile's pale, dangling body was so large that its head almost touched the floor. Cornelius squinted at the boy, as though unable to comprehend how he had managed such a thing.

"Who knew?" he muttered in astonishment. "The clumsy one is sometimes useful after all."

Ivor lowered the creature, clearly surprised at the old man's words that bordered on a compliment. Rin had assumed that the thing in Ivor's hand was dead, but the second its front scaly legs touched the floor, it found the purchase it needed to lash its tail. The sudden jerk of its thick and muscly hind quarters wrenched it free of the boy's grasp.

"Oi!" Ivor shouted, as though the creature had performed a most devious trick. "Grab it, Magnus!"

But even as he yelled out his brother's name, the last flick of the lizard's white tail was all that could be seen as it disappeared back into one of the steaming pools. There was a long moment when no one spoke, and Rin was sure everyone else's eyes had also flicked from Cornelius's shaking head to the empty-handed boy who was already wincing.

"Mm hm, Cornelius should be expecting as much. Perhaps we will not call him clumsy anymore..."

While the old man paused in thought, Ivor looked briefly hopeful, as though he believed his hard work catching the reptilian thing was about to change his status.

"Perhaps instead we should call him 'lizard-less'." The old man barked a short, sharp laugh.

Rin struggled to smother her own chuckle, not that she thought Ivor's lost meal was all that amusing, but there was something infectious about the old man's obvious enjoyment. She remembered Cornelius saying that the white, eyeless creatures were tasty the last time they had been in this place, yet she could see that he was willing to sacrifice the meal to savour Ivor's dismay instead. Smiling to herself, she sat back down, and was just about to close her eyes when she saw Lark slip the token's leather thong around her neck and tuck it away under her shirt. Rin quickly looked away, feeling as though she had been caught peeking at something scandalous or indecent.

Her fleeing gaze settled on Ivor as he poured the water from his sodden boots. Rin wrinkled her nose, knowing those would not be dry after a full day by the fire, never mind by the time he would have to pull them on again to leave. The shorter boy sighed loudly, seeming to be thinking the same thing. Then, as if he could feel Rin's eyes on him, he turned his head ever so slightly towards her and winked.

CHAPTER TWELVE
SQUALLS AND SCHEMES

When they emerged into the natural stone gallery at the surface, Rin struggled to open her eyes, squinting against the harsh brightness that flooded in through the mouth of the cave. After so long spent in perpetual dimness, Rin had become accustomed to its soft light and was not prepared to have this so quickly replaced by the brilliance of the midday sun.

Raising her hand to shield her watery eyes, she looked out over the valley. The sun was high, and no clouds marked the clear sky above them, yet it was colder than she had expected. Looking out to the mountains in the distance, she realised the luscious green from no more than a half-moon ago had been capped with white. Rin had seen snow before, but only an occasional fluttering of flakes that, more often than not, melted as soon as they touched the earth below. She couldn't imagine how many of those little flakes it must take to cover the top of a mountainlike that. Closing her eyes, she felt the sunlight touch her face, mixing pleasantly with the cold breeze in a way that she had never felt before. It was wonderfully crisp and fresh up here after the staleness under the earth.

The three brothers took a moment to complete their ritual, each one of them tapping three times on the stone at the entrance to the cave. Then Torsten moved to stand beside Rin, his eyes following her gaze out towards the mountains and horizon.

"There shouldn't be snow up there this early."

His voice held an edge that made Rin pull her gaze away from the peaks to study the taller boy's face. It was not the same carefree tone he had used to describe the mountains the last time they had passed this way.

"Is that bad?" she asked as a prompt, already knowing that he thought it was not good news.

"Hard to say for sure, but with everything else hanging by a thread, I would have preferred to see trees up there instead of snow."

He was talking as though he was still deciding how much of a problem that would truly mean for them when he suddenly seemed to realise Rin was staring at him intently, clearly trying to judge the scale of their trouble from each word.

He looked up at the clear sky and nodded appraisingly. "The summer season can be longer or shorter in any given year on this side of the Ashlands. In the summer, there is nowhere better: rich forest game, good fishing and plenty of growth – both wild and what we sow ourselves." He paused, scrunching his eyebrows. "The winters are bad, though. Harsh, but predictable, and we've had plenty of practice at setting aside stores and waiting it out." His eyes went to the snow-capped peaks again. "But the time in between, when the cold air from the mountain hits the warm air from the land down here... I don't know if the lowlands have ever seen that kind of storm before."

Rin didn't say anything. She had seen plenty of storms in the Dale – how much worse could these really be? She thought of two summers past, when it had rained for five days straight. The fat, heavy kind of rain that poured down onto the ground faster than the sodden earth could drink it in. There had been some pastures that had become so waterlogged that no one had been able to walk on them for months. Some of the village roofs had been damaged too, letting in water from leaks no one had noticed before. In weather like that, everyone stayed indoors, no matter what chores were left unfinished outside. It was dull and damp, but nothing that caused the kind of worry she had seen in Torsten's eyes. She noticed the tallest of the brothers was looking at her again, as though he could read the doubt she held for his concerns.

"I'm not scared to get a little cold or wet," she replied earnestly, trying to let him know that she took his warning seriously, but also that she was not some wide-eyed lowland girl, green to winter and afraid of a little rain.

He nodded, but there was still a dubious look in his eyes that caused Rin to reconsider the wisdom of her words.

"Come on," Lark called out. "You all see the white settling in up there. That's our window closing, and we need to be back in the Cove before it slams shut. Otherwise, who knows how long we'll be stuck out here waiting for the next one."

Lark was already moving, and Rin had travelled with her long enough to know she would not waste time looking back to see if they were keeping up. When they had come this way the first time, Ieuan and Tilly had been with them, and only now did Rin realise how much faster they could move without them.

They reached the same spot by the river in the late afternoon, and Rin was surprised to find the colour of the water so different from before. What had been rich, blue water was now closer to a silvery grey, and somehow Rin knew that what lay unspoken in such a colour was the promise of its icy touch. With every step that took them closer to the riverbank, the trees were thinning out more and more, and now Rin could see that the sky above had turned from bright sunlight to something much more ominous. There should have been plenty of daylight left before dusk, but instinctively, Rin knew it was darker than it should have been for such a cloudless day. She had never seen the sky above the Dale look so angry, and the strangeness of its unfamiliar expanse made it all the more foreboding.

Hesitating, she stood on the shore, watching the others dragging their little crafts out from under the scrub and pushing them onto the water, where they sat bobbing uncertainly atop the beckoning river. Then, Magnus was reaching out his hand, and once more Rin was hesitantly stepping into the small wooden craft.

Despite her trepidation, the strangely hued water flowed under the boat no differently than it had before. As she watched the riverbank race past her, she chided herself. She had enough real problems without dwelling on ones that did not yet exist. Ignoring her unease, she tried to focus on the forest that ran either side of the great river. Usually, she would have been captivated by the small flashes of white that marked the tail of some animal or other in flight, yet it was the sky above them that kept drawing her attention.

As the river flowed faster, she saw the familiar frothing peaks that marked the rougher water ahead. Rin braced herself this time, so when their shouts went out, she was expecting them. Knowing what was coming did not stop her stomach from dropping in a way that felt neither comfortable nor natural, but it did somewhat lessen the horror she had felt the first time they had made their speedy descent down the watery channels. She closed her eyes and, this time, they obliged her, staying shut until she felt the downward rush broken by the scudding of their little boat against the waves of the ocean below.

As her craft lurched upwards, Rin cried out, her eyes snapping open against the unexpected motion. Already, she could see the water here was different too. This was not the same ocean they had paddled against the last time. She gasped as suddenly their boat crashed down on the other side of a wave, and she heard Magnus grunting behind her as he paddled hard. Rin had never seen waves like these; they dwarfed their little boats.

"Stay low and in the middle of the boat," Magnus shouted to her, his words only just audible over the crashing water. "This is going to be a bumpy one."

She looked over her shoulder, trying to see his face, his words only just audible over the crashing water. She hadn't noticed the wind picking up when they had been on the river. Had the trees acted as a shelter, or did the weather here really change this quickly? The boat slammed down hard as it crested another wave, and Rin's hands grasped tighter to the slim wooden sides. The wind seemed to slap at her, carrying the salty spray into her face. Only then, as she spat out the seawater, did she realise her mouth had been hanging open in shock. Her head swivelled as she tried to locate the others amidst the valleys of peaks and troughs. Where were they?

She was starting to panic, imagining that the other small boats had surely been toppled or flooded by one of these endless walls of seawater. For a moment, she considered standing up to get a better view, then the boat was tilting upward again and she knew she wouldn't keep her feet. Seconds later, the craft rattled hard as it crashed back down on the other side, and she realised Magnus was no longer rowing.

"What's happening?" she called out, fighting the urge to wrench the oars from his hands and row them herself. She was certain they were being dragged further away from the land with every passing second.

"The tide is carrying us in, not pushing us out," Magnus

shouted back, his brows drawn together in concentration. "Won't be enough to take us to the shore, not against the river water spilling out from above, but we're in position. Watch out for the hooks – with this much swell, they can miss the boat sometimes."

Rin was amazed to see the calm in his expression, so far from her own feeling of panic. She took the oar he handed her and tried to prepare herself to fend off an ill-timed barb if she needed to.

"Where are the others?" she yelled back, realising that he had not yet seen the full extent of their problems.

At her question, Magnus looked over his shoulder, then smiled. "Storm protocol." With his thumb, he gestured behind them. "One line. Everyone stays three boats apart at all times."

Rin blinked, partly because another blast of sea spray was raining down on her and partly in disbelief. Trying to peer blearily through the spray, she shook her head. *They have a protocol for this?* She couldn't imagine people were out in these waves, in these little log boats, often enough to have a protocol for it. Not for the first time, Rin realised she had aligned herself with madmen.

She was still looking behind her when the thudding and crunch of wood made her jump. Sure that the boat was beginning to break apart under the rolling swell, she clutched her oar tighter and turned, but instead of splintering wood, she saw the shine of silvery metal. The Cove's hook had seated itself perfectly, and once more it began to drag them forward. So much of their journey back to the Cove had been familiar, yet even more had been different. Now Rin found herself longing for the safety of the large ships, dry clothes and a warm meal.

As they passed through the mouth of the Cove, the noise of

the waterfall crashing from above drowned out all other sounds, but now Rin could hear something happening on the shore. Last time, once they had cleared the current of the falling water, their boats had been pulled along smoothly, gently gliding to the shore. This time, they were still moving quickly, but they were jerking and butting against the smaller waves inside the walls. Everywhere, people were rushing frantically, not just down at the shore but over walkways and on the decks of the ships, too. Some had their arms piled high with ropes or bundles of cloth, while others barked orders in the frayed tones so often used by those with too much to do and not enough time to see it all done.

Rin noticed him first.

The large, scruffy mutt sat nearly as tall as the girl next to him, as they waited together on the shore. They were the only figures that stayed still and unflinching amidst all the chaos that swirled around them. Rin watched as, twice, rushing figures with bundles so high they almost couldn't see over them came close to colliding with the girl, who did not move from her spot. Only a last-minute warning snarl from Scratch caused those people to change their courses, stopping them from running right into her.

Rin heard a splash and immediately noticed the empty boat that was being pulled alongside her own. Reece had left his pack and shirt in the little vessel and, unhindered by either, his lithe body cut through the choppy waves faster than any of the log boats could. Rin felt her heart catch in her throat as the sopping-wet boy reached the shallows and pushed himself to his feet. Others on the shore had turned to watch him, too, but Reece seemed oblivious to all but one of them. He ran now, and as his feet reached the soft sand of the shore, Tilly was running too. His hands reached out desperately to touch her, to know that she was really there and could not be taken from him again in some cruel trick. Her hands reached out in reply, moving upwards to hold his face close to hers.

There was a sort of desperation in their kiss, and Rin saw how hard it was for Reece to pull himself back from it to whisper something to the girl. In response, Tilly reached out to touch the small piece of metal he wore around his neck, staring at it, before throwing her arms around him once more and kissing him again. Rin guessed that, most likely, there would be a lot more kissing to come, and she found herself looking away – not because she thought it was a shameful thing, but because it made her own heart ache more keenly.

Magnus and Rin's boat reached the shore first, followed by Reece's empty craft, then Lark's, and lastly Ivor and Torsten's. The older girl jumped from the little vessel onto the sand well above the tide line, careful to keep her boots dry. Picking up her brother's shirt and pack alongside her own, she looked at Rin and rolled her eyes.

"My little brother, always so dramatic."

Rin wasn't sure, but for a moment, she thought she had seen the hint of a smile under that disdain.

Before she could respond, Alyssa was beside them, but instead of her cheerful smile, her face was strained and worried. "Where are the others?" she asked, her voice catching as though in answer to her own question. "The boy – Ieuan – and the others? We were told to expect two more…"

Her thought trailed off as her gaze fell on Rin, seeing the tears that had prickled into the girl's eyes.

Rin had thought she was ready to answer such questions. She had known that, once they arrived at the Cove, she would be expected to account for those who were not here as they should be. She had repeated the words in her head over and over, in the order she was going to speak them to the council. She had carefully crafted her account, including only what was necessary, after which would follow her plan for getting him back. For getting them all back. But she hadn't been prepared for her honest pain to be so clearly mirrored in Alyssa's face.

Rin sank down to the sand, no longer caring about the wet that seeped in through her clothes, pressing coldly at her. She no longer cared who was or wasn't looking at her. She just wanted Ieuan back. She *needed* him back, right now.

Closing her eyes, she was about to reach for the only thing that could quiet such sharp pain, when she felt a hand touch her shoulder.

"I'm so sorry, dear." Alyssa's tone was softer than before. "Forgive my careless questions. I should know better." Then her hand was reaching under Rin's elbow and encouraging her gently back to her feet. "You can't stay here, though. There's a storm coming in. Might be nothing, but more likely it's something worse. As you can see, we weren't expecting them to begin so early this year."

Alyssa nodded her head towards the mass of people surging to and from the large ships atop the rocks, and Rin realised they were rushing to prepare themselves for whatever was coming. When Rin stood up, Alyssa tutted, looking at her wet clothes and then at Reece, who was still dripping.

"I'm afraid all the stores from the boat house have been sent up to the ships already. I fear that, like before, they will not want to be delayed in hearing whatever it is you have to say."

Reece's face turned from love-struck joy to something less certain as he took Tilly's hand in his own, holding it against his chest protectively. "Yes. No more waiting," he agreed.

Rin saw the girl's lip tremble slightly, but her eyes never left him, and she nodded resolutely too.

The big ship was warm as they entered, and the dry clothes were clean and soft against her skin. Rin had expected there would be others already here to meet them, but the room was empty, apart from the clothes and a pot of hot stew. Rin smiled as she saw that someone had provided a dish for Scratch too, filled with bits of bone and scraps. *No wonder the big mutt is looking so healthy*, she mused.

"Good," Magnus said as each one of them took a bowl and a seat at the large table. "Before anyone else gets here, there is something I've been meaning to say."

Rin stopped chewing, thinking back to the two piles of paper in the two different packs. She nodded for him to continue.

"I know you've all considered it, so let's get this out in the open while it's just us." Magnus lowered his voice. "We were betrayed, and the only people who knew of our plans were here in this room when we made them."

As his words hung in the air, Rin tried to keep her face from showing her shock. Of course she knew they had been betrayed – her father had told her as much – but by someone from inside the Cove? Someone in the Alliance? The idea was hard to accept, yet as she considered it, she knew Magnus was right. Not just anyone from the Cove, but someone who had been here while they had made their plans together. Someone who had pretended to help them, all the while knowing they would alert the Capital the moment they had the chance.

"And just what do you have planned in that crafty head of yours, Magnus?" Lark asked. Out of all of them, she seemed the least concerned by his news, twirling her spoon lazily in her hand between bites.

"You'll know when you see it, Lark. For now, it's best I don't say it aloud. It will make it that much more believable when the time comes." Magnus's eyes flicked to Rin, then back to the others. "Just guard your words carefully until we find out who it was that set us up. I think it would be wise for us not to tell them *all* we've done since we left here last, or what we plan to do next."

Scratch growled and Rin looked at the mut, then quickly around the room. Reece ignored the creature lying on the floor behind him and Tilly, but when he opened his mouth to speak, Magnus raised his hand to his lips suddenly, tilting his head towards the door. Rin couldn't be sure, but she thought she caught the glimpse of a shifting shadow in the thin strip of light that shone beneath the panel, as though something, or someone, had moved close to the door.

Reece held his tongue, and Rin was sure that he had seen it too. After that, no one spoke. Even though they did not see any further signs of listeners at the door, the lingering feeling that they were being watched remained. As time stretched on, with no sign of Fischer or the rest of the council, unease began to settle over the group.

Rin soon became aware of a thrumming sound from somewhere outside, a rhythmic vibration with each flurry of wind as it buffeted the walkways and ships. Rising, Rin left her empty bowl to look out of one of the small, round windows. It was dark now, and many of the lanterns along the walkways had gone out, while the ones that remained lit were dancing furiously on their tethers. Each new gust threatened to rip the little boxes of glass and metal off their hangings and the shadows they cast were cut short and became distorted by the motion.

The door burst inward on its hinges and crashed against the wall. Instantly, Scratch was on his feet, barking. The violence of the combined noise made Rin jump as she turned to face the fury of whoever had used such force. Instead, she saw Fischer smiling at her, followed by Jace and several of the other council members, who were scrambling to get through the door and out of the wind. It was only when Fischer fought to push the wooden port back into its frame that she realised it was the gathering storm, and not his hand, that had slammed it open like that. The bustling energy that entered with the swirling winds filled the room with jostling and Rin had a feeling that, finally, she would leave here with a plan to get her friend back.

While the masts outside creaked and strained against the force that howled past them, Fisher banged his hand down on the table, drawing everyone's attention to the start of the meeting.

"Welcome back," he began, still catching his breath a little. "I am not alone in saying we were unsure if we would ever see you all again." Fischer stopped suddenly, seeing the look on Rin's face. "Ah lass, of course," he said sadly, "and hear my apology as I mean it. That was not right to say, as you are not *all* here."

Rin nodded, only slightly mollified, but enough to let the moment pass.

The accountings after that were brief, each one clearly heeding Magnus's caution, as they retold only what was already expected from their mission. All within the council knew they had planned to retrieve enough information on the chips to be able to remove not only Tilly's, but also those of all the other Tavi still imprisoned in the Tunnels, so there seemed little point in keeping it a secret that Ieuan and Gibb could be added to the list of names they would be liberating from that dark place. Not one of them spoke of the tracks or of Cornelius, and when asked about Marta, Magnus merely said they had not been able to find her in the Void. No one had questioned that.

"While your 'stories' are all very *interesting*," Jace sneered,

"I take it you have something more to offer us than just your heartfelt, and no doubt exaggerated, tales of adventure?"

Rin had to stop herself from reaching over and wiping that sneer across the table. It was only the warning in Fischer's voice that stopped her from doing just that.

"Boy, you are only here by the grace of my good name, but if you can't keep a civil tongue in your head, I will throw you out that door myself."

From the white stretching out over Fischer's knuckles, Rin judged that this was not an idle threat.

"Rin did it," Magnus growled, barely able to contain his urge to react to the taunt. "She got all that there was to take, and some more besides that." He paused as he drew the stack of papers from his pack and slid them across the table. "We're not sure what you'll find in there, but we're hoping to free Tilly of her chip tonight, if we can."

Fisher squinted at Magnus as though he heard the words but did not see the sense of them. "Now is not the time to be hasty, lad," he said, carefully picking up the papers as though scared to damage a single page.

"At least tell her it *can* be done," Reece said, suddenly desperate, glancing from her anxious stare to Fischer's reserved studying.

The bearded man's mouth tightened, but he did not argue. He began laying out one page after another, forming a larger pile to one side, the contents clearly not relevant to the task at hand.

Other members of the council were moving in behind him, and Rin could tell by their darting eyes that every one of them was trying to read each line alongside the bearded man. There was muttering amongst the group and, twice, the larger pile was searched and then re-stacked. Rin could feel the excitement and tension of the huddled group, and not for the first time, she found herself wishing she could read the hidden meanings penned in the swirls and scratches on the page.

She looked across at Jace with suspicion as he walked back to his seat, finding it hard to believe that anyone could have read all those words so quickly. The others were taking much longer, and something about that bothered her. She was almost sure he could not have looked at more than half of those pages.

The sly boy shuffled impatiently on his wooden chair as another round of muttering came from the council.

Suddenly, Rin felt the energy shift.

Fischer's shoulders sagged as he looked up from the papers slowly, forcing his eyes to meet Reece's, then Tilly's.

He shook his head. "I'm sorry," he said, as though speaking softly would somehow lessen the blow. "This work, it... it's incomplete."

"No!" Reece slammed his fist against the table. "No, it *has* to be there."

Tilly whined and Scratch growled a low warning.

Reece quickly un-balled his fists, opening his hands in apology, showing Scratch that he had regained control. "It just *has* to be there, Tilly."

Rin was surprised again when it was not Fischer who reassured him, but Jace.

"Don't worry, we have everything we need." Jace peered at the rest of the council, seemingly confused at their response.

"Stop playing with the boy, Jace," Fischer bit back at his son, caught somewhere between defeat and irritation. "There are codes, but without a cypher, we don't know anything about how they might work."

"There is no need, father." Every person in the room was

staring at Jace now. "Each chip is its own cypher. Every one of them has a code on it. Each code tells you how many times to turn the key in each of its six locks. A lock for each of the pins that puncture the tissue around the spine. It's really quite simple, if you have both a key and the ability to read numbers." Jace smiled at them all, pleased to have explained what they could not.

Reece's eyes grew wide with surprise, then he sighed loudly. Rin had never seen such conflicted gratitude on a person's face before.

The same was not true of Magnus. "How do you know that, *Jace*?" he asked coldly.

"It's all right there in the papers. Haven't you read them yourself, Magnus? You *can* read, can't you?" The insult was thinly veiled at best.

"I can read some. Not well, but some. But I do have a new friend who can read much better than I can. Why don't you show me and the rest of the council just where you saw that written?"

Magnus was looking at Jace from under his brow and Rin could tell that such a look masked a conclusion he had already drawn.

"Alright," Jace replied, as though indulging a spoilt child.

The other council members parted to make space for the boy, each of their faces holding the same look of confusion as Rin's own. Jace's finger ran down each of the upturned pages in turn, and as he moved closer to the last sheet, the other two brothers stood, spreading out. Rin knew this was no accident; she could see now that there would be no access to the door that did not involve tangling with one of them. It seemed Jace had realised that too, as sweat began to bead on the boy's forehead. He grabbed the larger stack of papers just as the council had done twice before him, shuffling through them.

"Ah, here it is," he said, snatching up a page, an odd look of relief spreading across his face.

Magnus scowled, and for the first time Rin saw the doubt on her friend's face.

"Allow me to educate you, *Magnus*," Jace continued, moving towards the stockiest of the three brothers.

Rin couldn't say how she knew what was about to happen, but the cry left her lips a second too late. As Jace held up the paper for Magnus to read, the red-headed boy instinctively leaned in closer, only for Jace's fist to punch him squarely on the nose. Rin's voice was lost in the commotion of screeching chairs and a chorus of pain and alarm, but it was too late. Fischer's son had managed to wrench the door open, causing the papers to swirl and scatter around the room as the boy fled into the darkness of the storm.

"Don't let him get away!" Magnus shouted thickly, his nose streaming with blood.

"Grab the papers!" Reece almost screamed, panic-stricken at the thought they might lose even a word of what was needed to help Tilly.

Rin and Scratch reached the door first, with Torsten and Ivor only seconds behind, just as a crack of lightning split the sky above them. Scratch had turned back before the thunder had time to rumble out behind it, knocking the two brothers backwards into the cabin. Rin ignored the flash and rumble as she sprang out onto the deck and, for the first time, felt the full force of the storm lashing at her face.

Leaning forward, she pushed against that force, shocked by the strength with which it pushed back. With her face turned into the wind, she could hardly breathe as it ripped the air from her lungs. A second crack lit up the sky, rippling off the cliffs around her, and suddenly it was as though that second jagged bolt had torn a cloud in two. Rain began to pour unlike any she had ever seen. It fell not in the large, lazy droplets she recalled from the Dale, but in sheets of jagged pellets that stung as they bit at her skin.

She raised her arm, trying to shield her eyes as she looked for a trace of where Jace had gone, but there was nothing but storm swirling around her. Black darkness, broken only by the crackling of lighting and a wind that sucked all meaning from the sounds in the air. Making her decision, she turned back into the cabin, almost colliding with Ivor and Torsten.

"Where would he go?" Her question was lost in the noise of the room. Swiftly, she turned, slamming the door shut. "Fischer, where would Jace go?"

The man was still seated, never having moved from his chair during the chaos.

"Fischer!" Rin shouted again.

"I— I don't know. I don't know where he would go," he replied finally, raising his hand to cover his mouth. "I don't know who that boy is at all."

CHAPTER THIRTEEN
STORM IN EARNEST

Another wild gust hit the side of the ship and Rin flinched as the great wooden vessel shuddered under its ragged strength. She thought of Jace, somewhere out in the storm, and wondered if a young man without shelter could survive long in the midst of such violence. The pale look on his father's face made Rin think perhaps not.

She looked at Magnus in a question, but the boy shook his head.

"We have to let him go," he said through gritted teeth.

Rin opened her mouth to protest, but he carried on.

"I doubt he'll get far. He'll have to find somewhere to hole up and wait it out, same as the rest of us. If we don't find him, at least he doesn't know anything new enough to betray us to the Empire a second time."

Rin heard the council's murmurs at that, even above the creaking of the ship's deck and the howling of the wind.

"Tell us what you know, lad." It was not Fischer who spoke, but a tall, thin woman whom Rin recognised as Retta, one of the smugglers who held a seat on the council.

"There isn't much more to say tonight, not outside of what we've already told you. Only that we are certain someone from the Cove warned the Capital we were coming." Magnus looked at Fischer directly, as though to leave no doubt that this was truth. "Not just when, but how and why, too. That's the reason Ieuan isn't here with us now. They *wanted* us to have those archives and they *wanted* to ensure we'd come back to try and take the Tunnels. They need us to launch that attack and start removing the chips, because they need an excuse to re-open the Generation Project."

"How did you know it was him?" Fischer asked, unable to bear using his son's name.

Rin sensed that this was the time Magnus had told her would come. She reached into her pack and withdrew the small stack of papers they had removed from the others. She didn't need her friend to tell her what these last few pages would say.

"I'm sorry, Fischer," Magnus said, his voice full of regret. "The Alliance has a friend who once worked for the Capital. He was pretty certain that there would be contingencies in place."

Rin was relieved that Magnus was still being cautious about how much he was willing to share. She knew Jace had friends amongst the council, and she was not yet convinced that they had found all the rats on this ship. She scanned each face in the room, wondering just how deep such dark plots ran; looking for anything that might give away another who had betrayed them . She paused, and only when Magnus nodded his agreement did she reluctantly pass Retta the last few pages.

"Truthfully," Magnus continued, "I thought it would take longer. Our friend reasoned that if we removed those few pages, you would be forced to accept there was no way to remove the chips. We thought you would need time to study them and to debate, then, when we were all finally forced to give up, whoever it was would appear to stumble on the answer as if by chance. Whoever it was would need to ensure the Alliance could complete all of what Alfredson had planned for us."

Rin felt her muscles tense when Magnus used her father's

name, and then she was almost spitting the words, "Only someone who had read these last few pages, or who had already been told how to do it by the Capital, would know how to use the codes."

Magnus nodded, but held out his hand, requesting calm. "His arrogance made him reckless. He always was too impressed with his own cleverness," he added sourly, dabbing his nose on his sleeve to check if it was still bleeding. "If I were a betting man, I'd say that our friend was right. Jace knew long before we made it back here that we had been successful in retrieving those archives from the Capital. I'd say someone told him exactly which papers we took. That's why he was so shocked tonight, when they weren't all there as he expected."

"Why didn't you tell us?" Reece snapped, outraged that his friend had put Tilly through such heartache as part of a ploy.

"I'm sorry. Cornelius thought it would be more believable this way."

Reece's eyes narrowed until Tilly slipped her hand into his, shaking her head. The boy turned at her touch and his eyes held hers for a moment, then his shoulders dropped. Rin could see he was fighting to let his anger fade.

Retta had been studying them, watching their interactions play out but offering nothing in return. Finally, she lowered her gaze to scan the pages Rin had handed to her. The woman's eyebrows lifted higher with each word that passed under her eyes, and the moment stretched out uncomfortably while the room watched on.

Finally, she answered them. "It would seem they speak the truth, Fischer," she said, regretfully. "And Jace's actions didn't look like those of a man whose conscience is clear."

Fischer pushed back his chair, shock freezing his face. "I... I need to find my son." His words were slow, as though he was confused. Clearly stunned by what had transpired.

"I don't think that's wise. He made his choice, and that storm is not for—"

"He's still my son, Retta." Fisher's tone was powerful this time, but not angry.

"And that is the problem," the tall woman said as though he was forcing her to say the thing that she would rather have avoided. "No one can doubt what you have done for the Cove, Fischer. You know I voted for you to chair this council myself. But until we find out how deep the rot runs, we cannot keep letting our kinfolk run out of that door. Not when it is us who will pay the price if the Empire's reprisals reach the Cove."

Fischer scrunched his eyes shut, as though his next words pained him. "What are you proposing, Retta?"

The woman looked over at Tilly, a mixture of respect and compassion on her face. "Well, for starters, that girl has waited a long time to get that chip off. Since no one is going to be doing much of anything until this storm passes, I suggest that we study the rest of these papers and then do exactly what we intended to do when we started." She paused, looking at each one of them in turn. "Alfredson wants a war with the Tavi, that's clear enough, and if a fight with the Empire is coming, we're going to need every last one of us ready and able to stand against them to survive this. That starts with removing Tilly's chip."

Retta's words hung in the air for a long time, and they frightened Rin. War was not a word she had ever heard used to describe the present. It belonged to history; to the Immutavi Plague Wars; to the Resource Wars. Not to something that could happen now or in the future. Every other person around the table seemed to be contemplating the same reality: that a conflict with the Empire, which they had always sought to avoid before now, would be inevitable if they started freeing the chipped Tavi.

Rin looked around, finding herself forced to accept the silence. No one had raised an objection to Retta's proposal, and Rin knew that no one was going to. For a moment, she felt suspicious. *Is this woman working with Jace? Is she pushing us towards a fight that will only further the Empire's goal?* She shook her head, knowing that couldn't be true. The tension in the room told her this was a pot that had been a long time over the flames and was now finally boiling over.

There was something else in the people around her, though. Not just resolve, but a stubborn acceptance of the path ahead; an edge of rebellion that felt dangerous and exciting. What was happening now was not happening because Rin's father had set a plan in motion; it was driven by their passion – a focus and purpose that stole their fear and hardened them somehow. She could see it on all of their faces as they began to sort through the new stack of papers, placing them in the correct order amongst the others and then leaning in to decipher the text. Whether they were being dragged into this plan or stepping towards it willingly, the people in this room no longer wanted peace. They wanted their kin back, and – for the first time – they believed they might finally have the power to take them.

Rin was tired of feeling helpless when it came to the words held on those pages, and as hard as she tried, she could not find that renegade spirit they all seemed to be sharing. She felt like an imposter in their midst. What drove her was not the same as what these others sought. Amongst the fear and her desire to run, all that held her tethered to the plan was the urgent need to have Ieuan back. She tried to close her eyes to rest, but sleep eluded her as her mind grappled with recent events. The inaction of it all grated on her, and even though she was sure Jace would be long gone by now, several times she considered fleeing into the night to look for him, something inside her bristling at being confined.

Occasionally, Rin's eyes settled on Reece and Tilly, sitting together on the floor at the far end of the ship. Scratch was stretched out beside them, his long back running along the edge of the girl's leg. He always seemed to be pressed against her, just close enough that neither one was in any doubt of where the other was. Tilly's head rested on Reece's chest and he was stroking her hair, periodically whispering words that Rin could not hear. Seeing that made the thing that squirmed inside Rin twist worse than ever. She found herself rising, desperate to be moving, hoping to find some way to appease the ill-contented thing within her. She strode around the table, ignoring the papers and their infuriating symbols, but all too quickly she understood that there was still nothing she could do but wait.

Frustrated, she found herself back at the small, circular window, looking out into the black and wild night.

The room inside the ship was warm. There was a stove fire built into one wall, where flames licked and devoured the logs that continued to feed it. Added to that warmth was the press of council folk, their bodies generating a heat of their own. Rin knew she should be grateful not to be cold on a night as foul as this one, and yet something about the closeness of the room was stifling. So, she had been pleased to find things were different here at her window, where the cool draft swirled in through unseen gaps in the wood and the old glass rattled slightly in the wind. She could feel its cold, reaching fingers moving the strands of hair closest to her face, carrying with it the smell of the salty sea and the scent of the slippery green plants that grew near the shore. She felt her skin prickle under its touch, but she knew her goosebumps were not caused by the chilled air.

There was something frightening about the ferocity of such a tempest that could reach her even here. Torsten had been right to warn her. This was not like the storms in the Dale. This was like winter and summer were at war with one another; a great clashing of wills, careless of the land and lives they trampled underfoot as they wielded great weapons of wind and lightning. Surely it had been a storm just like this that had brought about the Fall of the world

In that moment, the great wooden beams she sheltered behind seemed flimsy; incapable of withstanding such violence. Watching and waiting, she stood there wondering if the wind might tear the boat from the rocks with its next shuddering gust; wondering if the next flash that lit the sky might strike the deck above them, shattering the wooden vessel into a thousand tiny splinters.

Rin didn't know it was possible to fall asleep standing up, but when she opened her eyes again, she could see daylight breaking through the clouds. Her head was resting against the wooden side of the ship, still facing the window. As her eyes adjusted to the dim light outside, they widened: if she had thought the sea waves had been big when they arrived, she now understood they had only been small hillocks by comparison. Great shelves of water taller than oak trees were crashing down against the shoreline below, sending foaming spray high into the air. She blinked in disbelief as she heard some of it rattling down on the deck of their ship. She had not thought it possible that the spray could travel so high or so far. Pressing her ear against the wood, she closed her eyes, searching for the vibrating of the wind and trying to read meaning from it. It was still present, but she was certain it was lessening now.

Someone at the table cleared their throat. Rin didn't have to look around: it was a sound she recognised, a small cough that cleared fatigue and doubt from a voice that was about to say something of importance. She closed her eyes again, considering which one of them would speak next; wondering whether their words would bring her peace or add further pain to her situation.

It was Retta who spoke. "For those that have been able to find some modicum of rest, I ask that you re-join us now. For those who have not yet shut your eyes, I request your continued presence only a few moments longer." The tall woman mirrored Fischer's calm demeanour, but her voice held a thickness that gave away how she had been amongst those who had not yet slept.

It took only a moment for all those still left in the cabin to regain their seats. A few of the people around the table were yawning or stretching stiffened backs. Rin had expected that, as she struggled to swallow her own yawn. Then there were those others, the ones who seemed to have passed the point at which sleep should have claimed them, rubbing tired eyes and shuffling papers too loudly with a jittery energy that was a little unnerving.

"While we obviously have cause to doubt his motives, these papers do confirm what Jace has already told us. With the right key, we should be able to use the code on the chip to unlock each of the pins and release it from the spine." Retta paused, looking over at Reece and Tilly. "However, with what we now know about the Empire ceding us these archives, there is no way to be sure whether doing so will release the chipped Tavi or unleash some new horror."

Reece's eyes went wide and Rin could tell that he had not considered before now that the information they had retrieved might have been altered or designed to hurt them further still. For the first time since Rin had shown the pack to the eager boy, she could see the doubt in his face.

"The designs are clear. Each locked pin must be turned exactly the number of times noted in the code. Once we start turning any individual leg, we can't stop, and if any one of the six locks is not turned enough, or the slightest fraction too far, it is rigged to kill its host."

Retta's eyes lingered on Tilly. Rin had not needed that gaze to tell her who was meant by 'host'.

"We know what this tells us to do, and thanks to your key, we have the tools to do it. The question is whether we trust these archives. Whether we trust that Alfredson's desire to reopen the Generation Project outweighs the Empire's desire to cripple us further."

While Retta's words hung heavy in the air, Rin realised that, this time, there was no way to be sure. What did she really know about her father? About the man who had forced this life onto them all? She knew he was ambitious – that much was clear – and that he was self-serving and reckless, too. She thought back to that night in the Palace; the smug glee on his face when she had loaded the archives into her satchel. Had his satisfaction been a consequence of her furthering his plan? Was this just another time she was being used as a toy in a much larger game she did still not fully comprehend? Rin felt her body tense at the memory of hitting the water and the overwhelming pain she had felt that night. The thought of it caused her to inhale sharply, which drew the gaze of several around the table. Apart from those quick glances, none of them made any other outward sign of acknowledgment. Then, as she remembered lying in the muddy bank with archers' arrows trained on her, she felt overcome by a wave of certainty.

"It'll work." Hearing her own voice echo through the room,

Rin saw the concern on Reece's face. "He wouldn't have let me live that night in the Palace, wouldn't have let us take these archives, wouldn't... wouldn't have taken Ieuan to make sure we'd come back, just to hurt Tilly. All of this hasn't ever been about just one of us." She turned to Tilly. "He wants us to remove your chip and then all the other Tavi chips we can get our hands on. He needs us to be a threat again: a threat real enough to convince the Empire that he is right about the Generation Project." She looked at Reece, whose brow was creased, his eyes darting from side to side as though he was desperately searching for the trap his life had taught him would be there. "It'll work, Reece." Rin placed her palms down on the stack of papers. "And then we'll make him regret it."

Whether she had convinced the boy or not, Rin wasn't sure, but it didn't matter. Tilly stepped towards him and placed her hand on his chest, where the key lay under his shirt. The mute girl held his gaze and nodded, before slipping the leather cord up and over his head. Then she kissed him. Rin couldn't say why, but somehow that kiss seemed like more than just the touching of two people's lips. It was a kiss that said *thank you* and *I'm sorry* at the same time. Rin knew then that Tilly wasn't sure what would happen next either, but she had claimed the risk as her own. Whatever happened now would be her choice, her fault, and she would not wait for anyone's permission to do it.

Rin marvelled again at how far the girl had come; at the strength she held inside her. Rin was not sure if she would ever possess as much of it as Tilly did.

"If you are ready, Tilly," Retta offered, taking a deep breath, "we can do it now."

Tilly nodded, looking nervously around the room.

"They don't all need to be here," Retta added, clearly sensing the girl's hesitation. "It can be just us."

Tilly's choice was clear to them all. The council began to rise, each one nodding or touching the girl's shoulder in some sign of tenderness or salute as they filtered out onto the blustery deck. The three brothers smiled at Tilly, each with a look that Rin knew was supposed to strengthen the resolve she was clinging to. Then Lark turned to leave. At first, Rin thought she would say nothing, but in the doorway, the girls paused, looking back at them.

"You scream as loud as you need to – no one in this world ever listens if you don't."

For a second, Rin thought she saw concern crease Lark's brow, before the girl left.

Rin made to leave too, wanting Reece and Tilly to have this last moment together before whatever came next. But Tilly grabbed her hand, shaking her head. Rin looked back, confused, as the girl's fingers wove a pattern on her palm that she didn't even begin to recognise.

"She wants you to stay," Reece explained, seeing the uncertainty on her face.

"I... a-are you sure?" Rin stammered, shocked by the request.

Reece looked at Tilly, who nodded again.

"She's sure." Another flurry of hands passed between the two. "She trusts you. She says you have a strong heart." Reece tapped his chest the way Tilly had done only a moment before.

Rin nodded hesitantly. "Okay."

There was a sudden shift in Reece's demeanour as he turned back to face Tilly. "I can help too. I don't want to leave you to do this alone."

This time, there was no flicker of fingers. Instead, the mute girl reached over to take Rin's hand in hers again. This gesture was clear, even to Rin. She was telling Reece that she would not be alone.

The boy's brow creased as he squeezed his eyes tightly shut, swallowing hard. "Alright. But I'll be just outside this door, okay?" He didn't open his eyes, as though accepting her wishes was a thing too painful to look at.

Tilly kissed him again, then led him to the door. If the girl forcing Reece from the room was a surprise, Tilly's gesture for Scratch to follow after him made Rin begin to doubt her own presence even more. The shaggy mutt was hesitant, cocking his head to one side. One of his raggedy ears stood alert while the other flopped over questioningly, as though he was trying to understand what the girl was asking of him. Tilly reached down and the dog plodded over to nuzzle at her hand, then she half nudged, half guided the great beast out through the door before closing it quickly behind him. They could all hear his confused whine and the sound of his nails scratching on the wooden panel as he pondered how he had found himself detached from his friend.

Tilly closed her eyes for a second, causing Rin to wonder if the girl was about to change her mind, but instead she stepped towards Retta, handing the thin woman the key. Hastily, Tilly removed her shirt, placing her hands on the table before nodding one last time.

Together, Rin and Retta stepped towards the girl's braced body. Rin had never looked closely at a chip like this before. Sure, she had caught glances of them, or else seen them drawn on paper, but they had always seemed like evil things, not to be examined for long. Now, she could see the horror laid bare before her, and she felt even more keenly that she did not want to be so close to such vileness. There were six pins in total: three on each side.

Where the metal bit Tilly's skin, it had stayed angry and raw. As she imagined those pins piercing her own flesh, Rin understood why it looked that way. Tavi skin never stopped trying to heal; never stopped trying to reject foreign objects embedded into it.

Rin shuddered. She had not expected to see the scarring and the signs of damage caused by Tilly's fingernails on bare flesh alongside the chip. It would seem that those wounds had never fully healed either, and immediately, Rin realised the cruelty in that. It was no accident – someone had designed it to suppress her ability to remove any trace of such torment on her skin. Rin's eyes moved from the girl's skin back to the six pins that anchored the small black chip to Tilly's spurs, and as Rin leaned closer, she could see them. It was not clear to her if they were letters or numbers, but there was a pattern etched on there that could be the code they sought. Beside each of those pin legs was a slot just the right size for a small key like the one Cornelius had fashioned for them.

Retta reached out, placing her hand on the girl's back. "Alright, here we go."

Tilly's body tensed, a small squeak leaving the girl's lips.

The sound was answered almost instantly by Scratch's harsh bark from beyond the door. Rin moved around the table to look into Tilly's eyes and saw the determination fixed in them. They nodded at each other.

"It's okay," Rin forced the words out reluctantly. She wanted to stop this and spare the girl her pain, but she knew it was not her choice. "Keep going, Retta."

"Alright. The first number is a four, so if the papers are right, we turn the key in the first lock four times."

Though her voice was calm, Rin could see that Retta's hand was shaking as she moved the key towards the first slot. There was a faint tinny sound as metal touched metal, then Retta began to count each turn.

"One, two, three, four."

Rin held her breath as Scratch's barking grew more frantic. Nothing was happening, and Rin could see that Retta was starting to panic.

"I turned it four times," she stammered. "I... I was sure that number was a four."

There was a click, and a scream, and for a terrible moment Rin could only watch on, horrified by this reckless thing they had done. But the first of the chip's legs had begun to twitch beneath Tilly's skin and slowly draw itself clear of her flesh. Once it was free, it jerked quickly back towards the chip and, for the first time, Rin saw just how deeply the little wire leg had lodged itself into the girl's spine.

Tilly reached out her hand, desperately seeking Rin's.

"Do you want us to stop?" Rin asked, frantic with worry, almost hoping she would say yes and stop this for them all.

Tilly only shook her head.

"Okay," Retta said, relief flooding her voice. "The next number is a two."

Rin watched as the woman flexed her fingers several times, trying to rid them of their shaking, before she continued the torturous process.

With each pin removed came the weaking of Tilly's resilience. Arms that had been braced to hold herself up to begin with soon failed, and her upper body now lay face-down on the table. Tilly's hand still clutched Rin's, but she had drawn it under her chest protectively. Each time a pin was removed, the girl cried louder and louder. Scratch was beside himself, howling and barking, throwing the full weight of his body against the thick wooden panel of the door. Rin had been trying not to look, but she couldn't block out the thick smell of blood that invaded her nose, forcing her to acknowledge the reality of what Retta was doing.

Soon, Tilly let out what Rin hoped would be her last scream, and Scratch howled long and loud in a chorus to the sound. Rin felt the girl's hand loosen its grip and she opened her eyes, finally looking past Tilly's shoulders to see the final pin free itself from her flesh, retracting towards the chip. With this last awkward movement, the crooked, angular leg drew lazily back towards itself, reminding Rin of a dried-out carcass of a spindly-legged scuttler. She didn't know how Retta could force herself to touch the thing, but the woman was already calmly reaching down towards it.

"Tilly, it's done," Rin said, desperately trying to reach the girl through the veil of pain and fatigue that overwhelmed her small body. "It's over," she tried again. "Tilly?"

Silent tears streamed down the girl's face.

Rin looked up again at the older woman, who was still holding the chip. "Did something go wrong? Will she be okay?" The questions spilled out of her quicker than she had the patience to wait for them to be answered.

The door tumbled open, Reece and Scratch tripping over the threshold together, each as desperate as the other to reach Tilly. Rin guessed then that, while the screaming had been bad for Scratch, the following silence had been far worse for Reece.

"Tilly!" he cried, his eyes taking in the blood on Retta's hands and the girl's still and silent form, laid out on the table.

When Reece moved to touch Tilly, Scratch snapped at him wildly. If there had been any form of friendship between the mutt and the others in the group, Scratch had forgotten it in this moment. All were suspects to him, and all were a threat, until he worked out who had done this thing to his friend.

"She's alive, Reece," Retta almost whispered, her wide eyes never leaving the snarling mass of fur and teeth in front of her. Slowly, she placed the chip down on the table and began to back away from Tilly.

Scratch was still barking and snarling, clearing the area around the silent girl, who had begun to shake and tremble. When the mutt's furry back legs collided with Tilly's, she gave a squeak of fright and scrambled to push herself up off the table.

Rin's heart dropped. Tilly had squeaked – not cried out with words or curses. She remembered her grandmother's words the first night they had arrived in her hut. *She hasn't spoken. Not a word. I don't know yet if that's physical or something else.* Perhaps it wasn't the chip that had stopped Tilly's words. Perhaps it was that something else all along. She thought about the torture the girl had endured as they had tried to prise the information from her mouth down in the Lab. Maybe it had taken everything from her to stop the sounds that would end her torment but condemn her friends. Had her determination to stay quiet silenced her forever?

Rin was wrong though – it might have taken her words, but it had not taken everything from the girl. With a primal scream, Tilly grabbed one of the empty bowls from across the table and threw herself towards the chip Retta had left it on the table. Tilly's intention became clear just as an idea flashed across Rin's mind.

"Tilly, wait!" she cried out, but the girl was too consumed by her goal to hear anything.

Then, Rin was moving too, but she was hit with a sudden pain that flared up her arm. She heard Scratch's snarl but kept going, the power inside her roaring to life, dulling the sensation and giving her strength. The mutt's bite may have slowed her, but not enough to stop her from reaching the chip before Tilly did. She snatched it out of the way just as the heavy wooden bowl clattered down on the table where it had been only moments before. Tilly screamed again, the sound full of anguish, and Rin felt Scratch's teeth sink deeper into her arm, splitting her skin.

"Tilly, wait," Rin grunted, gritting her own teeth against the pain. "Please wait! I know how we are going to get into the Tunnels."

CHAPTER FOURTEEN
PLANS AND PROMISES

"This is madness." Magnus was shaking his head as though he thought Rin could not have said something more ridiculous if she'd tried.

Scratch's hackles rose again There was a trace of frustration too close to anger in the boy's voice for his liking. The mutt might have consented to let go of Rin's arm, but he still stood protectively over his friend, challenging anyone he considered a threat. None of the council members from the night before had waited to see how Tilly had fared under Retta's ministrations, and Rin had not missed the surprised look on the woman's face that indicated she had expected more from her own kin.

"I think it would be best if we sat down," Retta said, looking at the mutt meaningfully. "And we should all watch our tone."

At first, Rin thought she was referring to Scratch's sensitivity, until Retta nodded in the direction of Tilly, who sat at the end of the table, looking exhausted. Reece had wrapped her in one of the larger furs from the trunk of spare clothes, and she had calmed slightly, but still not said a word. Since Rin had stopped the mute girl from smashing her extracted chip, Tilly had only stared at the bloody device, her face fixed in a harsh scowl, broken only when she sniffed or wiped at a tear.

Taking a seat with the others, Rin turned back to Magnus. "But it *can* be done," she said, as pleasantly as she could muster with her arm still throbbing. "Retta told us – it's all there in the papers. How to remove *and* how to place the chips. Listen to me – we know that chip malfunctioned, because Tilly was able to think for herself and stay in control." Rin tried to stay calm as she looked at the horror on Magnus's face. She swallowed hard. "With a chip and a uniform, I could make it look real. We can get through the checkpoints and into the Tunnels without anyone knowing I'm there."

"It won't just look real, Rin. It will *be* real!" Magnus tried to keep his voice soft, but his disgust won out. "You won't be pretending, you *will be* chipped. We have no idea what kind of malfunction that thing has. No idea if taking it off Tilly and placing it on you might reset whatever glitch it has altogether." They locked eyes and then he was shaking his head again. "Torsten, tell her!"

The air was thick with the tension and, for a moment, only silence followed his plea.

"We haven't thought of any other way, Magnus," Torsten answered his brother hesitantly.

Rin blinked. It was rare for the three brothers to disagree on anything outside of their usual teasing banter, and that was even more true when it came to anything to do with the Tunnels.

"So you're okay with being part of a plan to chip Rin and sending her down into the Tunnels alone?" Magnus's voice was heavy with the revulsion he felt.

"I didn't mean..." Torsten paled at his brother's words. "It's just that, with the chip, they would let her straight through. They'd never suspect..." the taller boy started, but didn't finish, as he saw the disappointment on Magnus's face. "No, no... Magnus is right," he corrected himself, then looked at Rin as though he had never entertained any other idea.

Retta cleared her throat again, and this time, Rin was irritated by the noise. This was not a council meeting the woman could call order to; this was a thing no committee of strangers could stop her from doing. Rin turned to look at Retta coldly, and saw that the woman was taken aback by the anger on her face.

"The plan has merit," Retta began, cautiously, "but this is not a decision to be made without the support of the council. We will hold another meeting in due course, once we're better rested," she concluded, more formally than Rin would have expected for a woman who still had so much of Tilly's blood drying on her hands.

"They aren't resting." Ivor answered the question that was unasked in her statement. "They went with Fischer. As soon as we left the cabin, he called for volunteers to form a search party to look for Jace and most of the Council left with him right then." The look on Ivor's face made it clear that he had wanted to go with them. "It's still blustering out there, but for now it's eased enough that someone should try and find him. The sea swell is still too high for him to make it out over the ocean, but he might just be desperate enough to try and make the River Run climb."

Rin didn't know what that meant, but she could tell by Lark's scornful laugh that she thought it was a bad idea, bordering on ludicrous.

"He's not Tavi, Ivor," Lark said, chuckling scornfully. "He has more chance of growing wings and flying out of here than he does scaling the cliffs with the force of the river hammering down on him. Although... perhaps he might do us all a favour and try." The coldness of her assertion was chilling.

"It will be best for everyone if he is long gone," Retta cut in, frowning at Lark. "If we never find so much as a trace of that boy, so much the better."

Rin looked across at the woman, suspicious, and then she

realised the truth in what she was saying. Jace could not return here now, not after all he had done, but to consider actually killing him? It was not a thing Rin wanted any part in. What she *did* want was to return to the Tunnels as quickly as possible, and not to be derailed from that plan now she was so close.

"Retta, you can't tell the Alliance what we intend to do," Rin said calmly, feeling the edge of the thing inside her that made her voice cold and powerful. "We don't know if Jace was working alone or with others."

Retta shook her head. "I don't believe that anyone else—"

"You wouldn't have believed Jace was capable either, Retta," Magnus cut her off. "Not until you saw it for yourself. Rin is right – we don't know who we can trust anymore."

Retta stared hard at him for a moment, then eventually looked away. "You're right. I never would have believed anyone in the Cove could have done such a thing." Her words sounded to Rin as though they had the ring of truth to them. "But still," Retta went on, almost speaking her thoughts aloud, "it's not for us alone to decide what risks the Cove takes."

"Then give them the choice." Rin's voice was quieter than she had intended. "They can vote on whether we go back and make an attempt to evacuate the Tunnels, but no one outside this room needs to know the details."

"How do you expect them to make a decision without that information?"

"That is the choice I am offering." Rin let more of her strength surge into her words. There was no place for feelings or compromise in this. "They can trust us to get this thing done, or they can try on their own. Without my help."

"Without our help, too," Reece added quickly, looking at Lark, then back to Retta.

The woman bristled. "I see." She glanced at the three brothers, trying to gauge their position if she was forced to take this to a vote.

Magnus nodded his support for Rin

Retta's nostrils flared. "You are all very sure of yourselves to be proposing such ultimatums to the council." There was a hint of a warning in her voice.

Rin shrugged. "And if you're sure we are mistaken, you are welcome to go yourselves." As she spoke, she saw Lark flash her a sly, approving smile.

Looking back at Retta, Rin held the woman's gaze for a moment, before lifting her eyebrows in a way that questioned Retta's silence.

When she didn't respond, Rin added, "I thought as much. You will be the only one in the council who knows the details, and if we find out you have shared the plan with anyone, we will know who Jace's ally was after all."

The last was said pointedly. Rin didn't really think Retta was working with the Empire. The woman seemed deeply committed to the Cove, as if she was made of the wind and the salt spray herself, but the warning served its purpose. Rin had impressed herself with her threat, seeing that it very neatly solved the problem and left no clear way for Retta to tell anyone their plans now, without casting doubt on her own motives.

"You still need our help," Retta insisted, unable to keep the frown from her face.

"Not as much as you need ours," Rin answered cooly, intrigued to find that Lark was right – she was starting to enjoy being the wolf and not the rabbit. "Make no mistake though: with or without the Alliance, I will wear that chip and I will find Ieuan and Gibb. Your council only gets to vote on who else I try to bring out of there with them. You have until the sea is calm enough for us to leave. Then I will expect your answer."

Retta's mouth pulled itself into a thin line, marking her displeasure at the options presented. Rin acknowledged the look with a hardness of her own, and was surprised to feel things settle comfortably into place inside her. Tentatively, she loosened her grip on her flow of power, expecting the familiar anxious feeling to seep back in to replace it. Instead, to her surprise, she remained sure and steady. Whether she was about to rescue her friends or lead them all to their deaths, she wasn't certain, but she did know she had settled on an action that her soul could make peace with.

"Well, you have given me a lot to do." Retta rose from her seat. "And not so much time to do it. If you will all excuse me, it would seem I no longer have a moment to spare." Her words were brusque, but there was a grudging air of respect emanating from the woman now.

As the door closed shut behind Retta, Magnus turned to face Rin. "I hope you know what you're doing."

"Does anyone?" She was surprised at the strained laugh that escaped with her words. "But nobody knows those Tunnels better than you three. This is the only way to get any of us down there quietly." She squinted, considering a problem. "Either Fischer will teach me to read the numbers, or he won't, but once I find Ieuan and Gibb, it won't matter – they both know how to read, and all the numbers too. More down there are bound to know enough of them to use the keys to free me and others once we explain it to them." She saw the look that passed between all of them: the look that noted how her plan hinged on the certainty that she would find Ieuan or Gibb first. "If Marta has secured us passage out of the Void and Cornelius has set his powders to collapse the tracks behind us, then there is nothing we need to do but wait for the sea to calm and the council to make their decision. I will not wait for longer than that – they have spent too much time down there already."

The fact that no one argued with her last point only made her more certain that they should return sooner rather than later for her friends.

"It's not much of a plan," Lark said dryly. "Get in with a disguise, hope you find your boyfriend and his father, take off as many chips as you can, then make a break for it."

Rin winced. It did sound overly simplistic when she put it like that.

"Still," offered Torsten, with a smile, "we've had plans before that were based on a lot less than that."

"And we've had more complicated ones that changed the second we started them," Ivor added, as though finishing the thought.

The two brothers looked at Magnus questioningly.

"We'll need to find you a uniform that fits," the eldest of the brothers remarked. "Then we'll start running mock drills until you know the Tunnels so well you'll look like you've walked those checkpoints all your life."

Magnus said these words as though he still doubted the wisdom of them, but it was his agreement Rin needed, not his enthusiasm.

"Well," Lark piped up again, "now that all of you are so eager to dance this jig, let's hope the old woman has convinced the Partisan to let us come fleeing through the Stacks."

Rin glanced sideways at Lark. It was not lost on her that the girl's mind had strayed to the part of the plan that would take her closest to Fievel again. Rin knew better than to comment on it, though, especially not when they all finally seemed to be in agreement.

"Let's get some air and some breakfast," Magnus suggested. "We'll meet back here just after midday. I want to check with Alyssa to see how much time we have before we can leave."

"Why Alyssa?" asked Rin.

"No one reads the weather better than her. If she says it will be cold on the first day of the new moon, it will be cold, and if she says this is a gap in the gathering storm, or this is the end of it, she will be right about that too."

Rin nodded, making a note to visit Alyssa as well. To read the skies sounded like a skill she would also like to learn if she could. She shook her head then, knowing it was not a good habit to start lying to herself now. She would find Alyssa because she wanted to know about the woman's husband and son; two more faces she would search for in the Tunnels, regardless of the council's decision.

She stepped out onto the deck and felt the buffeting of the wind around her – no longer terrifying, merely fresh and invigorating after their confinement in the cabin. As she looked out, she could see the thrum of people bustling along the walkways of the Cove. She could see the rise and fall of hammers and the drawing action of saws as parts of the settlement broken by the storm were mended or replaced.

Straining her ears, Rin suddenly found it odd that this was not accompanied by the usual sound of people at work. Rin had never known the wind to whip away sounds like that. What little activity she could make out was almost drowned out entirely by the crashing of waves and the rushing of sand, amplified against the high stone walls of the Cove. The sea sucked at the shore with a rushing and frothing, like it was trying to swallow great chunks of the land in its churning jaws. She had been right to be worried the previous night. It was not just the hunger of the sea against the land, or the odd missing step that had been torn from the walkway by the storm. The roof of the boathouse now lay at the opposite end of the shore, smashed against the rocks.

Turning in surprise, Rin noticed one of the smaller ship's masts had also been sheared in two before smashing down onto the deck below. She hoped no one had been hurt, considering how much force it would have taken to crash through the thick boards of the deck like that. There had been no word of injury or death as far as she knew, but perhaps such news would take time to travel to a stranger such as herself. She thought of Alyssa and Geira again, and hoped both of them had been well sheltered, as she had.

Almost as soon as the thought crossed her mind, she was met with relief as she saw the woman and her child shuffling along a walkway just above, handing out steaming cups of something from a familiar black kettle. The girl waved and then both of them were moving towards Rin.

"What a mess," Alyssa said wearily as she approached.

"I didn't know there were still storms like this, so long after the Fall," Rin replied, cringing at how naïve she sounded.

"Oh my dear, this wasn't like the storms from then. There haven't been any whirling-swirlers in these parts since the Fall itself."

Rin's eyes widened.

"Then again," Alyssa continued, "this wasn't the worst storm we've had, even in little Geira's time. I've been telling the council for months that we needed to get ahead of the winter maintenance. Some of these repairs should have been done last squall season. It's really a mercy no one was hurt, or worse." She tutted, as though Rin were among those who had failed to patch or mend before the storm.

"There were storms worse than this one recently?"

This time, it was little Geira who answered Rin's disbelief. "Yup! Once the little ship used to sit on the rocks down there at the edge of the shore. Then the last big storm lifted the whole thing up, people and all, and stuck it there."

She pointed to a ship that sat far above the water. Rin had assumed it had been there since the earth had risen up from the sea during the Fall, and was shocked to discover that wind and water alone had moved it so far.

"Those were dreadful winds, much worse than these. Geira's father, Shep, and seven other men went out into the dark that night to secure it to those rocks," Alyssa continued the little girl's tale, looking over at the ship, still wedged in the rocks, as though picturing Shep's hands tying knots to steady it. "The council held a dinner in the big ship for all of them after the storm passed. They say my husband saved at least twenty lives that night." She paused to pass Rin a cup of the warm broth. "And now, when it's their turn to go out into the night, they debate and argue about whether they will support one young girl and her five friends. How quickly they forget what Shep did for them, now that he is the one who needs rescuing."

As the silence grew between them, Rin felt something twist inside her. She knew she was about to offer something that might get her or someone she cared about killed, and part of her still cared desperately enough about living to halt her tongue for just a moment longer. She sipped the hot, thin soup, her eyes meeting the little girl's from above the rim of her mug, making her swallow the scalding liquid too quickly.

The words seemed to drag themselves out of her mouth, unbidden. "It doesn't matter what the council says, Alyssa. We won't leave anyone behind if we can help it."

The woman closed her eyes, then suddenly pulled Rin tightly into a hug. She had to tip her mug quickly to stop it sloshing over them both.

"It's not fair of me to ask," Alyssa said, and Rin was not sure if it was a tear or some of the broth that fell on her shoulder.

"You didn't." Rin let that be the last heartfelt thing she said, before desperately reaching for the current within. She knew this was not her time to fall apart.

Alyssa straightened her back. "When you find him down there, he will help you get the others out – our son, too. Shep has more courage in his little finger than the whole council put together."

There was no way to know if Alyssa's husband and son would still be alive in the Tunnels. Rin had not even dared ask if they were Tavi, knowing what it would mean for them if the answer was no. She pushed that notion aside: if they were still there to be found, she needed Alyssa to believe that she would be the one to find them.

Realising Geira was watching them, the woman wiped both cheeks before adopting the worker's tone of one who had a great deal to do, and who felt the day was running away from them.

"Well, there is plenty to be done today. This storm may have blown itself out, but I fear it will be the first of many this season. The council will see the sense of your plan, I'm sure of it. That means there will be a lot to prepare for if we are going to accommodate all these new mouths in the Cove this winter." Alyssa looked out towards the waves still crashing against the shore. "With the wind blowing from the north like that, it'll be two more days before anyone is going out over the sea. But by midday on the day after tomorrow, we should have poles enough for every able body to take to the water. We'll need every one of them, too, if we're going to catch and dry enough fish to see so many people from the Tunnels through the winter."

This could have sounded like a list of chores the woman was reeling off, and yet it didn't. Instead, it sounded like the determined planning of someone who would make sure they were ready for what she didn't dare hope they could bring about. Rin knew that feeling well – of forcing yourself to focus on what you could control and achieve, as a ward against what was uncertain and bleak.

The rest of the afternoon passed in a blur in their cabin, as Magnus walked her through what to expect at each checkpoint, time and time again. Then they began to act out the interactions she could expect to encounter from the guards, and after she had mastered each basic sequence, occasionally one of the three brothers would throw in some new problem or unexpected alteration that she had to try and navigate. All, of course, within the confines of the acceptable behaviour of a chipped Tavi. Even though this was all make-believe, Rin had twice felt a real, rising panic when they had surprised her. Each time, she had struggled to imagine her way out of such traps without blowing her cover.

On one occasion, Torsten and Magnus had disagreed about the best course to take if she was challenged by an Empire guard that wasn't Tavi – one who was capable of asking more probing questions. Her responses were to always either remain mute or to adhere to a handful of pre-programmed phrases, no matter how ill-fitting they may seem to their questions. This all depended on whichever false limitations they chose for her in this role. They were getting louder as they tried to instruct her in the stilted, robotic speech typical of the guards who were programmed for such work, and it was only when Tilly approached that they quieted their disagreement.

"What do you think, Tilly?" Rin asked, still hoping the girl might answer in words, given enough time.

Tilly's hand twitched, and she covered her mouth with her palm. The first few movements Rin could not decipher, but her vote for silence was clear enough.

Rin wanted to ask more questions, but the knock at the door caused them all to start. Could the council have reached their decision already? Rin caught the look on the other's faces, each of them thinking the same thing: if this really was the response from the council, it had come much faster than they had expected.

The door opened and Retta stepped through, leaving them no time to wonder if such a quick response was good or bad.

"Good afternoon," the woman began a little stiffly.

Rin only nodded back. She and the others would wait to hear what the council's answer was before deciding if this day would be a good one or not.

"Your terms are hard to like," Retta continued.

Rin raised her chin slightly, in a gesture that said she would not change them now that they were set.

Retta paused to take in the girl, then smiled. "But they are not impossible," the woman conceded. "You have the agreement of the council and the full support of the Alliance."

Rin tried to mask the sigh of relief that emptied her lungs. No matter what she had been willing to do, she was glad she would not have to face angering both the Empire *and* the Council with her actions.

The smile Retta gave her this time was genuine. "Just tell us what you need."

CHAPTER FIFTEEN
RETURN

Though the wind no longer howled the way it had the evening before, it still felt ominous as it whistled in the rigging of the ship above them, darkness threatening to consume the Cove as night fell.

Retta had not been exaggerating when she had offered the full support of the council, and only now did Rin truly appreciate how much she had been willing to gamble when she had been prepared to do this alone. Earlier in the day, supplies for the trip back to the capital had been delivered to their cabin, neatly stowed in fresh packs. Rin knew that if she had asked for a guard uniform too, one would have been found and tailored to her before the dusk turned to true night. She had not, though, still unsure how much of their plan she was willing to share with their new allies.

Yet despite Rin's unwillingness to share their plans with anyone outside her small group, the council had offered more than just supplies to their cause. Retta had been clear and precise when she had detailed the coordinated chaos that would fall on the Empire on the night that Rin and her friends would attempt to enter the Tunnels. The Alliance's intertwining network of people, whom Retta had simply referred to as 'hidden hands', would be there to assist them by fuelling confusion in the hope of distracting the guards. If all went to plan, there would be further pockets of resistance waiting to help once Rin and the others broke free of the Tunnels, blocking alleyways and setting off smoke to cover their tracks and lay false trails as the large group passed through the Void. Once they were clear of the Ashlands, a second party would meet them at the riverbank to help bring everyone down the channels together.

Rin knew all that was going to take some serious time, and as she listened to Retta, she closed her eyes, sending out her wish that Cornelius would be able to collapse the tracks behind them. It wasn't just that Rin found it hard to trust the odd little man who lived under the earth – the same man whose misguided work had been used against them for decades – but the way Retta referred to them as 'the survivors'. Those of them who made it back to the riverbank to be met by the council would be those who had *survived* this madness. It was a word that was hard to have echoing in her ears as she tried to make plans to ensure that she and her friends would be counted among them.

As Alyssa had predicted, by the afternoon of the second day, the sea had settled to nothing more than a few choppy little tufts of blue and white that licked at the shore. Rin wondered if she had been overly hasty to announce that their departure must be no later than today. Perhaps one more night to run through the plan, to really be sure that she could remember which alleys she must avoid when they broke free, would have been wiser. She was tired, and the cold sea air felt sharp against parts of her skin that it touched.

Looking down, she saw a flurry of bodies marking the shoreline below, and she knew then that she did not have another night to waste sheltering in the great wooden belly of the big ship. She could not let the people of the Cove see her waver now. She had said they would leave on this day, and so leave they must.

Rin was afraid, though. Afraid that she was already too late to save Ieuan and Gibb; afraid that she wouldn't be able to find Alyssa's husband; afraid she wouldn't be able to save *any* of the Tavi stuck in that dark place; afraid she would get them all killed. She was ashamed then, as her last thought was only for herself: she was afraid of the pain; that once again she would know suffering like she had known the last time she had taken on the Empire.

When she looked up, she realised Retta had been watching her, and instantly she grasped hold of the flow inside her and relaxed her face. They must believe that she was certain; if she gave them any reason to doubt her now, they might not follow her.

Rin wasn't sure which of the many tasks it was that had stolen all her time, but all too soon, the people of the Cove were gathering on the shore to wave them off. She felt like she had been crowned harvest queen as she walked through the throng of bodies that stretched from the walkways to the sand. People seized her hands, shaking them, praising her or else pleading for her to bring home some name or another that she knew she would not be able to remember. Each time another hand patted her on the shoulder, or another pair of eyes met hers with that same look of desperate hope, she felt the panic rise in her.

It was only when she felt her teeth begin to chatter together, and a weakness in her knees that threatened to make her stumble, that she seized hold of the flow within her in earnest. Instantly, it soothed her, drowning out all doubt and uncertainty as raw strength and calm steadied her. She could look at those faces before her now. It wasn't that she didn't recognise the sadness their features held – reminding her that she held their last chance at reunion with a loved one they thought lost – but she could now separate herself from it. She could understand it, but she could no longer feel the weight of their sorrow added to her own burden. The thing inside only cared about *her*, what *she* needed, what *she* could do to bring about the change she wanted.

When she grasped it as tightly as she did now, she found she could filter out the noise around her, transforming the throng of voices clamouring for her attention into distinct, singular sounds that she could choose to individually tune into. That was when Reece's voice reached her, and she found herself seeking his form in the crowd.

"Tilly, please. Please stay here." Reece stood on the shore, pleading with the girl, who was standing in one of the small log boats in the ebb.

Rin saw Tilly shake her head and Scratch huffed out through his nose in agreement, jumping into the boat.

"I don't want to lose you," Reece pleaded, his words revealing the panic and frustration battling with one another.

Tilly's hands moved, first pointing at Reece, then the shore.

"I can't stay. I promised Rin I would go back with her, but it makes no sense for us both to go, Tilly. It's a risk we don't have to take."

Tilly squinted at him, considering his words. Then she pointed to herself and the boat, then back to him and the shore. Rin was pretty certain that meant: 'You stay, then, and I'll go'.

Reece groaned, gritting his teeth. But before he could say anything further, Tilly stepped out of the boat. For moment, Rin found herself shocked at how easily she had been dissuaded from going with them, and Reece clearly felt the same, freezing for a moment before his shoulders relaxed and he reached out to her.

"Thank you. I need to know you'll be okay and I don't trust that I could keep you safe a second time if—"

Rin never heard what he thought he was keeping her safe from, as Tilly promptly ducked under his outstretched arm and rolled around his side until they were back-to-back. Rin clutched tighter to the current of ability inside her, and it was then she noticed the smile on the smaller girl's face. Instinctively, she knew what would come next. To anyone else, the move would have happened seamlessly. Rin felt her own shoulder drop in anticipation only a fraction of a second before Tilly's did. Silently, Tilly reached behind her, seizing Reece's head in her hands and then simultaneously kicking out behind her, buckling his right knee. The momentum drew them both downward, but where she dropped forward onto one knee, he fell backwards, pulled downward by both his weight and her arms. Then, as fluid as water, she half-turned, catching him and laying his back against her bent knee, keeping him just out of balance enough that he clutched at her arms to steady himself.

Had it not been for the small blade she held a finger's breadth from his neck, Rin thought the boy would have easily slipped her grasp. But the knife was there and, had they been fighting for real, all three of them knew this was a move he would not have survived. Yet instead of the movement being followed by a flash of silver or a spurt of blood, as if to make her point final, she leaned forward and kissed him. Rin saw the boy's eyes go wide and Tilly's cheeks puffed out as his laugh left his own mouth for hers.

Rin looked away, her eyes falling on the large mutt in the boat, who wrinkled his nose, yawned wide, then settled down to sleep.

"That's going to take him some getting used to," Lark commented, as she stepped past Rin and made her way to the shore.

Rin supposed she was right. For a long time, Tilly had taken care of Reece when they had been trapped in the Labs, but afterwards, *he* had been the one who had carried the responsibility of protecting them both. She wondered how long it would take them to learn to share that task.

There wasn't time to think for long about how it might change the love they had previously known, as an increasingly loud murmur began to sound behind her and she turned, seeing two familiar figures cutting through the crowd: the broad shoulders of Fischer and the slender height of Retta. They were muttering to each other in a way that made Rin tense, although she couldn't say why.

"We didn't find him." Fischer said the words before they had come to a stop, and Rin knew he could only mean Jace. "Don't ask me how, but I don't think he's in the Cove anymore."

Rin couldn't tell if he was relieved or angry not to have found his son. She would guess that most likely it was a little of both. Her eyes flicked to Retta, and she wondered if the woman stood a half step behind Fischer to indicate that he still held his seat as the head of the council, or if she was just so used to doing it that the habit was no longer conscious.

When he realised Rin had no questions on the matter, Fischer went on. "I apologise for my absence over the last few days. I did not mean to ignore my other responsibilities here. Retta has told me some, and informed me that 'some' amounts to all that she can say on the matter." He looked over at the woman, perhaps still hoping she might say more.

Rin was grateful that Retta had held to their agreement.

When still no one answered, Fischer sniffed hard and went on. "Well then, I think – or truer to say, I hope – you have all that you need?"

"You have given us everything we asked for." Rin knew that wasn't exactly an answer to his question, but it was all she was willing to give. The fact that Jace was still out there bothered her. She didn't know what they would have done with the boy if they'd found him, but the fact that he was still out there and that hers was not the only plan at play on this day caused her unease.

Fischer lunged towards her, and it took all her poise not to strike out at him defensively, but as his arms wrapped around her in a hug, he muttered, "You don't have to do this."

Rin stood stock still with her arms pinned to her sides. She knew he had meant to give her permission to abandon their dangerous cause; that this was not a plea to try and stop her. Yet his words irritated her. Mostly because she knew he was wrong. She *did* have to do this thing. There was a part inside of her that would never stop twisting and squirming if she walked away from it all now.

When she didn't answer, Fischer let her go, holding her at arm's length and looking into her face, and Rin felt a little pleased that the edge of hardness she forced into her eyes had shamed him slightly.

That look was one of the many things that flitted through Rin's mind on an incessant loop as they travelled back towards the Empire. Fischer's face, Gibb's face, Alyssa's face, a man she'd never met rushing out into a storm to save others from its fury. She wondered about Marta and Fievel, too; whether they had convinced the Partisan to help. When her mind was calmer, she walked through the plan step by step: each checkpoint; every variation; every complication that they had acted out in the cabin. If someone gave her paper and a pen now, she could create a drawing of the Void alleyways so detailed it could be used as a map.

More than anything, though, she thought of Ieuan. When the fear would grow almost unbearable, a terrible blend of foreboding and excitement that flooded her system and set every nerve to jangling and itching inside her, she would think of him. She would bring his face to the front of her mind, trying to push away all other warring thoughts, and instead imagine only the relief from her torment that she would feel when she stood beside him again. How it would feel when she took them both far from that twisted, dark place.

Rin knew she was doing it, and she was vaguely aware that her friends had begun to worry about the time she spent this way. She did not care. Drawing back into herself again, she let the river of ability drown out the true depth of her feelings. It was too much to expect her to laugh and joke with them while fear gnawed and lashed at her this way. Whatever they thought about her, resisting its pull was beyond what she could tolerate. They didn't understand what it was like for her. Rin knew it would be too tempting for anyone to ignore the draw of such a powerful thing. To feel the constant terror and keep stepping towards it anyway, without the strength inside her, was too much.

Ignoring their attempts to engage with her, she was almost unaware of the earth passing under her feet as she let her attention be drawn intently to the smallest details. The batting of the wings of a bee as it buzzed from flower to flower; the change in the sound of the river as it bent to flow around stones and unseen creatures that dwelled on its bottom; anything that meant she did not have to wallow in this time of waiting, when all there was to do was guess at what could go wrong.

Even though she tried to hold herself steady in this detached place, she had felt a few times now a prickling on her skin that made her feel as though she was being watched. Each time, it was Jace's face that streaked through her mind, yet when she focused her senses to seek out the cause of her unease, she found nothing.

What use did the Empire have for a boy like Jace? And why

would the son of a smuggler, who knew more than most about the atrocities of the Senate, wish to align his purpose with the Empire's? Those were the questions Rin kept coming back to. She had met enough people like Jace to know that there must be something in this for him; some deal struck that promised Jace enough to turn his back on all of those who had known and cared for him.

Rin shuddered. Somewhere out there was a boy who had already gambled her life once for his own gain. Not knowing why made it impossible to know what he might do next.

They did not have to cross the Ashlands again, instead camping in the mouth of a mountain cave, before following Cornelius's cairns down through the now familiar shafts once more. Each time Rin saw the next one, she looked behind her, fully aware that if she could follow these markers, so could someone else. Squinting into the dim light, she strained to hear anything that might indicate if someone was trailing them, frustrated rather than relieved when she couldn't sense anyone. She looked over at Scratch, surprised to find him looking back in the same direction. Were his instincts telling him the same thing? Or was he just mirroring her out of an old habit, hopeful she had seen some prey he could snatch away for himself?

Time took on its usual lack of meaning under the mountain, and Rin found herself almost looking forward to seeing the curt little man again. While he was undoubtedly rude, and more often than not abrasive, there was something about him that Rin liked.

Lark was the first to step out of the shafts, calling out for the old man as they emerged into his comfortably furnished cavern home. But her calls were only answered by the bubbling and popping of the lava. A large pile of the little chip keys had been left on the table and, assuming that Cornelius had left them for their return, Magnus walked over to scoop them into his pack. Rin followed him.

"He's been busy," Magnus commented, pointing towards the single piece of paper left beside the keys.

All the rest of Cornelius's papers had been shoved to the other end of the table, leaving this single parchment clearly marked as different from his other projects. On it, he had drawn an arrow that pointed towards the hole in the wall they had made when they burst through from the tracks only a few days before. None of them had to wonder where the old man had gone.

"He must already be laying the explosives to collapse the tracks," Torsten suggested, his tone apprehensive, as though this idea altered his enthusiasm for entering the place again.

Lark raised one eyebrow in a disdainful look that clearly said she thought this was obvious to them all without Torsten's narrative. Then, suddenly, it was as though Rin could see clearly for the first time in days. She recognised Torsten's need to say the words stemmed from his urge to avoid doing the thing – it was something Rin had needed to do many times before. It might be her alone who would be entering the Tunnels in a few nights' time, but all of them were risking something on this last mission to the Capital. It was only natural that they were afraid.

She felt a prickling sense of shame as she recalled her own behaviour over the last few days. She had pushed her friends away for her own solace, but in doing so she had left them to wrestle with their fears alone. She knew now how uninterested and unmoved by their struggles she must have appeared.

Rin caught Magnus staring at her and he nodded, his eyes soft and kind as though he could read her thoughts.

"There's no need to stop here," he said gently. "Let's keep moving. Ieuan has waited long enough."

There were not many words Magnus could have spoken that would have cut through Rin's self-pity and fear, but he had chosen well. The resilience inside her that only moments before had almost been exhausted solidified once more, and she set her mouth into a firm line, nodding back.

Together, they all set off along the tracks.

Rin had worried they wouldn't remember the turns, but each time they found the next lighting contraption with ease. She began to trust that the three brothers had a better head for direction than she did, which was reassuring when she thought of the twists and turns they had mapped out for her to take once she was in the Tunnels. They had chosen not to camp in the same spots as before, passing the place where, just out of sight, the Gen1's corpse still lay. The constant squeaking and pattering of small feet let Rin know that, soon enough, only bone would be left behind by the scavengers. That was not a thing she wanted to be reminded of while she tried to rest.

As they turned another corner, familiar mutterings drifted towards their ears.

"Has to be done. Terrible waste, but has to be done. Can't leave it open now. Can't risk them coming down here after them. Can't risk them finding Cornelius."

The old man was not speaking to anyone in particular, but as they drew closer, Rin found herself in agreement with his rambling thoughts. She already knew they could not leave the route open once they had taken so many freed Tavi through this place, but she still felt apprehensive about permanently removing this safe passage through the Ashlands.

The thought of that gave her cause to regret its loss. Her thoughts were interrupted by Lark, whistling a tune that Rin recognised as the one she'd heard the night they had descended in the upper-downer.

The old man's mutterings were cut short as his reply trilled out in answer, echoing around the hollow stone passages in an eerie, reverberating melody.

"He's in a good mood," Lark said cheerfully.

Rin couldn't tell if the girl was being snide or truthful, although she thought the first more likely.

As they approached the old man, he squinted, confused for a moment.

"The quiet one is back?"

Tilly smiled at him and nodded.

"Did it work?" There was a hint of concern in Cornelius's voice, but Rin knew he was more concerned with the quality of his work than with her welfare.

Tilly nodded again, then stepped forward and kissed his cheek.

Cornelius froze, blushing head to toe before smiling back at her. "Good. Yes, good. Cornelius made many more just like it. Good that it worked. Did the bra— Did *they* find the keys he left for them?" he blustered, looking at the others.

"We found the keys and your sign, old man," Lark answered, letting her amusement at his awkwardness saturate her words.

"Good. Good." He was nodding quickly, then suddenly his face became suspicious. "They didn't let the clumsy one hide any more of Cornelius's good things, did they?"

Lark laughed as Ivor's mouth opened and closed wordlessly. It took them all a while to reassure Cornelius that his home had survived their latest visit unscathed, but eventually, they were able to set up a camp for the night. Once they had eaten, Cornelius began to detail the work he had set himself since they had left.

"When the last one of you has cleared this section, you must take the first fuse that looks like this" – he held up what looked to Rin like a pleated section of wire and twine – "and place it in the lava flow from the closest light trench." He looked at each one of them in turn to see that they understood, pausing a moment longer on Ivor, as though sceptical that his nod meant he was truly following the plan. "Each explosion will set off the next. *Bang*, then the next, *bang*, then the next. It will be bringing down the stone walls of the tracks in the compartments one after the other. Hot earth and hard stone all flooding into what was Cornelius's good tracks." He paused, looking longingly at the walls and roof above as though still lamenting the loss of his network. Then, shrugging, he went on. "Anyone left behind in these sections will be trapped or crushed, so the brats must make sure everyone has reached this section before they detonate the first charge." His eyes narrowed and his voice changed to a more simple and condescending tone as he turned to Ivor. "That means, you all go *past* here *before* you place *this* wire in the hot orange stream."

It was the serious nod he finished with that Rin felt was the most insulting.

"What if there are more Gen1 down here?" Reece's question broke the mounting tension between Cornelius and Ivor.

"Won't be. Cornelius saw the one you killed. Saw where it was, so found out how it got down here. Sealed up now. Won't be any more getting down here, unless another rift makes a crack. But Cornelius will watch. Keep a check and make splits to keep the rifts away from the tracks." Once he was sure they had understood how to ignite his network, he turned to the challenge of the Tunnels. "Have to go off all at once. Six of them. All at once." He held up six fingers. "Fuses are all the same length and must be lit at the same moment. *Exactly* the same. Then, the brats will have to run. Have to run fast, too." He pulled another drawing from the brown leather satchel slung across his body. "*Here, here, here, here, here* and *here*," he went on, pointing to each of the six points in turn. "Support shafts run straight from the Tunnels down to the sewer system. Won't even need to go into the Tunnels if they place them there. If they light them at *exactly* the same time, the whole lot will come down."

Cornelius had a feverish look in his eye that would have been unsettling had Rin not shared his enthusiasm.

"Then they all got to run and get out from here," he said, circling on the plan what looked like a ladder that would lead them back to the surface not far from the wall that marked the boundary of the Void. "Whoever is here has to be the fastest. Got furthest to run."

His last point felt to Rin like a warning, but she watched with mounting excitement as the old man began to pass out small contraptions of tubes and wires to each of them. The plan was real, now. Rin would go down into the Tunnels and bring out anyone she could, then, when they were clear, each of the others would light their fuse and the Tunnels would be brought down for good.

When Rin settled down on her bedroll that night, she felt better than she had in weeks. By this time tomorrow, she would be back in the swamp, and she knew being on that familiar ground would bring a feeling of strength with it. She felt closer to Ieuan than she had in all the days that followed her flight from the Capital. Heading towards this fight filled her with fear, but she knew now with certainty that it had been much harder to leave him behind than it was to risk everything to get him back.

CHAPTER SIXTEEN
THE STACKLINGS

It was on the second day of their journeying through the swamp that Rin noticed him lingering near to her. Torsten was not one to speak when he had nothing to stay. Usually, he was more than happy to let Magnus lead, or else chuckle along with his younger brother's tales and jibes. Yet today, whenever she looked around, Rin found the taller boy's eyes on her. At first, she had tried to ignore it, thinking she had misread his intent, but as they made camp that night, she knew that whatever was on his mind would make its way to her ears sooner or later.

"What is it, Torsten?" she asked him, her irritation at his hovering finally getting the better of her.

He blinked quickly, as though still unready for the thing he had been working up to saying for the last two days. "We... we're nearly at the meeting point," he stuttered, poking about in the fire as if trying to stir life into it, even though it had already come to a flame just fine.

Rin nodded. "By tomorrow, we should be in the right place. Then we'll have to wait for one of them to appear to meet us."

She knew she was telling him things he already understood, but she also knew that was how it was done best. You couldn't just leave a person to flail in the magnitude of silence when there was something that struggled to be said. She knew how it felt when there seemed to be too many words to choose from, and that sometimes another person could add a few of their own to help move things along.

"Yes. One of them should meet us. Fievel probably... or Marta."

Rin felt the impact of the old woman's name and took a deep breath. *So, that's what this is about.* Torsten wanted to speak to her about Marta. Now she found herself wishing she hadn't helped him get to his point. Rin knew she needed Marta's help to finish what they had set out to do, but it wasn't easy to accept the help of someone you were still so furious with.

"I'm not saying you shouldn't be angry. It's not my place to tell you how to feel. All I thought to say was that you should give her a chance to exp—"

"Explain what?" Rin cut him off, her temper rising to a simmer. "Explain how she lied to me my whole life? How she could look into Gibb's face, the face of her only friend, and let him live his life surrounded by the same vile dust that killed his wife? Or maybe she will explain to me how she could let him raise his son in it?"

Torsten couldn't look at her, but now he seemed determined to finish what he had set out to say. "You've always been Tavi, Rin. Before and after you had the spurs, it was always in you. But you've only had to suffer the burden of it for the last few turns of the moon." He winced as though an old pain still troubled him. "The rest of us... we've been suffering since we were children, since our spurs grew in." He pointed over his shoulder before looking up at her from beyond the flames. "Someone held Marta down, probably more than once, and tried to cut them from her back. When they couldn't stop them growing, they would have turned her away from her home, probably in the hope she would die quickly... or at least disappear quietly."

Rin stared at him. Was he guessing about what had happened

to Marta, or was the story such a familiar one that he was able to add those details on his own? She wanted to say something, to add anything more in defence of the anger she felt, but it was not her words and instead Lark's that answered the boy.

"That gives her an excuse, does it?" There was a temper in Lark's voice that matched Rin's own. "What happened to the old woman was so awful that it wipes away all the responsibility for whatever she chose after?"

Torsten turned, only now realising Lark had been listening. "You know that's not what I meant."

"No? So it was not the point of your little story to get our Rin here to bend her morality to accommodate Marta's lack of it?" Lark shook her head as though the idea disgusted her. "This Empire is littered with stories like that old woman's. None of us should get to hide behind that as an excuse for what we've done."

Rin nodded. The girl's words made sense to her – they echoed the grudge she had been holding on to since she first heard the level of the old woman's deceptions. It felt good to have someone else sound her feelings out for her.

"Lark," Torsten made to argue, "you know it wasn't that simple—"

"It *was* simple," Lark cut him off again. "The old woman found a Tavi brat half dead on her doorstep and she chose to risk everything to keep her safe. Nothing else mattered to that old woman. She was prepared to risk her life and her friends' lives. More than that, she was prepared to let everyone else die if that's what it took to keep Rin's secret. To keep her safe."

Torsten squinted at her, confused as to when his point had become hers too. He opened his mouth to speak, but she continued.

"It was harsh, but damned if I don't respect the old swamp

witch for it."

The sharp change in Lark's allegiance left Rin dizzied. Just a moment before, she thought the girl had been ready to fan her anger at the old woman, then just as quickly, the rug had been pulled from under her. Clearly, Lark admired what Marta had done. Once more, Rin found herself questioning what kind of person she might become if she continued to follow the path she had started down.

"It was wrong," Rin said flatly.

"Oh, no doubt from where you stand it would seem that way, sure." Lark paused, then shrugged. "Where you stand as a child no more, as a girl turned almost to a woman, who had the chance to grow up free of the Capital Tunnels, uncut and whole. I'm sure from where you stand it's downright dastardly. But I wouldn't hold your breath waiting for the old woman to apologise for it. I wouldn't, if I were her." She smiled coldly, turning to Torsten. "And I wouldn't want someone trying to justify my choices with sad stories either. We decide what we do. It's one of the few things no one else can take from us, and I think the old woman made her decision a long time ago." She pulled a ration cracker from her pack, casually snapped it in half and took a bite, before adding, "You can't save everyone, Rin, and a wiser woman than me knew that it's not the words you say or the ideas in your head that let you sleep at night. If you want peace in your heart, you'd better be damn sure that your actions match up with your intentions, not with your justifications."

Torsten face was scrunched, as though this conversation hadn't gone at all the way he had planned, but Rin was less sure. Like it or not, she had heard what he'd had to say, and no matter how hard she searched for it, the sharp edge of her anger towards the old woman had dulled, if only slightly.

It was nice to have Scratch back in their company as they made their way closer to the fence. It was hard enough to look out for guards as they picked their way through the swampland that paralleled the chain link border; the last thing they needed was to worry about swamp dwellers too. Lark had told Rin the truth that night she had awoken from her tea sleep: every time they crept to the edge of the thick foliage, they found yet another pair of guards stationed along its boundary. Rin wondered how far the Void stretched in this direction and how she would be able to cover such a distance with a trail of people. She was starting to wonder how much further they would have to go when Lark came back from taking their bearings at the fence.

"I can see chimneys up ahead. Not too much longer and then we can head eastwards. Looks like we should be in the right place just before the dusk comes down." There was a glint in Lark's eye that Rin didn't think had anything to do with being closer to re-entering the Void.

There was no need to make a camp while they waited for dusk, nor did they want to leave any trace that they had stopped in this place, should anyone come across it by accident. Instead, they sat in silence, every one of them straining for the sound of their expected arrival. As the light began to fade, the tension in the group began to rise, although no one wanted to put into words their concern that the twilight was fast becoming night.

There was a loud splash, followed by cursing.

Ivor's laughter rippled out into the darkness.

"We're over here, Fievel," Magnus called out to the boy, who continued to curse and splash towards them.

When they finally caught sight of him, he was sodden from head to toe.

"I have been here every other day for the last week," he complained, "and then *this* day, of *course*, when there are people actually here waiting to meet me, I fall in that darned pool!"

Rin was holding onto the strength within her so tightly that she heard the sigh of relief leave Lark's mouth. For a moment, Fievel only stared at Lark, his shoulders tensed in apology, his face hopeful. Rin wondered if the girl who secretly wore his token hidden under her shirt might soften under such a look.

Lark met his gaze, but if there was anything warm hidden in her features, Rin could not discern it. Ivor chuckled again, and Rin was pleased that the sound filled the silence between the two.

"What kind of pool?" Rin asked suddenly, not sure if Fievel's fall was amusing until she found out how serious it might be.

"A deep one," the boy replied, picking a thin trail of slime off his ear, "but it wasn't pink and I didn't see any bubbles either."

He gave her a sheepish look, and Rin smiled back, relieved that the boy had at least learnt a little about the swamp since they had last seen him.

It was dark by the time Fievel had led them from the swamp and out from under the Stacks, the worst of the Clag having long since settled for the evening. When they came out of the narrow burrow that connected the two places, Rin was jarred by the instant contrast. The swamp had been dark and gloomy, but here, strings of warm lights stretched from wall to wall in bowed lines across the valley. Rin had never seen lights like them. It looked to her like someone had reached up and plucked stars from the night and strung them onto twine. Adding to their glow were oddly matched paper lanterns hung randomly over the high walls of bric-a-brac, all of them different colours.

The ground underneath those lights had been flattened out, and people were gathered in small groups on the hard packed debris. One girl was cuddling a small child wrapped in blankets while the woman next to her chattered animatedly, occasionally stirring a pot of something that steamed over a flame. Three men sat around a small table, shuffling little squares of paper. They would laugh loudly when one of them showed the drawings on theirs, or else cheer and clap when another would scoop up several more of the rectangular cards from the pile. Where the swamp had been absent of human noise, here the hum of the generators and the chorus of people talking blended into a seamless clamour of activity.

Rin paused, listening hard. There was music. Not like the kind they played in the Dale for dancing, but a kind played on a small metal box that could fit in the palm of a hand, with little holes to blow into. As her nose caught up with her ears, Rin realised the smells were different too. She had grown used to the scent of wet earth that prevailed in the swamp, but here the smells changed quickly. One moment she could smell rich, peaty smoke as it drifted out from the slanted roof openings that jutted out from around the escarpment walls, next the scent of sweet treats and savoury food mixing in the air. It was pleasant, and it reminded her how long it had been since she'd last had a decent meal. Far beneath, and almost hidden, her keen senses caught the tang of rusting metal and the foulness of the clag. It was an old smell that permeated the earth around them, but it wasn't strong enough to win out over the others unless she focused on it.

Rin wondered if the people of the Stacks were in the

middle of some kind of festival, as the place seemed to hold an air of excitement. It seemed impossible to her that those who lived in the Void, so close to the dangers of the Empire, would know such joy and levity on any normal night. Not when she had been expecting a place that mirrored the dreary alleyways and undercurrents of tension that she had felt in the rest of the wasteland.

"They seem so... happy?" It was not the question Rin had meant to ask, but the strangeness of the place had forced the thought from her lips unfiltered.

Fievel followed her gaze , as though only just noticing the people around him. "It's good to be in the Stacks at night."

"Why?" Rin countered, confused as to why the change in light would affect the mood of this little haven they had carved from the wreckage of the old world.

"No one bothers us at night. All the guards will have returned inside the uptown walls long ago, and the Partisan makes sure there's no trouble around here." Fievel smiled, his joy mirroring the faces of those who lived in this place. "It wasn't always like that. Not that I remember the time before, but the ones who are old enough all tell the same tale. Squabbles and fighting, thieving, the usual things that happen when you cram too many people with too little space and barely enough to feed their children." He shrugged in a way that asked what else they could have done.

"But the Partisan changed that?" Rin asked, sceptical that one man could have such an effect on so many others.

"That's what they say. He came recounting stories from an old book, one they used to read before the Fall. Every week the people from around here would come to the Hall of the Partisan, and when they left, they saw life in the Stacks a little differently." His hand reached instinctively for the token that was no longer around his neck.

Rin's eyes narrowed. That sounded too much like the tales the Empire priesthood had told her in the Dale, and she wanted no part of such sermons again.

"He must have quite a way with words," she replied, in a non-committal tone that prompted Fievel to finally notice her disquiet.

"Hmm, I suppose he does. But it's not just that. The Partisan brought order to the Stacks too. You either abide by the rules here, or you leave, and he has plenty of strong men like Boone to see that you go when you're told to."

Rin nodded. While the idea of tales from an old book troubled her in a way she couldn't put words to, the enforcing of rules by strong men was a danger she was more familiar with. She was not yet convinced as to whether the Partisan was indeed a good man or a threat, but there was no denying that the people who lived here seemed happy, and safer than most Void dwellers. That was not a thing to be discounted in times like these, and certainly this man had cared for Fievel in a way not many others would have. Suddenly, she felt guilty. If they were caught using the Stacks to escape, they would be putting everyone who called this place home at risk.

She looked down at the thick, ashy dust that stuck to her boots. *No more danger than they're already in.*

"Will he help us, Fievel?"

"Oh, well, erm... well, he hasn't quite... decided yet."

Fievel's long pause showed his confliction at that truth, and Rin realised he must have been hoping the Partisan's help would have been more forthcoming.

"Marta has argued a good case, but it's no small thing to ask. If he does give his help, he knows it's all of us he puts at risk."

"Right." Rin's heart sank. She didn't have time for days of debate and talking in circles.

"Marta tried her best," Fievel continued, "but he says he won't give his answer until... well, until he's spoken to you."

Rin stopped walking. She hadn't expected that, and suddenly felt unprepared. Ieuan was the one who had a way with words; who could say the right thing at the right time, in a way that made a difference to the person who heard them.

"What does he want to talk to *me* for?"

"Well, I think that he wants to help... I mean, I think even that he *will* help. But it keeps coming back to the terms. There's something he wants you to do... I wouldn't like to put words in his mouth, though. I think I might say it all wrong. Better you hear it from the Partisan himself, really."

Fievel's words jumped from one point to the next, and none of them made any real sense to Rin. She could see that he was anxious, though, and that did nothing to quiet her own nerves about such a meeting.

As the boy led them through the same maze of valleys and burrows that cut into the mountains of discarded waste that Marta had recounted to them all those nights ago, Rin realised she had been unprepared for the vastness and complexity of the Midden Stacks. There was no way they would be able to pass through here without a guide or someone to teach them such a route... and if what Fievel said was true, no one from the Stacks would take on that role if the Partisan refused to help them. They needed him on side.

The hall of the Partisan was exactly as Marta had described it, so much so that Rin almost felt as though she had been here before, and she found herself searching for the oddly attired man she knew would be the Partisan.

"Welcome to the hall of the Partisan…" The man began the greeting, just as Marta had also heard it from him on her first visit.

But Rin had stopped listening. Something was wrong. It was too quiet, and yet every fibre inside of her tingled. She seized hold of it so quickly and firmly that it was dizzying, and at once, she understood. Shuffling footfalls on the balcony above as they tried to hide their tread; whispering, too urgent to be as quiet as it should be; the bead of sweat on the man's forehead, despite the cool night air.

"*It's a trap!*" She shouted the warning, already turning on her heel, hoping she could make it to the door before the way was barred.

That hope died quickly as she heard a thick bar slide into place from the other side. Grabbing Fievel's arm, she flung herself behind one of the long, high-backed benches, and was relieved when she heard the heavy thump of other bodies beside her, letting her know they had all followed.

Crouching behind the wooden seat, she grabbed the boy's arms and forced him to meet her eyes. "What's going on, Fievel?"

"I-I… I don't know," he stammered, the tremor in his voice convincing her that *that* much was true.

A volley of small stones hammered down around them.

"Damn it," Rin hissed, knowing that, given enough time, one of those stones was going to land where it shouldn't, and someone would get hurt.

She waited, listening to the hands fumbling with slings above them.

, When the last rock rattled to the floor beside them, she stood up, leant over, and wrenched hard at the bench behind them. The few nails that had been holding it firm to the floor were long since rusted and gave way easily.

Rin toppled the loose bench into the next one, creating a protective wedge above them.

"Guards?" Lark questioned as a third volley rained down noisily above them.

"I don't know. I didn't get a good look." She bit back her irritation. If the Partisan had betrayed them, Rin was determined she would make him pay for it. Staying beneath the shelter of the benches, her eyes scanned the parts of the room she could see, ears straining to hear the dangers hidden in the parts she could not. "We need to get up on that balcony."

"Well, what are you waiting for?" came Lark's familiar drawl. "If you don't enjoy the view from the floor, just ask the good fellow where the stairs are and I'm sure they'll escort you straight up."

Rin ignored her. "The rocks are bad, but unless one hits you in the head, we should be able to fight our way past them. But that's what they *want* us to do." Her voice had taken on a familiar, detached tone, mirroring the eerie calmness she felt when she allowed her ability to flood her mind and body. "There is a second wave of attackers waiting up there. The rock slingers are just a distraction to push us into springing the real trap." She surprised herself as the words left her mouth, but she knew they were true.

"Damn it," Reece spat, and Rin noticed Lark pushing Fievel a little more behind her, and a little further away from her brother.

"The balcony is too high. Even if I could make it, it'll take too long to climb one of those columns." Rin shook her head, annoyed by her own limitations. "If they do have bows up there, they'll have me skewered before I reach the top. You three" – Rin pointed to the brothers – "remember when we fought, that first time we met? I need you to throw me up like you did Ivor. If we time it right, I might reach the wood at the bottom of the balcony." She nodded as though they had already agreed.

"That's a lot of ifs, Rin." Magnus's brow furrowed as he tried to think of another way.

"And we'd practised that a hundred times or more, too," Ivor added, in a tone that told her he did not think her plan was possible, never mind wise.

Another volley prompted them all to duck, Ivor instinctively drawing his shoulders to his ears.

"They're waiting to see if we take the bait," hissed Rin. "If we don't do something soon, they won't wait forever, and there are more of them than there are of us."

No one had an answer for that, but each one of them still seemed desperate to think of some other option.

Ivor looked up at the distance. "Keep your knees bent, right until the last second when you push off. See the looping flower pattern along the bottom of the balcony?"

Rin followed his gaze and nodded.

"We can get you that high. Fix your eyes on a single point and that's what you grab for. Don't take your eyes off that mark. Don't think about missing it."

Rin smiled, inclining her head in thanks.

"Ivor," Magnus cut in, "I don't think we should—"

"We have to," Rin bit back, not taking her eyes off Ivor. "We do it now, or we find ourselves outnumbered and, if it *is* the guard, who knows how many chipped Tavi will be among them."

Magnus looked like he wanted to say more, but then they were moving. Rin stretched her neck from side to side and rolled her shoulders, loosening them. It was not a necessary action, but it felt good to sense the strength rippling through her as she did it. She didn't know how many there might be up there, but the balcony was narrow, so at best they could only reach her two at a time. Hopefully she would be able to take out enough of them for her friends to escape before they overwhelmed her.

The three brothers crouched around her, their hands clasping together, making a basket under her feet.

"On three," Ivor whispered. "One, two... *three*."

Rin was flung upwards. She kept her knees soft until the very last second, then pushed off with all the strength she held in them. For a moment, she had the urge to close her eyes, only then doubting the wisdom of her plan, but Ivor's words rang in her ears and she kept her gaze firmly fixed to an ornately carved flower. Her fingers scraped hard against the wood and certainty replaced fear as they found their mark. For just an instant, she hung there, making sure her momentum wouldn't rip her free, before she began to climb. Hand over hand, she pulled her body upwards, and in seconds she was over the balcony lip.

A Capital baton swung towards her head and she lunged forward, rolling underneath before kicking out at the legs of its wielder. As the man dropped to the floor, she grabbed for him, pulling him down harder and cracking his face against the single wooden bench that mirrored the ones below. She barely had time to register his guard uniform before a boot struck out at her face. Instead of letting it shatter her nose, she caught it, wrenching the wearer's ankle sharply away from the rest of his leg. There was a crack and then a scream as, rolling to her feet, Rin turned to face whoever would come next.

"Stop!" a voice rang out, loud and hollow through the high arches of the room.

Rin raised her hands to her face, ready to strike or block the next guard. She was not about to start taking commands from the man who had betrayed them.

"Stop! That is enough!" the man called again.

This time, his words were strange enough to reach Rin through her urge to fight, and when those she had assumed would try to kill her stepped backwards, she found herself lowering her fists.

"Forgive me, Rin. Just a small test. Nothing personal, you understand. It would seem Marta was not wrong about you." The man's voice had now taken on the jovial tone of a storyteller. "Please, if you will come down and join us, you and I have a lot to discuss."

CHAPTER SEVENTEEN
CHIPPED

Rin stood there on the balcony for quite some time, still unsure whether to trust the man's words. The sight of all those Capital uniforms compelled her to keep fighting, but the smiles on the faces of those who wore them confused her.

The large man she had felled when she first set foot on the balcony groaned awake, pulling himself up to sitting and rubbing at the large bruise that joined the space between his eyebrows.

"It's alright, lass. Might not seem like it from where you're standing right now, but the Partisan is a good man. I think you'll want to hear what he has to say," the man said groggily, tenderly feeling across his brow for blood or broken bones.

"You think I should go down there?" she asked, unsure why she should care what this man thought, given he had only moments ago attacked her. And yet... there was something in the way he was looking at her – the way they were all looking at her. Was that... *adoration* in their eyes?

There was no threat in such a look, but it made her distinctly uncomfortable all the same. The felled guard only nodded, as though no longer trusting himself to speak. She looked over the edge towards the group that had gathered below, all of whom seemed to be examining her every move.

It was only then that Rin understood. Marta must have told them what she was; what she was capable of. Whatever the Partisan's terms might be, he had wanted to be sure she could hold up her end of the bargain before he agreed to anything.

She thought of the rattle in his voice as he had shouted up to her, urgent and laced with a fear he had tried to conceal. Such a voice had sounded to her as though it was convinced, but there was more than just *his* face turned up to stare at her.

A woman opened the door to the stairs and beckoned her to go down them. Rin cast one last look over the edge of the balcony, squinting down at the crowd below. She wondered if she had convinced them all. A drop from this height would be painful, even for her. She pulled away from examining those thoughts. It was easier to remind herself of the higher falls she had survived relatively unscathed than it was to focus on the one she was considering now. She looked back at the woman by the stairs. Did it really matter how she got down there?

She made her decision. She would not waste any more time with needless demonstrations and endless questions. If not all of the people down there believed that she had the ability to do whatever it was that she was about to promise them, it was better to make them certain now. Steeling herself and taking a deep breath, she felt a nervous shiver run up her back. She let the strength of it flood her again, calming and powerful. Quickly, she turned and, in two short strides, she leapt over the thick wooden partition that separated her from the open drop.

She heard the gasps from the Hall below as she cleared the balcony, then felt the slap of the stone as she landed hard, bending one knee to absorb the impact, forcing herself into a crouch. A sharp, stabbing pain ripped through her feet, and her teeth rattled together, but she refused to let any sign of discomfort creep onto her face.

Raising her chin, she met the stares of the people gathered in front of her. She had to admit, the mix of horror and awe on their faces was satisfying, and once she was sure neither one of her feet had snapped under the impact, she took a savage pleasure in the feeling.

Now, as she looked at each one of them, she knew she had done enough. If there had been any lasting doubt before, she saw no trace of it now.

If the trap had been a surprise, what Rin and the others encountered in the next room was far more disturbing. As the Partisan showed them through to the side room, Rin found Marta bound to a chair, with a look on her face that made Rin unsure if it would be safe for the Partisan to remain so close if they were to untie her. Rin saw the man startle at the old woman's scowl, but when he spoke, his voice was calm, as though this was the kind of thing a person found themselves recalling every day.

"So, Marta has informed us that you are planning to evacuate the Tunnels, Tavi and Civi prisoners alike, then destroy the route behind you?"

The question was a direct one, and Rin found herself not sure how much she was willing to say in front of a man she had no reason to trust and every reason to be wary of. The moment the door had opened and she had seen Marta bound, every instinct in her wanted to rush to the old woman's side. Only her uncertainty had kept her frozen in place, and she had instead found herself watching the Partisan intently, as Torsten moved silently towards Marta, unpicking the carefully tied knots that secured her. As she was freed from her chair, Rin felt relieved to see the old woman was not hurt.

The Partisan was studying Rin with a similar intensity,

seeming to read the distrust on her face. "It would seem that whilst you have passed our tests, we have not yet passed yours." He nodded as though considering how best to balance the scales of such a problem. "Fine, I won't ask you to share your plans, and will instead entrust you with mine."

His words didn't sound like a question, but the way he raised his eyebrows made it clear that he would not continue without a sign of agreement.

Rin nodded, her eyes flicking to Lark's for only a moment. She wished she had not sought the older girl's reassurance.

"Good. Very good. So we will help you, Rin. We will make sure you and any you bring out alive will have a safe passage through the Stacks."

Rin's eyes narrowed as she waited for the catch she was sure would be there.

"Why would you help us?" It was Magnus who eventually broke the silence. "You know what she is. What we are. What makes a man like you want to help us now?" There was a bitterness to his question that made the words sound like an accusation.

The Partisan stared at him a moment, then spread his hands. "Marta has explained the dangers of the Clag – that alone should be reason enough for us to help those who are trying to rid us of it, should it not?"

"And you just believed her?" Lark asked in her familiar way, almost pleasant, but still holding its sharp edge. "No little tests or rocks hurled at *her* head, I take it?"

"You must be Lark. I have heard a great deal about you too." The Partisan looked at Fievel warmly, with only a hint of pity in his gaze. "My sincere apologies for the rough nature of our appraisal, lady," he replied in a voice that mirrored hers, holding its charm but with no hint of remorse for his actions.

Rin felt the last of her patience leave her. If he could be direct, so could she, and she was growing weary of these continuous games they all sought to play with her. "You said that 'should be reason enough', not that it *was* reason enough. Why did you test us? What is it you want me to do?"

"Very perceptive," he said, smiling more earnestly at her. "We didn't know about the Clag until very recently, but we've had our own people imprisoned down in the Tunnels for much longer than that. Of course, we have tried to find ways to get them out before, but our attempts have always been hopeless. Marta here was right, though. You *are* different." His eyes lingered on her. "And I am starting to believe her when she says you will be our only chance to see those they took under the ground returned to us."

Rin looked at Marta and felt the anger ripple inside her again. More of the old woman's lies. Clearly, she had chosen not to tell him that the Clag would be so thick and concentrated down in the Tunnels that it had most likely already killed anyone who had been taken more than a few seasons ago. Rin avoided meeting his eyes, trying to decide if she should continue that lie. She might, if it would help her get Ieuan back. She could pretend to this man that she would seek out his kind as well as her own.

She shook her head, in answer to a question no one had asked, shocked that she had even begun to consider such a thing. It wasn't right. Even if she could lie to him now, when they emerged from those Tunnels it was likely that not even one of the Partisan's people would be among them. What would happen then? If he thought that she had tried to trick him, he might very well refuse to take them any further.

Taking a deep breath, she hardened herself to the reality of the situation. "I will bring out any who are still alive down there, Partisan—"

"Excellent!" he cut her off, clapping his hands.

"But," Rin pushed on, "you need to know that many of the ones you seek have most likely passed over to a place not even I can bring them back from." She hoped he would understand her meaning and not make her say it any more plainly.

"Ah, you think I don't understand." He looked at her with a gentle smile that held both respect and pity. "I understand, child. Some of our people taken long ago will not return, though I believe there is hope that some taken only a moon or so ago might. You misjudge us, though. Some of those we seek to get back are Tavi, like you."

He was right – Rin *had* misjudged him, and so had her friends. A murmur ran through the group behind her.

"You have Tavi living in the Stacks?" Rin asked in disbelief. She had not thought it was possible that there were other places like the Cove, where the Empire's lies had not been as quickly swallowed as they had been in the villages.

"That's right," he said quietly, looking from under his brow at them all. "It is not something we talk about. Not that we're ashamed, mind," he added, seeing Lark prickle at his words. "But it wouldn't be wise to let those outside of the Stacks spread tales that could do us harm here, either. Would it, Boone?"

Rin followed his gaze to find the man she had fought on the balcony, and realised the angry bruise on his brow had already lessened from a molten red and purple to a more ruddy brown. So that was what Fievel had meant, when he said the Partisan had strong men who could make sure a person left when he told them to go. Boone met her eyes and winked, and she knew instantly that her suspicion was right.

Rin turned to look at Fievel, her eyes narrowing. She should have realised sooner that the boy had known other Tavi before them. Why else would he have encountered their group of 'murderous monsters' in the swamps and, instead of believing they were the stuff of dark legend, befriended them? She drew her eyes away from the boy and looked back towards the Partisan.

"So that's it? We get your people out with ours, and in return, you help us all through the Stacks to reach the swamp?" It seemed too simple, too neatly aligned with her own plans. She had known for a long time now that she would not leave anyone behind in that place if she could help it.

"That is all," he confirmed. "I take it you have a plan?"

"We do." Rin didn't need to look at Magnus; she could feel him tensing up at the idea that she might tell this man anything about what they were going to do. He needn't have worried. She knew her tone did not invite further questions on the topic.

"I see." The Partisan seemed to understand her intention. "In that case, is there anything else you need from us?"

Rin was about to dismiss this offer when she remembered there was still something they had not yet secured. "I need a guard's uniform. Can you get me that?"

"We'll have one here for you before supper." He smiled at her, taking the request as a sign of an agreement between them.

He looked so pleased to be able to provide what she had requested so easily that Rin considered asking for something else, just to irritate the man. She had not fully forgiven the assault he had staged on their entrance to his Hall, but she let the idea pass for the moment. Her wish to wreak vengeance on the man was short-lived. She did not have enough space inside her left to hold on to any more grudges without losing focus on the one that was most important to her.

The Partisan had not been exaggerating, and less than an hour after he had sent a runner to seek out the item, a freshly pressed uniform had been presented to her.

A second knock at the door caused Rin to startle, but seizing hold of her power, she instantly detected the smell of hot soup and fresh rolls that wafted in from under the door. She had not had fresh bread like this since she left the Dale, and she felt her mouth watering at the memory.

She froze. Would this be the last meal she ate before they put that chip on her? Would this be the last thing she might eat ever again?

There was so much that could still go wrong, but one way or another, by the time the next night crept over the land and the darkness was thick enough to hide her, she would go down into those Tunnels.

She would get Ieuan out.

As the group settled into supper alongside the Partisan and some of the residents of the Hall, Rin soon became aware of a disagreement within the room. There was something in the sharpness of Tilly's hand gestures and the stern look in her eyes that told Rin her conversation with Reece was not a happy one.

"Tilly, no," Reece begged. The desperation in his tone caused the breath to catch in Rin's throat a little. It was heavy with a fear too close to her own. "You can't."

The mute girl's hands weaved sharply in response; some actions she did twice, others she let hang in the air a long time before making the next.

"What is she saying?" Magnus asked Reece, trying to help

both of his friends.

"Not here. It's about the Tunnels," Reece murmured, taking in the room. There were a few unfamiliar faces that, although they had not turned toward him, showed too much of an interest in the bread in their hands, or the grain in the wooden table, to not be listening to their words.

Magnus nodded. "We need to be alone for a moment," he announced to the room.

A few faces looked longingly at their supper before they made to rise, but the Partisan waved them back to their seats.

"Please use the quarters in the back," he said, gesturing to another door of plain dark wood. "They are comfortable, and quite empty."

Rin and her friends left their own steaming bowls, but each one of them took their bread. It was too much to leave hot buttered bread behind when you didn't know if you might not have another meal to eat.

"What did she say?" Magnus asked again once they were alone.

Reece paused, holding Tilly's gaze, and Rin knew he was considering telling Magnus he didn't know. If Reece did not share Tilly's words for her, who else here would be able to discern the things the boy did not want her to do? She guessed he was considering that, if he did not tell them to Magnus or the others, he would have a better chance of stopping her. Rin saw uncertainty flicker across the girl's face and she felt her chest tighten. If Reece did not share her words, he would be stealing her voice, just as the Capital had done. Reece seemed to come to the same conclusion in much the same time, scrunching his eyes tightly shut as though the pain of it had stabbed him and the words left him with a groan.

"She said we need to put the chip back on her. Not on Rin."

Rin blinked and shook her head, as though those words could not possibly have been intended to mean what she thought she had heard. "No." She looked at Tilly, only to find the girl nodding calmly back at her. "No, Reece. Ask her again."

"I think that she said..." Reece started to talk again, then trailed off, holding up his hand to rub at his tightly closed eyes.

Tilly walked over to him and slipped her hand over his. Her touch caused him to flinch, opening his eyes instinctively to see her smiling softly at him.

Reece cleared his throat. "She said Rin should wear the guard uniform, and that *she* should go in as the chipped Tavi. Not in so many words I guess, but I think she was saying that without a Tavi prisoner to escort down, one guard wandering around through checkpoints would gather a lot of attention. But one guard escorting a chipped Tavi wouldn't even be worth questioning." He looked at Tilly from under his brow, seeking approval for the words he had chosen for her, and then seeing her nodding again, he shut his eyes once more. "Tilly has a point," Ivor said finally, when no one else had offered to refute her idea.

"Shift changes are always done in large groups, so that rules that out," Magnus argued, as though trying to think his way through a problem that he already knew the answer to but didn't want to accept. "Rin could be going down there alone to escort one out."

"Perhaps," Ivor conceded, "but usually the guards on shift would know if one was coming out, or there would be a writ from the Lab to send one up. It's possible, but suspicious. Tilly's right, Magnus. The most plausible reason for one guard to be heading down into that place would be to bring a Tavi prisoner in. Fewer questions, less interest in them."

There was another long silence as they each considered the magnitude of this change in the plan. If Reece had been hopeful that the others would put an end to what he obviously considered to be Tilly's madness, it was clear now that they would not. Rin saw Reece's jaw tighten. If someone was going to do this thing, she knew he could not bear it to be her.

"Then I'll go," he offered, voice firm.

Tilly shook her head, the shapes she made with her hands seeming softer and more apologetic now. Rin didn't know what those meant but she thought she could have guessed even before Magnus spoke.

"She knows those Tunnels much better than we do." He looked at Reece, then seemed to speak his next words as though, even now, he was not convinced it was right to voice such a thing. "We would never have made it out of there without her. If anyone can help Rin down there, it's Tilly."

Rin had expected Reece to keep arguing, but instead, the boy's legs gave out on him and he sagged to the floor. If he had kept arguing, Rin might have been able to bear it, but she couldn't stand this. They couldn't expect her to accept Tilly's help now, not when Reece was so broken by the mere idea of it.

"I'll go alone," Rin said in a way that she hoped would put an end to it, but Tilly was already shaking her head.

Rin furrowed her brow; she had gotten used to people doing what she told them to do, and this was an inconvenient time to be reminded that they did that because they thought she was right, not because they had to.

Tilly's closed fist first touched her chest, then spread out her fingers in front of her in a sweeping motion. Finally, she held Rin's eyes as her last gesture pointed down.

"She says she's going down there with you," Reece choked

out, though Rin had not needed the translation.

She stood, looking into the determination on the girl's face, trying to think of what she should say, until she realised it didn't matter. There were no words that would stop Tilly from doing this thing, just as there were no words that would stop *her* from doing it. Rin felt a lump growing in her throat as she pulled Tilly into a tight hug. She didn't want the girl to be in danger; she didn't want anyone else she cared about to get hurt, or worse. Yet some part of her was relieved that she would not have to go into that place alone; that someone else would be there to help her find Ieuan.

"That leaves us one person short for lighting Cornelius's fuses," Lark said flatly, as though she had been completely unmoved by their exchange.

Torsten turned to answer her. "Fievel could do it? He could be fast enough if he was positioned at the point closest to the exit, and I'm sure he'd do anything to help."

"No," Lark said in the same flat tone. "And if anyone here so much and *mentions* it when he is in the same room, you'll have to find someone else to light mine, too." She smiled sweetly at Torsten.

Rin's brow creased. How did Lark always seem to find a way to get what she wanted? She'd made a note to herself to keep an eye on how she did that, but for now, it didn't matter. Rin already had a name in mind for the task.

"Ask Boone."

"Well now, that is a *much* better idea," Lark said, as though oblivious to the fact she had all but threatened them a moment ago. "You think he'd be fast enough?"

"He's fast enough." Rin paused, and then, seeing no reason to keep it a secret, added, "He's Tavi."

The others around her nodded, unsurprised.

"You think he'll do it?" Torsten asked, doubtfully.

"I think so." Rin couldn't say what made her so sure, only the hint of something honest in the man's face and the way he had smiled at her made her think it was true. "If the Partisan will allow it, that is."

"Then I think that's settled," Magnus concluded.

Rin couldn't tell if it was sadness or apprehension that made his words sound so hauntingly final.

When they re-entered the room beyond their private quarters, all the sounds of eating stopped. Tension began to seep into the silence, until the Partisan cleared his throat meaningfully and, at his warning, everyone began to eat again.

"The food is getting cold and you could all use a good supper and some rest before tomorrow," the man added, his eyes squinting at them as though he was trying to decide the nature of what had just happened behind those doors.

Rin knew that his words made sense, but he might as well have told her to catch the moon in her hands. She might be able to force down some of the soup, it did smell very good and it had been a few days since she had eaten a proper meal, but rest? Rin knew there would be no more rest for her until this was done. Sure, she could stretch out on her bed roll alongside the others, but she could already feel the thrumming inside her. A thing held so taught it could snap or tangle at any moment.

No, there would be no escape into sleep for her tonight.

CHAPTER EIGHTEEN
THE TUNNELS

As Rin had expected, Boone agreed instantly to their request, and when the Partisan held no objections either, their plan was set. The morning dragged on as though each minute was an eternity to be endured, and then, as the sun had begun to dip behind the Stacks, making the Hall of the Partisan feel cold, Rin waited with the others while Marta took Tilly to the room she and Fievel had set up for tending the sick. Even at that distance, they could still hear the girl's screams when Marta placed the chip back into her flesh. Rin felt her skin bristle in disgust as she forced herself put on the uniform of the Capital's guards, imagining what terrible things had been done by the last wearer of the grey garments.

Then, it seemed as though time had sped up much too quickly, and Rin found herself standing with the others at the edges of the Void, with the safety of the Stacks far behind them. She looked up through the thin veil of cloud stretched out above them. The moon was almost full, but through the Clag it looked as though it was veiled in smoke. It was much paler than she had even known it to look before, and what little light it did cast made an odd halo of colours against the hazy night sky. Rin thought that on another night, when she did not have such risks to take, it might have looked beautiful in its way, but tonight its odd shimmer filled her with fear.

The uniform was tight at her neck and she kept fussing at the collar, trying to loosen it.

"You can't keep tugging at it like that," Lark chided her. "Chipped Tavi guards don't squirm around like that."

"I feel like it's trying to choke me," Rin muttered through gritted teeth.

"So we're all clear then?" Magnus interrupted before Lark could reply.

Rin knew they were all as ready as they could be; that he was not really asking because he doubted anyone. He just needed some way to say goodbye, a way to define this as the moment they would separate, with no way to be sure who among them would meet again.

"Rin and Tilly will go in, work a little imposter magic, pop off a few chips, and once they're finished, and get clear of the Tunnels with all our new friends, the Alliance will send word. Then they'll signal to us by banging on the covers at the surface above each of us. When we hear the first thump, we get ready. When they hit the covers a second time, we light the fuses and run."

"Did I miss anything, or are you going to make us go over this another pointless time?" Lark waved her hand as though such a thing was merely a formality and they would all be back in the Cove in time for fish stew and honey cakes. "I mean, if we keep wasting time here, there's every chance they'll all be dead and we can just go home."

Rin's expression darkened. If it hadn't been for the way the girl's eyes twitched nervously, Rin might have hit her. But she could see Lark was afraid, and as she had come this far only to help her get Ieuan back, she could ignore a certain amount of the girl's savage tongue if it strengthened her for what she had to do.

"Those are some dark words, lass," said Boone, shaking his head, one hand patting his chest. "Not right to say it when we're asking for more than just luck to pull this off."

Rin wondered if Boone wore a token under his shirt like Fievel had, but soon her attention was drawn to Lark, who was laughing and shrugging her shoulders. Somehow, his scolding seemed to be what Lark had needed to hear, though Rin could tell that her scoffing was a more forced than normal. There was no doubt about it, though. The more uncomfortable she made the man, the better Lark seemed to feel.

A short while later, they parted ways, and Rin was not alone as she moved through the alleyways of the Void. Though she had to move a little slower, Rin was still glad to have a friend with her. Tilly's face was fixed and determined, but there was a red rim to her eyes that Rin could not pretend she didn't see. There would not be enough time in all the world to make this up to Tilly; there were no words to tell the girl how much this meant to her.

They had no trouble reaching the wall, and Rin was surprised by how easily Tilly made the climb up. At the very top, the girl pointed into the distance and nodded, and Rin followed her finger, knowing what she would see.

Rin had never set eyes on the Tunnels before. She had a picture in her mind, painted for her by the three brothers, but it was not what she had imagined. That departure from expectation rattled her, as she realised she really had no idea of the reality she was about to face.

The entrance was set far back from the wall, towards a part of the Capital that not even the poorest uptown homes overlooked. Even from here, though, she could see that the entrance's mouth was wide and built into the sloping earth of the Capital. It was well lit, and she could see guards standing on either side, keeping watch for ones such as her. She couldn't see far into the mouth from where they were, but around the entrance the rock seemed a rusty red colour, and there was a heavy coat of Clag that stained the ground with its foulness. Thick, black pipes ran along the roof of this first Tunnel in pairs, and harsh white lights buzzed at intervals along the walls that disappeared within, leaving no clue as to what else lay beyond.

Tilly tugged at her arm, and Rin realised she had been staring longer than was wise.

Rin had been frightened for so long now that she had forgotten what it felt like to exist without that gnawing in her gut. As she walked towards the cave mouth, she let a small stream of her inner strength wash over her: not enough to numb her, but enough to feel her heart steady in her chest. All of a sudden, she found herself fighting not to smile. *Not tomorrow, not soon, but now. Now* was the time to take back what they had stolen from her, and she would not wait a moment longer to go in and get him.

They had practised, and she knew that she must not smile, so she worked hard to let every muscle in her face relax. Placing a hand on Tilly's shoulder, she marched her prisoner forward, struggling to keep their pace even and measured when everything inside screamed at her to run and fight her way through to Ieuan.

As they approached, one of the guards at the mouth of the Tunnels called out, "Stop where you are!"

Rin could tell from the way he said it that this man was a Capital guard, not a chipped Tavi guard. She kept her eyes fixed straight ahead, as though she had not heard him.

"Why are you here?" another man asked suspiciously.

Rin fought the urge to acknowledge this question too, keeping her expression vacant and her eyes fixed on the entrance.

The guard standing beside him answered instead. "Damn it, Mirk, you know you gotta ask them right. No point in just saying any old thing to them. If she's a talker, you got to ask them right, and then they say the answer. All's they can say is the answer, and they can only say it if you asks them the right way." He was rubbing the top of his head in a way that suggested this was a thing he had explained often enough already.

"Well, what is it I'm meant to say again? Wait, don't tell me, I'll get it."

Rin cursed inwardly. This man was an idiot, and he was drawing far more attention to them than she would have liked.

"Oh yeah." He cleared his throat. "What business you got in the Tunnels, guard?" he asked in a much more formal voice.

Rin almost wanted to laugh at the absurdity of it, but she did not. Still, she stayed silent.

"Wait, that was it, warn't it, Gren?" Mirk asked, scratching his nose.

"No that wasn't it, you moron. Ask her 'what business brings you to the Tunnels?' and say it *just* like that, mind."

"That's what I said!" the man whinged. "She probably just ain't a talker is all."

"No, that ain't what you said. What you said was—"

The man was cut short as Tilly lunged forward, and Rin had to stop herself from grabbing the girl's shoulder. Tilly fell hard on the ground and squeaked, letting her shirt fall off her shoulders a little and exposing the chip now nestled back into her raw flesh.

"Crikey, they're making them a bit rough these days, ain't they?"

Rin realised then that Tilly had made it look as though *she* had shoved her to the ground. *What is she doing*? They hadn't practised this.

Not knowing what else to do, Rin remained motionless, her eyes pinned to the same spot she had picked the moment they had been questioned.

"What I was going to say," the man continued, as though the girl lying on the ground was of no consequence to him, "was that it weren't what you said, but it don't matter now anyways. That one's a cattle pusher. You can ask her questions all day long and in any old way you like, and you won't get so much as a cheep out of her." He shrugged. "Cattle pushers don't talk none to no one."

"Cor, Gren, is that what they teach you up in that guard school?" Mirk asked, seemingly awestruck by his colleague's 'knowledge'.

"Yeah, they teach us a fair bit up there," Gren replied, making a smug sound as he sucked air through his teeth. "Chipped Tavi guard escorting a chipped Tavi like that, bound to be a cattle pusher taking one of them things down to the Tunnels for good. Best place for them both, really."

Rin seethed. *Thing*. Tilly was not a *thing*, and neither was she cattle. She felt the muscles in her jaw start to tighten and then instantly forced herself to let them go. These two were not her target, and making them sorry for their ignorance would not help Ieuan.

There was a pause, and Rin was not sure how to get things moving again, but the man called Gren spoke again.

"Well, you've seen her chip, and no doubt that other one is just as braindead as the rest of them. Wave them down already and hurry up. Gives me the creeps looking at them for too long."

The younger man did as he was told, and as soon as he gestured with his hand Rin bent down and grabbed Tilly's arm. Half dragging, half guiding her back onto her feet, she pulled the girl into the Tunnels.

She had not expected the heat that hit them as they entered.

The sudden change in temperature combined with the smell of the Clag was almost suffocating, and for a moment, Rin wanted to abandon their plan and run for the safety of the open night air. She felt Tilly's shoulders stiffen under her fingers and, almost imperceptibly, squeezed her friend's shoulder.

The rest of the checkpoints went more smoothly. The guards seemed lazy and complacent, and Rin guessed that Tunnel duty was reserved for those guards who were not bright enough to be entrusted with other tasks. Chipped Tavi and Tavi guards would not be expected to require much handling. Still, something nagged at Rin. *This all seems too simple.* She had once before fought her way into a place, only to find out that her father had been waiting for her arrival all along. Her eye twitched as her mood darkened. If that was so, and if her father had made it easier for her to get down here this night, she would make sure he lived to regret it.

The deeper they descended, the thicker the Clag became. Rin's eyes began to burn and she found that she could taste it now too, the gritty dust crunching between her teeth. If she thought it was bad here, she knew from what Magnus had told her that she wasn't prepared for what awaited her beyond the last checkpoint. She had been counting the turns and checkpoints as they went, just as she had done over and over when they had practised. She knew they had reached it before she even saw the door.

Two guards stood waiting by the great metal wheel that controlled a heavy iron panel, set on hinges as thick as a man's body. Wide seals ran around the door's edges and, while they may once have been black, they were now as ruddy as the Clag-coated rock that surrounded them. A small, rectangular window was set in the middle of it and, occasionally, Rin could see something whipping by. It wasn't a colour she could discern as different from those around it, but rather, for a second, she could tell that there had been the faintest suggestion of movement; of something denser behind the glass. A faint rushing sound accompanied it, like a river running quickly over rocks.

These guards did not ask her any questions; Rin supposed no one who made it down here managed to do so without passing the other checkpoints. It was no longer worth checking what another guard had already checked five times before. Besides, why would two Tavi girls seek to break into such a foul place? As soon as the two guards had seen Rin's uniform, they had groaned audibly, their shoulders dropping. It would seem that opening the last checkpoint was something they would prefer to avoid, too. That was not encouraging.

As the door creaked open, the Clag bloomed into the room, swirling on the air that rushed through the Tunnels. This she had expected: it had been part of Cornelius's ventilation system, with its great bellows originally designed to suck the pollution from above into his botanical lungs before breathing out the purified air. Within the Tunnels, she knew they would face a number of sections like this. They were pressurised chambers designed to cool and squeeze the air tightly, causing it to rush faster and faster through those sections, dragging in the air from other compartments and then forcing it into the chambers deep under the ground.

It was one thing to hear all that from Cornelius; it was quite another to feel the rush of chilled air that hit her in the face. Not just cold, but thick with the dust of the Clag. If Rin's hand had not been on Tilly's shoulder, she was not sure how long she might have stood looking into the maelstrom before her, but as Tilly's feet moved, Rin found herself forced to step in unison with her. The air rushed past them, and even if Tilly had been able to speak, Rin doubted she would have heard her.

The brothers had recounted over and over again the turns she was to take here, yet she let Tilly lead her now, once more feeling a wave of gratitude for the girl who had accompanied her into this nightmarish place. Had she been alone, she wasn't sure she would have made it this far.

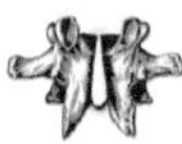

They'd had no problems getting from the Void into the sewers below. Sewers were not usually heavily guarded places, and the Capital ones were no different in that respect. Now, all they had to do was wait.

Reece looked up towards the Capital often, although there was nothing to see but the stone roof above them. Part of him was still unsure how they had ended up here, with Tilly chipped and back in Tunnels. It felt like everything he had worked for since he'd got out of the Lab had been for nothing. But the way she had looked at him when she had refused to let him talk her into staying behind on the shore... in that moment, for the first time since he'd rescued her from that awful place, he had seen the old Tilly come back to him.

He shook his head like he had just thought something terrible. He loved her no matter how much of her had come out of those labs. Still, there was a part of her that had remained trapped until that moment and he just hadn't realised how much he had missed that fierce part of her. He had made the mistake of forcing her to do what he thought was best before, and it was Rin who had told him he would have to choose whether or not to keep making that mistake. He snorted, as though he had any choice in the matter at all, not with the Tilly who had gone back into the Tunnels this night. That Tilly would not be forced into anything, not even by him.

"What are you smiling about?" Boone asked, watching the boy incredulously.

"Honestly?" Reece rubbed his eyes, "I think I might be going mad."

"Ah." Boone nodded solemnly. "Well, they do say madness is a sickness, and they call those with the heartache 'lovesick'. So, to my way of thinking, the two go hand in hand." He chuckled. "Love is a type of madness all of its own, and don't I know it."

Reece raised an eyebrow questioningly. "I'm not sure, but I think we both just agreed that I'm mad."

Boone laughed louder. "And long may it last, boy."

Reece nodded at that.

"This is your post," Lark interrupted them, rolling her eyes and slapping Boone on the back. "Closest to the exit. Light yours and get out. Don't wait around until you see us – just get moving."

"I wouldn't dream of it," Boone said, dryly.

"I mean it. All of you. Light your fuse, then get out. I'm the fastest so I'm taking the furthest post." Lark glanced at Magnus, who looked like he wanted to argue with her, but they all knew that she was right. Without Rin, Lark *was* the fastest of them. "The last thing I need is to have to climb over the top of one of you on the way out."

"We know the plan, Lark," Reece said softly.

He knew his sister too well to think that she meant her harsh words. What she really wanted was to ensure that if *she* didn't make it out in time, none of the others would get themselves trapped down here, waiting for her. As for his own wants, he wasn't yet sure whether he would wait for her or not, so there was no point in arguing with her.

Besides, she always seemed to know when he was lying.

Once Rin and Tilly cleared the first of the pressurised chambers, they could finally stop to catch their breath. The Clag was still thick here, and Tilly ripped away a long strip of her shirt and tore it in two, offering a piece to Rin. She took it and then watched as the girl tied it over her face and nose. Rin copied and found she could instantly breathe a little easier. It made the already warm air in this compartment warmer, but her lungs no longer burned with each breath, and after a few swallows, she thought she had cleared most of the grit from her mouth.

The Tunnels here were smaller and more roughly cut into the stone. Rin could see dark brown water pooling in places, and here and there wooden beams had clearly been hastily added as supports for walls.

"Which way now?" Rin asked.

Tilly shrugged, then pointed to her eyes and down the Tunnel in front of them.

Rin nodded. Of course – now they had to start sweeping the Tunnels. They would start removing chips when they found someone who wore one, and Rin just had to hope that, somewhere in that search, they would find Ieuan and Gibb.

The Tunnels here were dimly lit, and Rin knew that was on purpose. The lights were the same as they were at the checkpoints above, but there were far fewer of them and they did not seem to shine as brightly. They would not likely waste so much power on lighting the way for Tavi and traitors. That left whole patches of darkness that overlapped each another before the next bulb.

As they walked, Rin found it was better to stay focused on that next patch of light ahead, rather than the darkness in between, and she had been doing just that when she tripped over something.

A body.

Rin stared in horror. The girl was alive, but barely. Her body was thin, and the guard's uniform hung on her bony frame. If it had once fitted well, the girl must have wasted away to almost half her original size now.

In such a weakened state, she offered no resistance when they turned her over to look at her spine, which was almost as prominent as her spurs. Now, faced with the dangerous task she had only seen Retta do, Rin suddenly lost all confidence in her ability to count numbers well enough. She couldn't do this.

No. She *had* to do this.

Taking the key in her hand, she looked over at Tilly, who nodded her head encouragingly, shaking it occasionally if it looked like Rin might make one turn too many.

The emaciated girl did not make a sound as each spindly leg pulled free of her skin. Only as the chip fell away did Rin hear her gasp.

"What... what have you done?" the girl croaked, her voice dry and cracked from lack of use.

"There's no time to explain. Can you walk?" Rin asked, desperately hoping the answer was yes.

"I... I think so?" she replied, blinking back her confusion. "Where are we going?"

"Out."

They moved on as a three after that, becoming four and then five. Every time they found another chipped Tavi, Rin would ask if they knew Ieuan or Gibb. Each time, she was met with only more questions – 'who are you?'; 'what do they look like?'; 'are they Tavi or Civi?' – and each time she found herself no closer to finding them.

Most of those they found were in better condition than the first girl, and a small few seemed in decent health. That was useful. Now, when a Tunnel branched off, some of them would move down that track alone and then they would regroup with any they had found at the point they had spilt up.

It didn't take long before some in their number were sound enough in body and able to read numbers, and so Rin gave them keys and explained how to use them. Now, their group began to grow much more quickly. Some of the guards had to be held down by two or three others as, chipped and programmed as they were, they fought to keep their Tavi kin away from them.

Rin found her thoughts darkening as they continued. They had only found one living person who wasn't Tavi, and when he coughed, she could hear the rattling of damage done deep in his lungs. She was beginning to get desperate. How long had they been down here? *How many Tunnels are left and why haven't we found them yet? What if we never find them?* Rin clutched on to the power inside her, letting it soothe her fraying mind. She had to stay calm; she couldn't let the others see her panic. They trusted her and she would need that trust to get them all out of here.

As she turned down the next Tunnel, she saw him.

"Gibb!" Rin called out his name before she could stop herself.

"Get away from me!" he shouted back, swinging a wooden beam in front of him like a weapon. "What have you done with my son?"

"Gibb, it's me!" Rin was shocked. He looked terrible. How

had such a short time withered such a strong man so quickly? She remembered that he had been sick with a fever from the razor-grass before they had brought him down here. Even so, she could hardly believe this man, who needed the support of the wall to stand, was Ieuan's father. "Gibb, it's Rin."

"Rin?" he replied croakily, dropping the beam as though that name cut through his confusion. "Oh gods, no. They got you too. Got you and turned you into one of their guards. Oh gods, no."

"No Gibb, it's really me." Rin's voice cracked as she struggled to swallow the hard lump in her throat that threatened to bring tears. "We're going to get you out. To get everyone out."

"Get us out? Get us all out..." He was muttering to himself, then suddenly shouted as though unable to hold any of what had been said before in his head. "Where is my son?"

"It happens," a voice behind her spoke. "Some of the Civis just crack down here. Their minds can't take it and they go somewhere else. Usually die pretty quickly after that, too."

"He's *not* dying." Rin bit the words out, as though saying them solidly enough could make them true.

"Hey. Over here!" Someone from the back was calling to her. A young Tavi girl. "Over here!"

It was hard for Rin to get to her, with the narrow Tunnel so tightly packed with bodies now. People tried to move aside for her to get past, but even then, it was difficult to move back through the throng.

"He says he knows where your friend is," the girl said, half propping herself up against a Tavi in a guard's uniform.

Compared to the others down here, this Tavi guard looked reasonably clean, like he had not long ago had his uniform washed and pressed. Rin looked at him, half in desperate hope and half in dread of what he might say next.

"They took him out a few nights ago," he said, panting slightly. "He started to get sick. Real sick. Usually no one cares, but they cared about him. They sent a few of us down here to pull him out." He looked away, as though disgusted that he had any part in such a thing.

"Where did you take him?" Rin asked, the pounding in her chest so hard now that she was sure they must all be able to hear it.

"They made us take him to the Lab." He couldn't look at her when he said it, shame eating at the part of him that was now back in control of his body.

"Thank you," she said.

The man squinted at her, confused.

"After we get everyone out of here, I'll get him out of there too."

The Tavi man looked at her with sadness in his eyes, but whatever depressing possibility he had been about to impart died on his lips.

"I need you to do me a favour," Rin added, relieved that he had chosen to keep his cynicism to himself.

"Anything?" the Tavi replied, desperate to do something to set right what had he had done.

"I need you to make sure that man gets out of here." She pointed at Gibb. "Make sure he gets to the Midden Stacks— no, to the Cove, if you can. But at least see that he makes it to the Stacks."

The man nodded. "I know where those places are, and if I make it out of here, I will make sure that man is by my side when I do."

"Good enough," she agreed, and they clasped hands, wrist to

wrist in a promise Rin knew the man would risk his life to keep.

Those who were more able helped those who were not as they passed through another of the fiercely pressurised sections and into another system of Tunnels. Left lobe, right lobe. Rin could not be sure they had searched every Tunnel, not every branch and pathway, but she was as close to sure as she could get. He truly wasn't here. All of her plans had been for Ieuan, and to come here only to discover, with sickening finality, that 'here' was not where he was...

She looked up and found Tilly staring at her. The mute girl nodded in agreement. Rin seized hold of the feeling within her as tightly as she could, tighter than she ever had before. Part of her had resisted drawing on its strength in its fullness, scared that holding onto it like this might mean she would not be able to remember how to let it go. None of that mattered now.

She would take these people to the surface. Then, she and Tilly were going to the Lab.

CHAPTER NINETEEN
IEUAN

Breaking into the Tunnels had required stealth and more than a little luck, but breaking out proved to be far easier. Rin didn't know if that was because she had drawn so much of the power into herself, or simply because she had an army of Tavi at her back. They did not bother to try and trick the guards this time: with so many of them set to the same task, even metal bars that would have held back three or four bent easily under their strength.

Rin didn't stop to see what happened to the guards who had once stood at those gates, but with her senses as heightened as they were, she did not miss the thudding and screaming that followed their exit. She ignored it. All she cared about now were the forms of Tilly and Gibb, and the Tavi ex-guard who carried him. Despite the sea of grey and ruddy brown clothing, they stood out to her, like she had marked them out, so desperate was she not to lose them amongst the others.

The air on the surface was cooler and sweeter than it had ever felt before, and ripping the cloth covering from her face, she called over to the man who was carrying Gibb.

"You know the Void, yes?"

"Yes. I'm not from around there, but I've walked enough of it in *this*," he said bitterly, gesturing to his uniform in a way that made Rin think he would rather go naked than wear it a moment longer.

Rin nodded, swiftly scratching a map into the earth. "Avoid

here, here and here." She looked at him to be sure he was following. "Then wait here for my friends."

"How will I know who they are?" he asked, cautiously.

"There should be six of them. If they all make it out." Rin heard the coldness of her tone, like someone else had taken over her voice. "There'll be a lot of explosions below ground, then they should emerge from here." She circled the point where they would exit the sewers.

"What should I tell them?" he asked, looking from Rin to Tilly.

"Tell them we've gone to get Ieuan," Rin said, scrubbing out her makeshift map.

She turned her back and left him and the others staring at her.

Rin had heard a lot about the Tunnels. In truth, she had spoken about little else for quite some time now. But the Labs? All she knew of those she had learned from Lark the night the girl had spoken to her under the stars, in a life that felt so different from the one she had now. What she did know was that this decision was beyond reckless. If she loosened her grip on her power even for a moment, she knew the part of her that was screaming at her to stop would grow too loud to ignore.

So she didn't loosen it.

Looking at Tilly, she did not see her friend anymore, only her guide. She saw the only one who might hold enough knowledge of this place to help her get Ieuan out alive.

The two of them sat, waiting under the starless sky, when they heard them, so close together that Rin would not have been able to tell there had been six different explosions had she not been holding onto her power so tightly.

The lights of the Capital flickered and went out, and for a moment, darkness bathed them all. Then a humming filled the air as, switch-by-switch, generators whirred to life. Tilly nodded and Rin found herself following her silent guide without question.

They moved down a shaft similar to the one Lark had described all those nights ago, and Rin could not help but check each section to see if the metal grates that had trapped Tilly were primed to trap them too. Although she could see the seam where they ran, none were triggered by their presence.

As they reached the bottom, Rin kicked at the covering that was screwed into the wall below, ripping it free from its fixings. It clattered noisily to the floor.

Tilly winced, holding her fingers to her lips, and Rin gave her an apologetic shrug. The smell of the place struck her; a chemical scent lingered in the air that she knew meant danger. She had smelled it on her father, but something in her subconscious recognised it too. The strangeness of this place was too familiar to be new to her.

She loosened her grip on the current slightly, urging any memory that might aid her now to surface.

Just like in the Tunnels, here the lighting was dim. There were red lights flashing on the doors and throughout the hallways, but no sirens sounded. Doors that Rin had expected to be locked pushed open easily, the number pads beside them dark and blank. Rin pointed to one and raised her eyebrows at Tilly. The girl opened her hand wide, then bunched it into a fist six times. Rin didn't know if she was getting better at understanding the girl or if Tilly's movements just appeared to confirm her own hope that the blasts had knocked out power to almost all the systems down here.

At first, Tilly led the way confidently, but as they entered the last corridor, she froze. Several doors lined this hallway, and Rin realised her guide had no way of knowing which of them might contain Ieuan. The chemical smell was stronger down here, which only added to Rin's sense of urgency. Not pausing to think, she stepped towards the first door, pushing it open to reveal a cold and sterile place. An empty metal bed was centred in the middle of the room, with thick restraints laid atop it. She shivered at the thought of those cold metal cuffs trapping Ieuan here, but he was not in this room, and she shut the door quickly. It was not a place she wished to linger.

The next two rooms were just as empty, but as she pushed open the fourth, she saw him.

Instantly, her hold on the power within fled from her. For a moment, she simply stared at Ieuan in disbelief, terrified that if she moved towards him, she might wake from a dream, or if she looked too closely, she might find it was not him at all.

His body twitched and air filled her lungs in a way she had not felt since before she had first heard he had not made it out of the Capital.

Then she was running to him.

"Ieuan," she croaked out in an urgent whisper, shaking him. Only then did she notice the thin tubes running into his limp arm. She whipped around to Tilly. "Should I pull them out?"

"I wouldn't do that if I were you." It was not Tilly who answered, but an oily voice that crept out from behind a darkened glass screen.

Instantly, Rin seized hold of the current again and faced the screen

"The boy turned out to be much more susceptible to the Clag than we had anticipated," Alfredson continued in a smug drawl.

"Quite interesting really; most likely a weak genetic component worth exploring there."

Rin drew her hands into fists, considering how much force it would take to break through glass like that.

"Oh, now now, let's not be hasty. As you can see, I went to rather a lot of trouble to keep your sweetheart alive. It would be a shame if I had to kill him now." There was cold delight in his words that told Rin that he would not truly consider it a shame at all. "I'm curious, did you have a plan? Or was it simply to barge down here and retrieve the boy?" He paused, and when she did not answer, he went on. "I have to admit, I was impressed. That was a very neat little evacuation you organised down there, and blowing up my uncle's lungs – now, that was a stroke of genius even *I* had not expected."

Rin was moving around the bed now, trying to decide if she should ignore his warnings and wrench the tubes from Ieuan's arm anyway.

"Although, while it *was* genius, it was also rude." He sighed. "And here I was, prepared to offer you a deal."

Rin stopped searching and turned her attention to the glass, where she could just about make out the shadow of the man who stood watching her.

"Ah, much better," he said, spreading his hands wide. "Now, about our deal. I have something you want, and as it turns out, you have something I need."

Rin's skin prickled. She did not think it would be wise to give him anything he needed.

"Oh now, don't be like that, child."

Rin looked at Ieuan, then at the door. The longer they stayed here, the more difficult it would be to leave.

"Here's my offer, girl. I will wake up your sweetheart and he and your friend over there can leave, but I am afraid, *not* with you. You, my dear, will have to stay."

Rin felt as though the fear might choke her.

"Now, you might think of course there is another way, that you might pull out those tubes and attempt to fight your way out. Very admirable. A little tactless, but it has merit in its simplicity. But before you consider doing that, I want you to place your head on his chest."

Rin looked at the murky glass, then back at Ieuan. This was all happening too fast, too fast for her to make a plan. She needed him to stop talking. She needed time.

"Go on, dear. Lean down and be sure to listen."

She looked at Ieuan lying there, his chest rising and falling as each breath filled his lungs. She shook her head, trying to clear her thoughts. He was still breathing; he was here, and alive. There was still hope. Her mind worked furiously as she leaned over him to place her ear on his chest. His skin was warm and, even down in this dark place, still held the faint trace of his scent.

That was when she heard it. *What was that sound?* Her head had rested against his chest often enough for her to know that something was wrong. Thud thud, and then – what was that swishing, like a breath but inside his heart? She listened again. *Thud thud, swish.*

"The irony is not lost on me that your great love should have such a weak heart," Alfredson chuckled. "But as I am a compassionate man, I will add something to my bargain. On the table there, you will see a syringe. Once he is awake, you can simply inject that into the poor boy. He will have a rotten few days, but then he will either die, or he will recover."

Rin looked at the needle, wondering what kind of medicine could do such a thing. Certainly nothing Marta had ever shown her.

"And if he survives, he will be stronger and better than he ever was before. Just like Jace here."

With that, he flicked a light on inside the room. Rin felt as though the floor was spinning. Fischer's son was staring back at her.

"Jace?" she whispered.

The boy smiled viciously back at her.

"Jace here was a willing participant in the trials. It's much quicker to turn loyal Empire citizens into Gen6 than it is to grow them from scratch. So, when the trials are officially sanctioned and complete, and once we find out why so many of the participants die during the change, we'll be able to supply an army of them almost overnight, giving power back to those who should rightfully hold it."

So *this* was what Jace had traded her life and the lives of those in the Cove for.

Rin looked down at the syringe, knowing Ieuan didn't care about power, that he wouldn't want her to change him like that. His heart, though? He wouldn't survive outside of here for long with a heart that sounded like that. But if she gave him the injection, what if it simply killed him?

She couldn't trust anything that came from Alfredson. She hadn't been listening for a moment, but he had continued his lecturing. Then she heard something that forced her attention back to her father.

"You see, I believe you are the missing link in my research. Something about your genome holds the answers I need." He huffed. "Terribly frustrating, waiting all this time for you to get back here. Now, come along, I'll have your answer please."

Rin's head was spinning. It was stupid to have come here

without a plan. She could already feel the defeat washing over her as she searched desperately for some other solution. There was nothing in the room that could help her, and she knew nothing about hearts or the kinds of medicine contained within that syringe. From what she knew of her father, it could all be lies... or it could be true. She had no way to be sure.

She had nothing, and then finally, she knew she had lost. She had come so far; been so close to rescuing Ieuan. But now... she had nothing left to bargain with.

"I need a minute to say goodbye." Rin choked on the words, trying to stop the tears that rolled down her cheeks. Picking up Ieuan's hand, she held it to her lips. "I'm so sorry, Ieu. I'm so sorry I left you down there. I should have been quicker. I should have got back here sooner. I really tried, Ieu."

Her voice cracked as she said his name for the last time. Pressing his hand tightly to her cheek, she tried to lock the memory of his touch into her mind.

"Oh please, you'll make me regret coming down here if you keep that up."

Rin's head turned to see Lark stepping into the room behind her, and for a moment, she could only stare in shock at the girl.

"Wha... what are you...?" Hope and disbelief warred in Rin's chest.

"Don't ask what I'm doing, dummy. I'm saving you three, obviously. Not because I like you, but if you think I'm traipsing back down here a *third* time to spring you loose, you can forget it. Best we all just leave now." She spoke as though she could not see Ieuan's unconscious body on the bed before her. "And pull out those tubes already. There's no way whatever *he's* shooting him full of will be doing your boy any good."

"Lark? Is that you?" Alfredson leered at her, like she was an additional prize he hadn't expected to receive. "Well, this really *is* a pleasure. I didn't think we'd be seeing you back down here again." He waved his hand nonchalantly. "It changes nothing, of course. Even with the two of you, you still won't manage to fight your way out of here. Not carrying *him* with you, and not when it is only a matter of minutes until they restore power to this unit."

Rin looked at Lark in alarm and the girl nodded, indicating what he said was true. Then she tilted her head subtly towards the tubes in Ieuan's arm. Rin only had a moment to decide, but if she had to choose between trusting Lark and trusting Alfredson, she would choose Lark every time.

"Are we bringing that?" Lark nodded towards the syringe on the table.

Rin hesitated. Taking it was not the same as using it, and she didn't have time to decide now. "Take it," she called over to the girl, pulling Ieuan's unconscious body into a sitting position and tucking her shoulder under his abdomen.

Alfredson chuckled. "You can't possibly think we are just going to let you leave."

"And *you* can't possibly think I came down here without a plan." Lark smiled sweetly, showing too many teeth to be entirely convincing. "I think you know me better than that, *Doctor*."

For the first time, Rin saw doubt on her father's face.

"Cornelius sends you a gift."

Whatever Alfredson had been about to say in reply to Lark's comment was drowned out by another explosion, echoing down the corridor and filling the room with smoke.

"We need to move," Lark called out, in a way that let Rin know they were already behind, as a second bang blew one of the doors off in the hallway ahead of them. "We need to be moving *faster!*"

"Jace, stop them!" Alfredson screamed, his usual composure vanishing.

Steadying Ieuan over her shoulder, Rin tightened her grip on every last bit of strength she held inside of her and pushed herself into a run. Things began exploding all around them, and the fragments seemed to move through the air more slowly than normal. She knew that Ieuan should feel heavy over her shoulder, but instead he seemed only an inconvenience, forcing her to occasionally shorten her stride and adding a slight clumsiness to her rhythm.

More bangs and she couldn't tell if they were in front or behind her anymore. Instead, she focused only on running, always moving upwards through doors that burst open or buckled under Cornelius's powders. She wanted to look behind her, to check if anyone was following them through this mayhem, but she couldn't spare a second for such a glance. The ground they ran over shifted constantly as more bangs sent debris across their path. Tilly tripped over a pile of rocks that had crumbled underfoot, but Rin didn't slow down. Catching the back of the girl's shirt, she pulled hard, wrenching her back to her feet without losing a stride.

They were still running when the cold night air reached their lungs, and they were still running while the sounds of guards and chaos echoed around them where the Alliance sprang their traps. The shouts of guards and chaos of smoke and noise echoed around them, but still they kept running. Rin had lost track of the turns now – whether they were headed to blocked alleys or towards safe ones, she didn't know. She only knew that, either way, she would not be stopped.

By the time they reached the edges of the Stacks, Rin felt

as though her lungs might burst and her legs felt heavier than she could ever remember. Lark waved her hand, signalling they should stop.

"Enough, there's no one behind us," she panted. "We can stop running. For now, anyway."

Rin didn't want to stop, but she wasn't sure if she could continue to force her legs to move that way much longer.

"I said *enough*, Rin. Gods, you're annoying sometimes," Lark snapped. "The Partisan's people have seen us; they'll be here with help soon."

Tilly moved over to Rin, hugging her tightly as the last bit of strength seemed to leach out of her. She set Ieuan down, leaning his back against a smooth, sloping rock, trying to imagine that he was merely sleeping, but she couldn't. The way his head slumped to the side, the limpness of his body... this was no natural sleep.

Self-doubt overwhelmed her. Had she done the right thing, pulling out those tubes?

"What were they doing to him?" Rin wasn't sure whether she was asking Lark, or if she was just unable to hold her thoughts inside anymore.

"Could've been something to keep him sick? There's a slim possibility that it really *was* something to make him better, but I doubt it," Lark said cooly.

Rin felt anger flare in her. Lark had told her to take out those tubes. *What if they were keeping him alive?*

Lark was watching her intently. "Listen, whatever they were giving him wasn't worth staying behind for. If he dies, it's better that he dies up here on the surface, holding your hand, rather than living down there as part of their experiment."

For a second, Rin wanted to hit her again – that wasn't *her* decision to make – but just as swiftly, she felt her anger seep out of her. It was the same decision Ieuan would have made, had he been able to choose for himself, and she knew it.

Turning back to Ieuan, she brushed the hair from his face, leaving a dusty smudge on his brow. Frantically, she tried to wipe it off, upset that she had marked him with the foulness of the Clag, but instead her actions only dirtied his face further. Realising she was only making it worse, she stopped, resting her forehead against his.

"Come on Ieu," she whispered, searching his face, desperate for any sign that he might have heard her. "We're out now, okay? You have to wake up." She didn't care that Lark could hear her. She didn't care about anything else now.

Ieuan made no sign of recognition, his chest continuing to rise and fall raggedly. If she closed her eyes and listened for it, she could still hear the odd sound his heart made. *Thud, thud, swish.* She thought of the syringe that she knew was tucked away in Lark's satchel, the thought bringing back the shock of the girl stepping out of the shadowy hallway to rescue them.

"Why did you come back, Lark?"

She shrugged. "Like I said, I wanted to save myself the journey back here when the others found out you were gone."

Rin tilted her head in response, trying to decide whether her reasoning could possibly be true.

"Oh fine." Lark rolled her eyes. "Cornelius knew blasts of that size would wipe out the power in the Capital, including the security in the Lab, and we both felt it was too good an opportunity to miss." Her face took on that dark look that made her appear slightly unhinged. "The fact that I happened to save you, and you now owe me, is just an added bonus."

"Thank you." Rin was grateful beyond what those simple words expressed, and she wasn't sure if there would ever be a way to repay a favour like that one. Even if she was still unsure whether what Lark had done had anything to do with her and Ieuan.

Rin had barely caught her breath before a group appeared from the Stacks. Some she recognised from the Partisan's Hall and others still had the thick ruddy Clag of the Tunnels on their skin. Hands patted at her back warmly, and several people she didn't know pulled her into hugs that felt far too personal coming from strangers. She wanted to shrug them off, but found she didn't have the strength or will to stop them.

She saw the Tavi ex-guard from the Tunnels was among them.

"Did he make it?" she asked.

"Gibb is with an old woman now. That one has a tongue that could cut steel, but I got the impression that if anyone could help him, it was her."

Rin nodded, too tired for words. *Good.*

She could have walked with the group as they continued their journey, but they insisted on carrying her as well as Ieuan. In the end, it had seemed easier to give in than to fight it. The time passed in a blur as she allowed her exhaustion to overwhelm her. She had only enough energy to focus on Ieuan, who still had not woken up, and she was determined not to let him out of her sight until he did.

As they reached their next meeting point, she saw Torsten up ahead. She felt something lurch inside her when she realised his two brothers were not beside him.

He reached up, helping her down from the crowd that carried her, and then hugged her tightly. Unlike those that had come before, this was a hug she returned full-heartedly.

"I suppose we'll have to stop being surprised by you one of these days." She heard the way Torsten's voice was heavy with weariness too.

"Where are the others?" she asked, her urgency to know outweighing her fear of his answer.

"Everyone made it. *Everyone*, Rin," he said, holding her face and looking into her eyes. "But we need to keep moving. Collapsing the Tunnels has left them in chaos. We took a big section of their Tavi guard with us too, but this isn't over. Sooner or later, they will realise what we've done, and then they'll come for us. Magnus and Ivor have gone ahead; they'll take the first of them into the swamp tonight." He looked out westward, towards the Void. "We need to get as far away from here as possible, before they realise where we're going."

Rin didn't waste time agreeing with the obvious, but then something jolted her memory. "It might already be too late for that, Torsten. Jace was with them." Rin watched as Torsten's eyes went wide, then narrowed darkly. "I think we have to assume he told them we're heading for the Cove."

"Let's hope they think we have to cross the Ashlands first, then." Torsten was nodding as he spoke. "There's still a good chance they don't know about the tracks."

Rin remembered the way her neck had prickled when they had entered the shafts before; the feeling that someone was following them. She thought that perhaps it was too late to hope that wasn't the case, but she said nothing. Whether the Capital knew about the tracks or not, it was still their best chance of getting these people back to the Cove. If she had hoped there would be time to rest, that hope had gone. There was no doubt in her mind that they needed to be gone from the Stacks before the dawn broke.

The alleyways of the Stacks were lined with people now. Some were those who had escaped the Tunnels and now drudged on, still stunned by what had happened, and some were the hopeful ones who were seeking familiar faces in the crowd below. Whether the survivors were known to them or not, the people of the Stacks offered water and what food they could spare into hungry hands. Now and then, there were shouts of joy, and Rin felt their happiness melt into her, unable to filter out their emotions from her own. Sometimes she would hear laughing, and all too often sobbing, as some were reunited, while others shared the news of those who had not survived.

A little boy with a thick smattering of freckles ran up to her. "'Scuse me, lady!" he called up to her. "'Scuse me, but the Partisan wants to see you before you leave."

She looked down at his face and found herself pleased to imagine that he might now have a chance to grow up free of the Clag.

"Don't worry, I'll make sure they find something to carry Ieuan on, and I won't let him out of my sight until you get back," Torsten promised her.

She still didn't want to leave, but there was no time to argue about it. She would hear what the Partisan wanted her to hear, then they would finally leave this place behind them.

CHAPTER TWENTY
ACTION, INTENTION AND JUSTIFICATION

Rin let Freck lead her back to the Hall of the Partisan. She had to admit, the small boy could move almost as quickly as she could, weaving through the narrow warrens of junk with surprising dexterity.

This better not take too long, she thought, irritated by the use of time she did not have to waste.

As they pushed open the door, the man standing in the Hall seemed... different. It was certainly the Partisan, but gone was the pomp and ceremony that surrounded his usual greetings. Instead, he held a frail girl in his arms, and was spooning small amounts of soup into her emaciated body. Tears poured freely down his face and he made no effort to wipe them away.

He paused to wave Rin inside. "Come in, come in."

At the sound of his voice, the girl in his arms groaned and, for the first time, Rin recognised her as the first of the guards she had found in the Tunnels.

"This is Megri – you have already met, I know." He raised another spoonful to the girl's lips, encouraging her to take another sip. "She's my daughter."

Rin didn't think she had any tears left in her, but she was wrong. She wiped at her face quickly as the salty droplet rolled down her cheek.

"What you have done is nothing short of a miracle, girl," the Partisan continued. "I'd hoped, but I did not truly believe this day would come."

Rin nodded, still not trusting herself to speak.

"And still I must ask more of you."

She stiffened, sensing the danger in his words.

"You are special, girl. Even more remarkable than I could have imagined. You have the power to set things right again. To stop the Empire once and for all."

Rin had not expected to hear that. She had been lucky to escape with her life the first time, beyond lucky to succeeded twice. '*They will all try to use you*'. Lark's words echoed in her head. She finally had Ieuan, and if they could make it back to the Cove, they would be safe at last. Safe to live their lives.

Safe to be *happy*.

The girl in the Partisan's arms coughed.

Would Megri be safe, though? Would the little boy with freckles be safe? Alfredson was trying to build an army of Gen6. The Empire had already shown what it would do with that kind of power.

She shook her head again. No, she was lucky to be alive, she did not need another cause to die for.

"I'm sorry—"

"Ah, but don't answer me yet," the Partisan interrupted, meeting her eyes with an earnest expression. "Of course, it would be premature to plan the war while the battle still rages. Go back to the Cove. Get well and strong. But remember this conversation, Rin. I believe you might be the only person left in this world who can stop this."

Rin left the Hall of the Partisan with those words burning in her ears. The last thing she wanted was to be involved in any more battles. She did not want a war. She wanted Ieuan to be well again, and she wanted to swim with him in the steaming pools inside the mountain and learn to cook fish stew.

By the time she rejoined the escape party, she was among the last of them to disappear under the Stacks and into the swamp beyond. Torsten had asked the people of the Stacks to find a long board to lay Ieuan on, and two men now stood ready to carry him onward at her signal. The boy groaned and Rin ran to him, unsure whether it was a good sign or a sign that he was slipping away from her.

"Ieuan?" she called his name softly, taking his hand in hers. "I'm here, Ieuan."

His eyes fluttered open, then closed again. Rin stood, silently waiting, but no more sound left his lips. She was just about to give up and wave them onward when she felt it. A small squeeze, slow and deliberate. Not the twitching of nerves or the unconscious reaction to touch, but a squeeze.

"It's going to be okay, Ieuan," she whispered. "We all got out. Gibb too. We're going back to the Cove. Just hang on, okay?" She wasn't sure if he could hear her, but she wanted to believe that he could.

She looked up at the two men who had offered to carry him, realising that one was the Tavi ex-guard who had taken care of Gibb. The other looked very much like him, only younger.

"I can carry one end," she said, looking at the younger boy who was still stained with dust from the Tunnels.

"We'll manage, won't we son?" the older man said, smiling at the boy. It was a smile that seemed to say *we can manage anything now*.

"Son?" Rin felt the word slip out. She thought of Alyssa, and that tightness in her chest came back.

"Yes, that's my boy," the man said, seeming confused at the tears that filled her eyes. "We can carry your friend. It's no trouble," he went on, misreading what had caused her sudden emotion.

"When I was in the Cove, a woman asked me to find her husband and son," Rin explained.

The man's breath caught in his throat. "My wife? My wife she... she's still alive? And my baby girl?" His voice trembled and one leg gave out on him, forcing him to kneel on the floor, looking up at her. "Is she... are they...?"

"Shep?" Rin asked, still unsure if this man could truly be him. She held her breath; it seemed to take an age before the man nodded slowly. Rin felt warmth rushing up from somewhere that had long been cold inside her, a smile pulling at her lips. "They're alive. Alyssa and Giera are alive."

"They're alive," Shep croaked, as though it had been more than he'd dared to hope for.

Rin let out a noise somewhere between a chuckle and a sob, scrunching up her nose as once more she felt the tears dampen her face. "They've missed you terribly, but they're alive. Alive and well."

The man gave a choking sob as his son knelt beside him in a heavy embrace.

There had been many reunions in those first few days. Free from the Tunnels, with food, water and Marta's care, Gibb had returned to himself. As soon as he had been able, he had sought Rin out. They had not had to share many words, both seeming to understand all they needed to about what had happened since their last meeting. Now, their shared focus remained on Ieuan, who still seemed to flit in and out of consciousness. Even when he was awake, he did not seem to Rin as though he was really there. He had squeezed her hand again, and his father's too, but nothing more than a groan had left his lips.

They had moved as quickly as they could without letting anyone get hurt, stopping only for a short time each night. Every evening, Marta and the others would join them, and the old woman and Fievel would spend hours discussing which remedy they might try next to restore Ieuan's health. Rin didn't know when her feelings had shifted, but she found she was no longer angry with the old woman. Perhaps it was what Torsten and Lark had said, or perhaps it was the way Marta was caring for Ieuan now. Either way, Rin did not feel she needed an apology anymore. She was not even sure that she had ever been owed one. Instead, she was just glad that her grandmother was here with her, still trying to help her, just as she had always done.

They always made sure they were moving before the sun had risen each morning. It was a hard march, and there was not quite as much food as Rin thought some of them needed, but with the fear of the Empire at their backs, no one complained. A few of the Tavi had picked up small cuts here and there, or had fallen into one pool or another, but without their chips they would heal quickly enough and caused Marta no real concern.

Rin felt secure in the knowledge that her friends were spaced out down the line each day, ensuring there was always one person evenly placed throughout the group who knew how to navigate the swamps. Shep and his son had proved themselves to be more than able stretcher-bearers, and alongside Rin, the three of them had taken turns carrying Ieuan.

It was as the dawn broke on the third day that Scratch's ears pricked up. Instantly, Rin turned her head in the same direction he had. Faint and distant, the sound nevertheless sent a shiver through her. *Dogs.* Her memory buzzed with the sound. These were not swamp mutts; mutts didn't bay that way. These were Empire hounds, and they were coming for them.

"Run!" Rin shouted, and she heard her call echo up the line ahead of her. She turned to Shep, who was still trying to carry Ieuan. "Put him down!" she shouted.

"No, we can make it. We've had word down the line it's not much further."

Rin looked around her. She couldn't see that far ahead through the thick foliage, but she recognised the place, and could guess that more than half of the group had likely made the climb down onto the tracks already. She heard the howling again, off in the distance, and knew that it didn't matter if they were close to the tracks.

They wouldn't all make it.

It didn't matter who carried Ieuan; without someone to draw the hounds away, not all of them would reach the safety of the tracks in time.

Rin nodded briskly, her voice taking on a commanding tone as she tapped into her inner strength. "You two take him with you to the front. Tell them there's no time to send everyone down the ladder one at a time. Get Lark to show the rest how to get down quickly." Rin was pleased Shep didn't waste time asking her what that meant; he was already adjusting his grip to start running again. "Don't wait for me."

There was reluctance in Shep's face, but he nodded. Wasting no more time, he motioned to his son and they began to run up the line, hurrying those at the back forward.

Rin found herself eagerly anticipating the feeling. She had spent long enough apart from it, and the strength and numbness it offered called to her. Greedily, she let it spread through her, not caring how much of it she drew into herself. She breathed the swamp air deep into her lungs, sensing that the hounds were closer than she'd thought, but that the scouts following them were further back. She needed to buy enough time for everyone to get down onto the tracks and then into a compartment that was safe from Cornelius's blasts.

Rin strained to hear, trying to decide exactly how far she was from the tracks. Then, she started to run.

First, she went back the way they had come, making sure her clothing and skin brushed against the nearest shrubs and trees, wanting to ensure that her scent was the freshest, so she could draw the dogs away from the others. Part of her knew it would not matter: she was sure it was her trail they would follow anyway.

Where earlier her muscles had ached, now fresh life surged into them, answering her call for speed and power instantly. She knew it was reckless, but there was something inside her that found this moment exhilarating: just her and the swamp. No one else to care about. No one else to slow her down. A part inside of her yearned to test herself this way against the hounds. Rin wondered for a moment if that should worry her, but worry was a thing so alien to the power within that she could barely understand it. In a detached way, she wondered whether she had been drawing on that strength too often of late.

She soon lost track of how long she had run for, but she always made sure to keep the location of the giant mechanical opening in her mind, and the hounds just close enough to be sure they were still following her. When she circled back to the mouth of the tracks, she was pleased to see no sign of the others. With any luck, they had already reached the first compartment by now.

Howls sounded behind her, closer than she had wanted them to get, and she could hear the voices of their handlers urging them on.

She grabbed hold of the safety rail and locked her legs around it. Then, taking one last look at a swamp she hoped never to see again, she dropped.

Lark had not mentioned the fact that it felt as though your stomach was trying to escape through your mouth when she had done it before. At least there was a glow from a lava trench below. It was no longer being filled from the wall, but there was enough light left in this one to guide her on.

As she landed, she saw no one.

She was starting to tire a little now and the footing down here was treacherous, but still she ran on. The first of them must have reached the bottom of the ladder not long after her. She couldn't hear barking anymore, but the crunch of boots on the small stones and the angry shouts of people had replaced them.

Not too much further, she told herself, but each new sound behind her told her she was no longer keeping pace. The gap between her and their pursuers was beginning to close.

"Hurry, child!" Marta's voice hissed from the shadows. "Hurry now. Just in here."

The last of Rin's strength flared as her leather boots bit deep into the gravel, pushing her towards her grandmother's voice. She flung herself across the line that marked the nearest edge of Cornelius's safe compartment. The last of the escape party was pushing on well ahead of her, but she could see now who it was that lagged so far behind the others. The pair of them were breathing hard, and Rin knew they wouldn't be able to carry Ieuan much further like that.

"They're not far behind me, Shep!" Rin panted. "Leave Ieuan with me and keep going."

The man looked like he wanted to argue, but then seemed

to think better of it. Hesitantly, he nodded, and they set Ieuan down gently. The man gave her one last look that asked if she was certain, and when Rin nodded her reply, he yanked his son by the shoulder and they both disappeared around the next bend.

"We need to blow it now," Rin called to the old woman.

"I know. Now where's that damn fuse?" Marta was patting around the floor desperately, looking for the thin braid of wire and twine. "Help me, girl!" There was real panic straining her voice.

"Looking for this?" a voice sneered from the darkness.

Rin turned to find Jace, holding something in his hand. Even in this dim light, Rin knew what it would be. The sight made the hair on her neck rise.

"It's not too late, Jace," Rin said cautiously. "You could still come with us."

Slowly, she moved closer to him. She had to reach him before he could pull the fuse free from Cornelius's explosives at the far end of this compartment.

"Oh, it's far too late, Rin. Or should I say, it's far too late for *you*."

In one swift motion, he severed the thread.

"No!" Rin lunged at him, catching him in the stomach and driving him into the wall behind.

Jace's fist struck downwards, hammering against her shoulder and shoving her to the floor. She looked up at him, shocked. Whatever they had given him in the Capital had worked – she had not expected such a force.

He kicked her hard in the chest, knocking the wind out of her, and she felt as though she had been kicked by a horse, not a man. Feeling the panic rise, Rin welcomed the power in – all of it, as much as she could hold – and as she saw Jace's leg draw back a second time, she knew she would kill him. Instead of rolling away from the attack, she rolled towards him. Catching the one leg still left on the ground, she wrenched at it, hard. The boy howled as he fell forward, extending his hand to catch himself, but Rin was already moving. Using the momentum to fling herself back onto her feet, she turned, ready to face him again, when she heard a loud *crack*.

The old woman's staff had collided with the side of Jace's head.

The boy did not rise.

Rin loosened her grip on the current, startled by how eager she had been to kill him in that moment. It scared her; the realisation that if she didn't maintain control over her power, it might compel her to do unspeakable things.

Marta bent down to pick up the fuse.

"What now?" Rin asked, as the voices began to echo louder behind them. "Can we reattach it?" Rin didn't know anything about fuses and this seemed like a very poor time to try and learn.

"No, my girl." Marta was speaking calmly now. *Too* calmly. "I think not."

"Then we keep running, right?" Rin knew even before the old woman shook her head that this was a problem they could not outrun.

"I've made a great many mistakes, Rin. The biggest was to think that you needed me to keep you safe. You are so much stronger than I have ever been."

Rin winced. She didn't want to hear those words. Not now. Not if Marta was going to say them as a goodbye.

She wrapped her arms around the old woman and pressed her face into her shoulder, suddenly feeling like a child again.

"Now, you must be stronger still," Marta whispered.

Rin pulled her face away, looking at the old woman in confusion. Then Marta shoved her, hard, and swung around so quickly that Rin did not have time to think.

The old woman dipped her staff in the bright glow of the lava. Almost instantly, the wood caught aflame.

"What are you doing?" Rin wanted to stop her, but from doing what, she didn't know.

The old woman ignored her, shuffling away as fast as her legs could carry her. Not away from the voices that hounded them, but towards them. Rin felt the cold stone under her hands and, looking down, she saw which side of the line Marta had pushed her towards.

Now she knew. The first bang ripped through tracks, then another and another. Dark, sooty dust filled her nose and she threw her body over Ieuan's in a desperate attempt to protect him. These were not like the bangs Rin had seen in the Lab; these shook the ground above and below her, as though the whole world might topple. Time after time, they rattled her, each one pounding in her chest, stealing the breath from her lungs.

When they finally stopped, she opened her eyes to nothing but blackness. Her ears were ringing, or at least, she thought they were. Either that, or the rock around her was still screaming.

She shook her head, trying to clear it. She would have to talk to Cornelius about what constituted 'safe'.

Focusing her senses, she realised she could only hear her own breathing and then, more softly, Ieuan's. Where was her grandmother?

"Marta!" Rin shouted, her voice hoarse. A few loose rocks tumbled around her, but no answer came. "Marta!" she cried again, more desperate now.

Rin didn't know how long she sat there, cradling Ieuan's

head in her lap, calling the old woman's name into the darkness. All she knew was that no one was answering her. Tears flowed down her face as she pulled Ieuan tightly to her chest, feeling the warmth of his skin against her and listening to his heart beating so awkwardly in his chest.

They found her like that – curled up in the dark and covered in dust and tears. She had refused to let go of Ieuan, and so they had carried them both away together. Rin was vaguely aware that they had tried to talk to her, but all she heard was the ringing of the earth and the thud and swish of Ieuan's heart. She had begun to tap the rhythm out against her leg, against the wall, against anything – *tap, tap, swish; tap, tap swish* – convincing herself that if she stopped tapping, his heart would stop beating, and she would truly be left here alone.

Tap, tap, swish. They carried the two of them along the rest of the tracks. *Tap, tap, swish.* They carried them through Cornelius's home. *Tap, tap, swish.* Along the rough stone of the shafts. *Tap, tap, swish.* Now there was a pattering; that was annoying. It was hard to focus on her tapping with that pattering above her.

Rin sat up, furrowing her brow in confusion at the interference. Steam was rising up around them and rain was dripping from the giant teeth above. *Ah, so we're back here.* She looked around – there were fewer of them again. Lark and Fievel sat by the fire, and she could see that Magnus, Torsten, Ivor, Reece and Tilly all laid out on their sleeping packs, although none of them slept. Ieuan lay motionless beside her on his stretcher. Rin blinked slowly, hoping the others from the Tunnels were back in the Cove by now. She lay back down.

"Rin?" Ieuan groaned.

Oh great, Rin thought, *now* I'm *going mad too.* At least being mad would be a pleasant change from being afraid.

Tap, tap, swish.

"Rin?"

She sat bolt upright, along with the others. They had all heard it, eyes darting between Ieuan and her. She scrambled to get up, knocking over the cup of water someone had no doubt been trying to force her to drink.

"Ieuan, I'm here." Her heart caught in her throat as he smiled back at her.

"Did we do it?" His voice was dry from lack of use and his words caught in his throat, making him cough.

"We did it, Ieu." Something between a laugh and a startled sob bubbled out of Rin. "We got them all out." She wiped the tear that rolled from his eye.

"Good." He smiled, then wheezed again. Concern flashed across his face. "You didn't let them change me, did you?"

At first, Rin didn't know what he meant. She looked at him questioningly.

"I saw what it did to Jace." Ieuan coughed again, and this time it took a moment for him to catch his breath. "That stuff is evil. I told him you wouldn't do that to me."

The syringe. Rin had all but forgotten about it, tucked away in Lark's pack. She watched as the smile returned to Ieuan's face, as though he had known all along that he could trust her.

"You're going to get better, Ieu. Then we're going to swim in those warm craters just like we talked about." Rin could feel her throat tightening against the urge to cry. She wanted him to believe he could get better; she wanted to believe it herself.

He didn't answer.

"Ieu?" Rin shook him. "Ieu!" She lay her head on his chest.

Thud, thud, swish.

It was fainter now. Too faint.

"He's dying, Rin," Reece said the words softly, as though somehow that would make them less awful.

"No! He has to get better."

"I'm so sorry," Reece said, covering his mouth with his hand.

Lark stepped close beside him, holding something in her fist. "He's dying, Rin, but maybe he doesn't have to."

She opened her hand, revealing the syringe in her palm.

Rin shook her head. *They all heard what he said. He doesn't want that.*

But what about what I want?

"What if it kills him?" she whispered.

"He's dying either way."

Lark's voice was not cold or mean now. Rin thought the other girl might be trying to hold back her own tears.

Rin picked up the syringe, then Tilly was in front of her, shaking her head. Rin instantly felt horrified that she had even considered it, dropping the needle as though it had scalded her.

In that moment, Lark lunged.

Even if Rin had expected it, she was not sure what she would have done. The tall, slender girl's hand snatched the syringe from the air and drove the needle deep into Ieuan's leg, plunging down on the handle the moment it pierced his skin.

They all stared at her, wide eyed, a mix of horror and shock across all their faces.

"You'd be amazed what people can learn to live with." Lark shrugged, and Rin thought there was a hint of an apology in there. "The trick is being alive long enough to get used to it."

She turned to Fievel, who was staring at her, his eyes wide. Lark lifted his token from under her shirt and over her head, placing it in his hand. Then she walked away.

Within the hour, it became clear to them all that Ieuan was too sick to move. Fever and delirium had followed the injection almost immediately, and Rin refused to leave his side. She still couldn't decide if she was angry with Lark or grateful. Angry that she had taken away Ieuan's decision, but grateful that she had not made Rin be the one to make that choice.

She wasn't sure when she had fallen asleep, but she awoke suddenly to the sound of a staff echoing against the stone floor.

"Marta?" she called out instinctively, but as Cornelius shuffled into sight, she knew how foolish that had been.

"Marta is gone, Rin." Magnus's face was full of concern. "You heard what Cornelius said before – anyone behind the line when those explosions went off would be crushed."

"Wrong," Cornelius said abruptly, as he dropped off a woven bag full of fresh mushrooms and hard ration biscuits. "The brutish one is wrong. Cornelius did not say she would be crushed, he said she would be trapped *or* crushed."

Rin stared at him. "You mean she could still be alive down there?" Rin felt a moment of hope and then, just as quickly, it turned to horror as she imagined the old woman trapped beneath all that rock.

He nodded. "Yes, or crushed."

"Well, which is it?" she asked desperately.

"Could be crushed or could be trapped. No way to know unless Cornelius sees a body."

The three brothers all stood and faced him with the same opened-mouthed horror that matched her own.

"Cornelius," Rin pleaded, "we have to be sure."

"Only one way to be sure." He shrugged, as though providing

an obvious answer. "Have to dig her out."

"Can it be done?" she asked doubtfully, remembering the earth that had rained down on her.

"No way to know until we try."

She wanted to go with him right now and start sifting through earth and rock herself, but she could not leave Ieuan alone.

"We'll go," Torsten said, reading the conflict on her face.

"We'll all go," Reece added.

Rin looked around the faces that were nodding back at her. She had to let them try.

They gathered some tools and left with Cornelius straight away, leaving Rin alone with Ieuan.

She pressed a cool damp cloth against his brow. All she could do now was wait.

EPILOGUE

They would always remember the day in the Cove when those they had thought lost were returned to them. The shore was lined with people, as boat after boat came ashore with their loved ones.

Not all the tears shed that day were for joy, but not all were in sorrow either. Those who recalled it to their children in years to come would speak of the reuniting of families, and of the great bonfires they had lit to guide them home. They would tell them how the food was plentiful, and how the joy in their hearts had moved them to sing old songs that many thought only the sea still remembered.

Then, they would light a candle and shed a tear for the ones who remained; who were still lost, never to return.

HERE ENDS BOOK TWO.

ABOUT THE AUTHOR

R. R. Boxall is the author of the YA Dystopian Fantasy Immutavi series. Growing up on the small Scottish island of Fetlar, her passion for books and fantastical tales took root in its rich cultural soil. She is currently living on Shetland's main island where she works as an Air Traffic Controller. When she is not in the tower, with her eyes turned to the sky, her imagination is wandering through unexplored worlds and extraordinary adventures.

Keep up to date with all things Immutavi by following
R. R. Boxall on socials!

Instagram: @rachael_boxall
TikTok: @rachael.r.boxall

9 781803 783413